KV-636-001

Mary de Laszlo worked for *Queen Magazine* in the 1960s. She also worked in Paris in the fashion department of *Jardins des Modes*, reporting on shows and the Paris collections. Mary is married with three children and now writes full time. She lives in London.

DANCING IN THE WIND

When plant hunter Randolph Graveson is paralysed in an accident, the only thing that keeps his mind alive is the hope that a new variety of peony he discovered will blossom. Then Cedric Hartford — a rival plant hunter — visits and his dog savages the roots . . . Determined to reclaim this peony, Randolph insists that his daughter Delphina return to Tibet to fetch it, and entrusts her safekeeping to his friend Arnold North. But hot on their trail are Cedric and his nephew, Lorin Courtney . . .

Books by Mary de Laszlo
Published by The House of Ulverscroft:

BREAKING THE RULES
THE WOMAN WHO LOVED TOO MUCH
DANCING ON HER OWN
THE BEST-KEPT SECRET

MARY DE LASZLO

DANCING IN THE WIND

Complete and Unabridged

ULVERSCROFT
Leicester

First published in Great Britain in 2005 by
Robert Hale Limited
London

First Large Print Edition
published 2006
by arrangement with
Robert Hale Limited
London

British Library CIP Data

De Laszlo, Mary
    Dancing in the wind.—Large print ed.—
Ulverscroft large print series: romance
    1. Plant collectors—Fiction
    2. Large type books
    I. Title
    823.9′14 [F]

    ISBN 1–84617–362–0

Published by
F. A. Thorpe (Publishing)
Anstey, Leicestershire

Set by Words & Graphics Ltd.
Anstey, Leicestershire
Printed and bound in Great Britain by
T. J. International Ltd., Padstow, Cornwall

For Minna — with love

Prologue

'You are the last person I would discuss my plant finds with,' Randolph Graveson spat contemptuously, towering above the stubby figure of Cedric Hartford.

'I know you've found something special, I just want to see it.' Cedric's features were clenched with determination; his pale eyes glittered dangerously. He moved a step closer to Randolph, his hand thrust out, as if he would seize him and shake his secret from him.

Randolph laughed, dismissing him with a toss of his head. 'Find your own plants if you can keep off the opium long enough!' He strode away from him, his tall frame majestic against the brilliant Tibetan sky. He held his head high, his heart singing. He had just experienced one of the rare wonders of plant hunting. He had found — he was certain as he could be — a new species of peony. It was his and his alone, and Cedric Hartford, drunkard, opium-taker and thief, would not take it from him. He turned again, triumphant in his joy. Cedric was right behind him.

'Just show me, Randolph,' he snarled at him.

Randolph laughed again, the joy of his find intoxicating him. His derision incensed Cedric further, who sprang like a cat upon him, determined to see this find. Randolph jumped away but his big frame dislodged the scree on the uneven path. He put out his hands to save himself but his body was too heavy and he crashed over the edge of the mountain.

1

1936

'Go and see if they have come yet, Delphina,' Randolph demanded from his wheelchair.

'Yes, Papa, I'll go at once.' She spoke with a false cheerfulness that fooled neither of them. His fretting during these last weeks for her to keep going into the garden to see if the new shoots of his peonies were appearing had become an obsession. He reminded her of a tethered eagle yearning for the freedom that would never come to him again. It was such an agony for her to see him so confined that she would do anything for him.

'I'll get my coat.' She dropped her hand on his shoulder, bent her head with its bright sheaf of auburn hair to kiss him. 'I won't be long.'

'Thank you, my dear. You didn't go yesterday or the day before with that rain, so they might surprise us today. They should be here, they really should by now.'

Delphina could feel how he was fighting to control his impatience. It lay curled inside his broken body like an electric current ready to

3

burst forth at the slightest provocation.

She scurried into the hall, snatching her coat from the cupboard and pulled open the heavy front door. Why she was hurrying so, if they were there they wouldn't go away. She hated upsetting him further so she always seemed to be rushing to do things for him. She knew she was in danger of over-indulging him and making herself a slave, and every evening when she sank exhausted into bed she swore that tomorrow she would be firmer with him. But every day her sympathy got the better of her and she scurried around him as busily as ever.

It was mid-morning in late February. The last few days had been dismal with rain but today with the glimmering of sunshine the air felt fresh and new. It was still too early in the year for the peony buds to reveal their leaves, unfolding like crushed butterfly wings, but the shoots might have started to show that they were alive. She ran across the lawn to the large border that ringed it; the earth was rich with loam dug in by Ely, the gardener, — or more likely Tom under his supervision — in the autumn.

She took a few steps into the bed then squatted down close to the earth. Gently she searched through the straw and scraps of dead leaves that the winds had trapped there.

There was nothing. Sick disappointment clawed at her. How she dreaded telling him that there was still no sign, that surely the plants were dead. Dead like his hopes, his life. Still her fingers moved on, searching, probing the earth. Then she saw one. Like a bright pink nose pushing itself out from the gnarled root in the earth. There was another, smaller beside it, and another.

She jumped up, excitement surging through her to run to tell him the good news, then she remembered that the frosts might come to damage the new shoots. She squatted down again and, carefully as if they were sleeping babies, covered them again.

'What is it, miss?' Ely the old gardener put down the wheelbarrow and straightened up slowly. 'It's not . . . they ain't grown?'

'Yes, they're there, but only on one root.' Her eyes were shining. 'Go and look, Ely, one anyway is alive.' She ran on into the house. This minute show of life would make her father's day, would go some way to relieving his feeling of uselessness.

Her glowing face told him all before she could speak.

'Take me to see them,' Randolph said, the grey pain lifting from his face. 'Call Carson, let me see them.'

'They're not many, just one or two tiny

buds, but they're there,' she said. 'Will they flower this year?'

'They are alive, that's the important thing,' Randolph said. 'They'll flower in their own time. Ah Carson, take me to the garden.'

'But, sir, there's a nip in the air.' His manservant glanced quickly at Delphina.

'Damn the nip, get me there,' Randolph bellowed, but his voice held a note of excitement not anger.

'Let me get your coat, a scarf, a rug.' Delphina ran to the cupboard in the hall.

'Don't fuss so, my darling, what's a cold when you'll never walk again?'

'Papa . . . '

'Come on, I'm impatient to see them with my own eyes. At least I've still got the use of them.'

They got him outside the front door and the gardener's boy Tom was sent for to help Carson get the chair down the steps. It was heavy work pushing the chair across the waterlogged lawn, the wheels leaving great welts in the ground.

Once arrived at the flowerbed it took more time to manoeuvre him closer. Ely put down some planks. Carson and Tom dragged the chair as close as they could to the flowerbed. 'Damn these bloody legs; take care the wheels don't damage the buds.' Randolph alternatively cursed and directed the proceedings.

Delphina winced at his impatience, trying not to think that last year he'd have run here alone, not been dependent on anyone.

Carson and Tom, with Ely holding the chair, half lifted and supported Randolph's heavy body while Delphina pushed back the straw again and he saw the new shoots of the peony that he'd brought home from Tibet.

Randolph stared at the tiny pink shoots for a long moment, before they eased him back in his chair. His gaze appeared far away as he saw again those creamy heads, golden as if the evening sun had left its light in them. He had come upon them quite by chance, hidden from view, among the rocks. His heart had caught with the sudden excitement that still hit him after all these years as a plant hunter when he found a new plant.

He'd heard the rumours that another plant hunter had found a pure ivory peony, so fine that its translucent petals had given the impression of holding the sun, but when he'd gone to look for it again he could not find it. But was it this one, here at his feet? Randolph was certain it was and he would not lose it, but bring it back to flower in his own country.

He'd taken a flower to press, then the next day, unable to resist one more look at it, had

7

returned to the plant. His trips were planned enabling him to return to the plants to collect the seeds when they were ripe, but this time it was as if he had had a premonition that he would not return. Next to the main plant was a smaller one. He'd dug out some fat portions of the root, wrapped them in his handkerchief and put them in the canvas bag he carried on his back.

Then Cedric Hartford had destroyed him.

It was a miracle and the loyalty of his guides that had brought him home. But he would never roam free in the foothills and mountains again. He was trapped forever in a wheelchair. The peony roots had been damaged in the fall, but Randolph had brought them home, a further feat of endurance as, he had been told later, Cedric had gone through his things determined to find any plants of interest and claim them as his own. He had grabbed the peony from its press putting it with his plants, but he had missed Randolph's old canvas bag, muddled up under his coat when he fell.

'That's hope, sir, ain't it?' Ely broke into Randolph's thoughts, his plain old face serious with conviction. 'Seeing nature at her work again after the winter, shows ye life never dies.'

Randolph did not answer, but Delphina

smiled at Ely's simple faith. 'It's always a miracle,' she said, knowing that Ely believed that with the new birth of spring his master would somehow regain movement in his paralysed body and be planning, with his usual vigour, another trip to some far off land to bring home more plants.

'Isn't it wonderful, Papa? Something to look forward to?' she said, with more eagerness than she felt. 'Do you think they will flower this summer?'

Randolph shook himself from his reverie and, with a great sigh in his voice, said, 'I don't know, my darling, but I would give all the world just to see them once again on that mountain, dancing in the wind with the sun in their petals.'

Carson, hating the cruel fate that had crushed his master, said, 'It's cold, sir, it will do you no good hanging about and getting a chill; let me take you back.' And before Randolph could protest he began to heave the chair round.

'Come on, boy, give me a hand,' he barked at Tom who, hands in pockets, was idly scuffing holes in the lawn with his feet.

'Mind yer feet, look at that mess.' Ely scowled at him. 'When you've finished taking in the master you come right back and smooth that out. Then you can clean all the flowerpots in the greenhouse; that should keep you out of trouble.'

The boy scowled. Randolph said wearily, 'Take me in then, Carson. Oh that the summer would come.'

A car came up the drive and stopped outside the front door. A thick-set, stubby man got out. He was about the same age as Randolph, with a heavy face, his weather-beaten cheeks folding in lines round his neck. His hair was dark with grey streaks, and grew like an unruly bush from his scalp. He walked briskly towards them, smiling.

Delphina froze at the sight of him. She glanced quickly at her father whose face was now livid, his eyes dark with anger.

'Hartford,' he spat the word, as if it was poison to be expelled as swiftly as possible from his body. 'What the hell are you doing here?'

'Randolph, good to see you out enjoying the spring air.'

'Why are you here?' Randolph's body may be broken but his voice was strong.

'My dear chap, I came to see how you were.' A tic of unease twitched at the corner of his mouth. He blundered on, 'I thought we could have a chat.'

'About what?' Randolph spat at him, hatred in his eyes.

'I'm planning another trip, to Tibet. I thought you'd be interested.'

Delphina bit back a cry at his insensitivity.

Randolph's face was terrifying in its anger.

'How dare you come and taunt me with your plans. No doubt you've come to find out where the best plants are to be found, being too idle to find your own. Well, you've had a wasted journey. I won't tell you where they are. Their whereabouts will die with me.'

'Papa . . . ' Delphina bent over him anxiously. She was afraid that not being able to move, this anger might provoke a stroke.

'I'm fine; leave me be, Delphina,' he said irritably.

'Hold on. I've only come to discuss it with you,' Cedric's mouth curved with a reptilian smile. 'I could bring you back any . . . ' He shrugged, as though he was offering a holiday souvenir instead of rare plant species some people might kill for. 'Something that might interest you.' He gave Delphina a conspiratorial smile as if to suggest he must humour her father.

His look filled her with contempt. How dare this man come here to humiliate her father when it was his fault that he was imprisoned in this chair? Before she could answer him, she heard the car door slam and a younger man came towards them. He was

11

tall and slender with thick blond hair, a duck-egg green scarf flung carelessly round his neck enhancing his slightly tanned skin. He walked towards them with an easy grace.

'This is my nephew Lorin Courtney,' Cedric said, as if they were all at an enjoyable party instead of in an angry little group on the lawn. 'He will be coming with me.'

'I want neither you, nor any member of your family to come here again. I ask you both to leave immediately,' Randolph ordered, not even bothering to look at the second man.

'Come, Uncle, let us go.' Lorin's voice was firm.

Carson snapped at Tom to take his place at the chair and began to push it towards the front door. Delphina put her hand on it too, but Lorin swiftly bent down and picked up the front of the chair saying, 'It's quicker if we carry it over the grass; it's hard going now it's so wet.'

'Put me down,' Randolph said, but at the same moment Carson said, 'Thank you, sir, that's very helpful.'

Delphina hovered around them, wanting to protest to save her father's pride, loathing Cedric for coming to gloat over his advantage over him.

As they passed the car there was a sudden commotion from inside. An enormous dog hurled itself at the sides and windows barking excitedly making Delphina jump. The dog, pushing against one of the doors that had not been closed securely, leapt out and, barking wildly, jumped round them.

With a reassuring smile, Lorin said, 'Don't worry he won't hurt you. Prince!' he called in a commanding voice. 'Here, boy!'

With great care he put down Randolph at the top of the steps by the front door then ran down them again calling the dog to heel.

Cedric said heartily, 'He's only young, just over friendly and been cooped up in that car too long.' The dog bounded up to lick him. Cedric picked up a piece of branch that had blown down in the wind. 'Fetch!' he called, throwing it away from him.

Prince yelped in delight and ran after it, bringing it back, lathering in anticipation of having it thrown for him again.

'Get me in, away from this circus,' Randolph said. Delphina saw how tired he was. His face was white as milk and he was shaking. His anger had drained him and he didn't want Cedric to see his weakness. She opened the door and Carson took him in.

Delphina stayed outside. She would ask Lorin to leave, sensing in him more consideration than his uncle possessed. She was just in time to see Cedric throw the proffered branch again, this time straight into the flowerbed that held the precious peony buds.

Before she was more than halfway down the steps, Prince had landed on the bed. Ely having just removed the planks was stacking them in his wheelbarrow. The dog's huge feet pounded the earth. He couldn't find the branch so he scratched frantically in the earth, thinking it under the ground.

'Stop it! Oh, please stop.' Delphina ran across the lawn, her feet sticking with every step in the wet earth. 'Come out, please come out of that flowerbed.'

'Get off you great brute.' Ely picked up his spade.

Lorin, seeing her dismay, ran after her, calling Prince to come to him.

She reached the flowerbed and sank down on her knees in the churned-up earth, searching with her eyes and fingers for the glowing red buds. She found them, snapped off by Prince's giant paws, lying there, useless now away from the root, which itself was now half out of the ground. She let out a low cry of pain. The precious plant that meant so much to her father in his diminished world was now completely destroyed.

Lorin saw at once what had happened. 'I'm

so sorry, were they very special?' His voice was concerned.

'Sorry Prince has messed up the garden; good thing he chose that bare patch. Still, your gardener will soon dig it over it again, won't you, old chap?' Cedric said jovially, coming over to them.

Anger seared through her, blocking out for the moment her agony of her father's pain when he learned of this violation. She sprang up, her face contorted with rage, her eyes sparkling like fire, her tawny hair falling about her flushed face. She cried out, 'Get off our land! Never, ever, come back here again.'

'My dear, how anger becomes you; what a fiery temper you have.' Cedric smiled as if to humour her, belittle her as an adult ridicules a child's tantrum.

In three steps she was on him; she wheeled back her hand and struck him full on the mouth. 'Go now, and don't you dare come back here to plague us again.'

She marched across the lawn not turning back, not wanting them to see the tears of sheer anger that were rising in her and threatening to spill over and course down her cheeks. Cedric had caused her father's accident and now he was responsible for breaking off the peony's buds, ruining the small signs of hope and new life that might have brought him comfort and excitement as he watched them grow. Her heart almost broke as she thought of how she would tell him.

Lorin was beside her, walking fast to keep up with her. 'I am so dreadfully sorry. Please tell me what kind of plant it was and I'll replace it.'

His voice calmed her a little, yet it did not stop her pain. Impatiently she wiped the tears from her face with the heel of her hand. 'The species is unnamed, it . . . ' Her voice died away as the thought caught her. Cedric Hartford must have come here to find out about the peony. Her father had told her how ruthless he was, how he stopped at nothing to steal from fellow plant hunters, urged on by huge sums paid to him by an unscrupulous benefactor. No doubt his nephew was in on it too, had come here to find out all that he could before they left for Tibet.

She took a deep breath and said as nonchalantly as she could, 'They are not the least important. But my father adores his plants. He has so little now to live for and was looking forward to seeing them bloom.' Her lips felt frozen as she spoke. Anyone remotely to do with Cedric was her enemy. 'So you can leave now. Goodbye.' She dismissed him curtly and ran up the steps to the front door shutting it firmly behind her.

She waited in the shadows of the hall, fighting to compose herself before going to her father to tell him of his plant's destruction. Cedric's arrival had caused him so much anger that another shock so soon might be too much for his system to cope with. Yet she couldn't hide it from him for long. All those months while he struggled to recover he'd waited for the moment that proved the roots held life, that he, despite his terrible fall had brought home a new species of peony. Now that he'd seen them growing, they'd given him something to hold on to, to restore his pride. Something to show that he was still one of the best plant hunters alive.

'You look all in, miss, let me get you some coffee.' Elsie, the maid, bustled past with a hot-water bottle. 'Must have been that dog, I said to cook, fancy bringing that great thing 'ere. Quite gave me a turn I can tell you, 'im bounding about like that.'

'I'm all right, Elsie, thank you.' She forced a smile.

The dog barked again and instinctively she glanced out of the window at the drive. Lorin had him by a leash, his strong arms controlling the beast's desire to run off again. At first sight he had seemed too slight but seeing him now his body tense against the straining dog she saw how he was like a dancer whose coiled muscles held an iron force. He turned and caught her gaze, but she jumped away from the window. She would not be seen staring at him like some soft-headed girl. He was Cedric's nephew and was going with him to find her father's plants. He would be as ruthless as he was.

She heard them get into the car, slam the doors and drive away.

For so many months now she had battled to save her father, to persuade him that broken and useless though his body was, he was still an important person in his field, even if he would never travel again.

Last January Randolph had set off for a trip to Tibet. She'd written the day in her diary and drawn a ring round it. January 3rd 1935. All her life he had disappeared on these trips, mostly to 'the triangle', Burma, China and Tibet, coming back with glowing descriptions of the savage beauty of the lands at the top of the world. Delphina was enthralled by his descriptions and, above all, his deep love for these far-off places and their people. She pored over his photographs trying to conjure up the true beauty of the great hills and mountains with their wealth of plants growing like weeds in the valleys and crevices, the flowers shining like bright jewels, bringing as much excitement to their finders as if indeed they were.

Her mother, Sophia, had not shared this enthusiasm. At her funeral, her sister Polly remarked to Delphina, 'I don't care what fancy names the doctors called her illness, Sophia died of a broken heart, pining for your father.'

'Oh Aunt Polly, that's not true,' Delphina had protested, but when she'd thought back she saw there was some truth in it. Her mother had adored Randolph. When he was home she sparkled, all beauty and gaiety, warming everyone around her with her glow, but when he had gone her light was extinguished. She closed in on herself. It was hard to say when her illness struck her. Gradually she became weaker and more listless until even when Randolph came home she could hardly rouse herself to greet him. She'd died two years ago when Delphina was eighteen.

She braced herself now to go to him to tell him of the devastation the dog had caused. As she relived that moment, she recalled Lorin's concern and a feeling of warmth crept unbidden into her, but she dismissed it angrily. How could she think he was kind being the nephew of that man who had caused her beloved papa to come home more dead than alive?

All the pent-up griefs and fears of the last few months crowded in on her: the day they brought her father home so weak and broken; his face, once so vital, now suddenly so old; his skin papery pale, with great ravages of pain cut into his cheeks; the terrible dead weight of his body. She wondered if it would not have been better if he had been killed, left to lie among the desolate beauty of the country he loved so much.

She thought of that now and the guilty realization that her freedom, too, had been curtailed. Kind and good though the servants were, it was her, Randolph looked for. Just as the door had opened after the death of her mother, and she'd been given a taste of freedom with parties and attentive friends, not to mention the interest of one or two young men, it had been slammed shut again and she must stay here confined with him. She hated herself for even thinking this when he, who had always been so free, was now trapped in his wheelchair, dependant on others, until he died.

But she couldn't go on putting off telling him about the destruction of his beloved plants. He might want to go out to the flowerbed again today to see them; she must tell him now. But perhaps they were not so bad, she thought with faint hope. She'd go and have a proper look though even as she went she accepted that she was just delaying having to tell him.

Ely, seeing her from the greenhouse where he was supervising Tom's cleaning of the flowerpots came out to join her. His face was grave, like a doctor with a depressing prognosis.

'Don't look good, miss. Dratted beast's claws tore into them badly.'

'Might they throw up new shoots?' She dreaded his answer.

Ely shrugged, sucked in his rosy cheeks. 'Wouldn't like to say, miss. There is one tiny shoot left but the root's 'ardly in the earth.' He shrugged again.

Delphina bent down and carefully looked under the straw. Ely had taken away the broken buds and the raw places on the root lay exposed. On one side there was a tiny rosy lump, barely more than a hint of a bud, but it was something. 'What do you think? Might this one grow and then next year the whole plant grow again?'

'Who knows, miss. It doesn't do to disturb the roots so, especially with a peony. We'll keep an eye on it. We can only wait and see. What does the master say?'

She averted her gaze from his concerned face. 'I haven't told him yet.'

'Bad business, miss, bringing an untrained brute like that to someone's 'ouse. Master didn't look none to pleased to see them men neither; not that there've been many visitors lately. Ah miss, it's a sad 'ouse now, what with your sweet mother gone and now this.'

'I know, Ely.' Delphina was touched by his expression. To cheer him and indeed herself up she said, 'But maybe that one tiny bud will shoot; we might get a peony after all.'

'That we might.' Ely did not sound convinced.

'I must go and tell him,' she said, with resolve, walking back over the lawn. She caught sight of a scarf lying on the drive. A picture of Lorin swam back into her mind as he'd walked towards them, this scarf round his neck. It must have fallen off in the scuffle with the dog. Mechanically she picked it up and unconsciously she held it to her face. A faint scent came from it; she felt her heart quicken then sense took over. How could she think anything of that man? She'd be playing straight into Cedric's hands. Perhaps he had brought him here to try and charm the whereabouts of her father's precious peony from her. She must not fall for that and betray Papa's secret. She was sure Cedric would stop at nothing to get what he wanted.

She let the scarf fall to the tips of her

fingers and carried it inside as if it was contaminated and hung it on a peg out of sight. Then, taking a deep breath, she forced herself to go into the dining-room to tell him.

'Where have you been? I hope not hanging round that odious man, his fawning nephew and that bloody brute of a dog.'

'They were dreadful; so rude to call just like that.'

'You can't expect better from his sort; the whole family are blackguards. That nephew will be just as bad, but I won't tell him where my plants are. He can go and look for himself.'

She struggled to find the words to tell him. He regarded her intently.

'Don't tell me that bloody dog savaged something in my garden,' he snapped, as if he could read her mind.

There was a sour taste in her mouth a sinking of her heart. 'I think we have to be patient a little while longer, Papa. The dog knocked off some of the peony buds, but there is one still there and . . . ' The words died as she saw the change in him.

Like a sudden storm, the anger whirled through him, deepening the creases in his face, darkening his eyes.

Delphina ran to him, putting her arms round him. 'Papa, please stay calm. There is

23

one bud left; it won't be wonderful this year, but it's still alive.'

Randolph began to shake, his eyes became glassy, his mouth clenched and unclenched as words coming out like cries of pain were wrenched from him.

She ran for the door and called for Carson.

'I'll ring for the doctor,' he said, his face ashen at the terrible sight of the rigid, twitching body of his master.

'Quickly, oh quickly.' Delphina loosened Randolph's collar, calling to him, begging him to come back from the hold of this seizure. If he died now she would hold Cedric Hartford and his whole family responsible for his death.

2

They dared not move Randolph from his chair. Carson stood behind the chair and held on to him to stop him falling on the floor. Delphina struggled to behave calmly as she fought to bring him back from his terrifying seizure. She was petrified that if she allowed the hysterics boiling in her to break through, it would hasten him to the grave.

Elsie, and Mrs Crane, the cook, fussed round with her.

'I'll get him a nice hot bottle,' Mrs Crane said, running as fast as her bulk would let her to her kitchen.

Elsie, hand clamped to her mouth as if to stop her screams from pouring from it, skittered about anxiously. One minute she brought a rug, another she proffered a glass of water, meaning well but more of a nuisance than a help.

Carson put his hand, then his ear to Randolph's chest.

'His heart seems strong enough,' he said.

'Is it a stroke?' The words were like blocks of wood in her mouth.

'I don't know, miss, the doctor will soon be here.'

Almost as he spoke, the sound of a car scrunching on the gravel and a motor dying came to them. Delphina sprang up and ran to the front door.

Her heart sank when she saw it was the doctor's son, Philip Stacy, getting out of the car. In her anguish she had no time to hide her dismay, and she saw a look of resignation cross his face. He had not been qualified long enough to prove how good a doctor he was. His father now in his sixties was renowned for his skill.

'Tell me what happened, Delphina,' Philip said gently.

'My father had a shock, a sort of fit . . . ' She stopped, too terrified of the seriousness of it to continue. He slipped his hand under her elbow and led her back into the house.

'Let me look at him,' he said calmly. 'Where is he?'

'In the dining-room. It happened there and we . . . '

He went straight into the room. He knew his way round the house as he had often dined here when her mother had been alive. Then he was studying to be a doctor and he'd come with other young friends to little dinner

26

parties her mother had insisted on giving for her.

'When I was young my house was filled with young people from dawn to dusk,' she'd boasted. 'Even if your father is not here, I want the house to be full of friends for you.' She liked Philip Stacy and seen how he looked at Delphina, admiration for her shining through his shyness.

'He'd be a good husband for you,' she'd said; then with a bitter curl to her mouth added, 'A doctor with a country practice does not travel to the edge of the world, leaving his wife alone for years at a time.'

Delphina followed Philip into the dining-room. Randolph had not moved. His head slumped, his limbs were clenched and stiff, his mouth open in a ghastly sneer, his eyes staring ahead as if dead. Carson stood aside but kept one hand on his shoulder in case he should fall. Philip opened his bag and began to take out instruments, all the time firing questions at them, his eyes never leaving Randolph's body. Then he began to examine him thoroughly, his hands guiding the instruments over him, listening, watching.

Delphina felt calmer as she observed him at work. He had qualified just before her mother had died and had only come to attend her with his father. But now she saw she need not be afraid, he was confident and in charge as he examined him.

At last he straightened and said to Delphina, 'He has had some form of seizure. It might soon pass, or it might have damaged his brain. We must get him to hospital.' He smiled at her reassuringly, but she felt as if blocks of ice were lining her stomach.

'No . . . ' she said, 'surely . . . ' She dared not put into words what she dreaded, as if giving life to them, they would come true. If they took him away, he might never come home again.

Philip understood her fears at once. 'Delphina, he needs skilful nursing that only trained people can give him. He needs more tests than I can give him here, so we can be sure how to treat him. His heartbeat is strong; do not give up hope.'

'It would be better, miss,' Carson took charge. 'I'll go and pack the master's case.'

'Philip, are you sure? Couldn't we get a nurse to come here?' The fear quivered in her voice.

'I am sure. Even my father would agree on that,' he said firmly. He squeezed her hand. 'Let me telephone the hospital, and try not to worry.'

When he had gone she went over to her father and wrapped her arms round his stiff frame. She could feel his heart beating against hers and the feeling comforted her.

'Papa,' she said, 'fight on, don't give up, please don't give up.' Yet even as she said the words, the truth, as painful as acid in her heart, came to her. Would it not be better for him if he died quietly now? Even though a short while ago she'd cried for her lost freedom, she wanted him to stay with her, even as this useless, broken body, imprisoned in a chair. But what of his feelings? His life now was so cruelly curbed by his paralysis. His only way of freedom was in death. Should she pray for him to recover from his seizure? Might he not be left worse, his mind unable to work?

Philip came back in to the room. 'An ambulance will be here soon.'

'Philip,' — her heart felt so heavy she felt it might fall through her body — 'he won't be . . . ' The words seemed to come from far away and it was difficult to choose the right ones. 'His mind will come back, won't it?'

'Delphina, let's get him to the hospital, then we can make plans.'

'You must only fight for him if his brain is undamaged. He would not want to live if that had gone.' Her voice had authority now. This battle she must fight for him. He must not be saved if his mind had gone.

'Come, Delphina, don't look on the black side,' Philip said, almost jovially, but in his eyes she could see he knew that her fears could be justified.

But, to her immense relief, just over a week later, Randolph was home again.

'If I am to die, then I will die at home,' he said, furious at being stuck in bed with nurses fussing round him. 'If only I could get out of this bed and leave you all. You will kill me here with all your treatments and your potions.'

Delphina though delighted to see his strength return, his mind undiminished, also felt guilty at his behaviour. During those first anxious hours the doctors and nurses had given her such reassurance and taken such care of him.

The staff nurse laughed at her apologies. 'It shows he's better. We don't take any notice.' She said more gently, 'The hard bit will be when you take him home. He'll not be an easy patient, but he should be kept calm, or it might happen again, and next time it might not have a happy ending.'

'I know,' Delphina said, 'I'm prepared for that.'

The day they took Randolph home was crisp and sharp.

'How are the peonies?' were his first words

as the car rounded the drive. He had not spoken of them since his seizure and Delphina had been dreading his questions.

'Well . . . it's early yet,' she said brightly.

'I wish to see them.' He fixed her with a penetrating gaze. 'Don't try and hide anything from me, Delphina. I lost the use of my body because of those plants. Yet the sight of them shining as if light was trapped in their petals like some Holy Grail, will never leave me. I want to know what has happened to them.'

'They don't look too good,' she said hesitantly, as if her words would throw his brain back into seizure. 'It seems — '

'Tell me straight out, girl,' he demanded. 'Don't fob me off with false hopes as if I was senile.'

'No, Papa. I don't want to upset you again.'

'Naturally I'm upset with that bloody man barging in here, coming to gloat over my disability. But tell me now, I insist upon it.'

She said fearfully as if each word was a knife to wound him. 'That dog must have damaged the roots, they haven't grown and the one tiny bud left has shrivelled and died. Ely wants to leave them in case next year . . . '

Randolph did not speak. He sat in the back of the car, staring ahead. Then he said slowly,

'Before I die I must see them growing again.'

'Maybe another plant hunter has found them, brought them back. Couldn't you find out from your colleagues at Kew?'

Randolph pulled himself back from his thoughts. 'I haven't heard of it,' he said. Then his face clenched, his eyes went steely and hard; his chin jutted out with determination. 'I will see them again before I die. I will bring them back, have them growing here.'

Carson opened the car door. 'Welcome home, sir.'

'Yes, Papa,' Delphina said soothingly, helping Carson to ease him out and into his chair.

'I will get them here some way or another,' he repeated firmly.

Delphina smiled at him. 'You have come home,' she said, 'enjoy that for now. I'm so happy you're back, Papa.' She kissed him, holding his hand as Carson wheeled him inside.

The days drifted on. Randolph seemed to spend a lot of the time deep in thought. Delphina, thinking he was perhaps reflecting on his second close call with death, tried to lighten it by suggesting she read to him.

'No, my dear, not just now,' he kept putting her off.

One morning when she came into the

study where he sat, he stared at her intently as if he was examining her, feature by feature, as if he was trying to recognize her, as someone once known.

A prickle of alarm touched her. 'What is it, Papa? Why do you stare at me so?' Had his mind been touched after all?

'Oh . . . sorry, my dear.' His smile was vague. 'It was just . . . well, you must go outside more; you look pale. You've been too much indoors with me. Do you still ride?'

'I have no horse,' she laughed. 'We sold Mermaid when mother was ill, and I hadn't enough time to ride her.'

'Then I come back broken to bits and useless. My poor child, what a life you have had, tied to one or the other of your parents. We should have had a houseful of children.' He looked sad, then before she could answer, said, 'Your mother should have stayed alive; how she would have enjoyed seeing me confined like this. Then she could have owned me completely.'

'Papa, she would have hated to see you so,' Delphina protested.

'She always wanted to keep me by her side, smother me with her love. But . . . ' he sighed. 'How beautiful she was, and how I loved her, but I should never have married her for I needed to be free.'

'You kept your freedom; you were always away.' Delphina thought of how her mother had faded, wilted like a flower without water when he had gone.

'I did, but it killed her. Didn't it?' He looked directly at her.

'Yes,' she said, 'I believe it did, or anyway Aunt Polly thought so.'

He sighed. 'Never let that happen to you, Delphina. Never have nothing in your life but a man. Whoever he is, he will let you down.'

She smiled wryly. 'Watching Mother all those years, I promised myself I'd never be caught like she was. She should have gone with you on some trips.'

'She would have hated it. It would have been too hard for her, the rain, the cold, and the sheer physical hardship. She could not have borne it. She belonged to the drawing-room, the bedroom. She was so beautiful, so fragile, like a hothouse plant,' he smiled sadly.

'I'm not like that,' Delphina said.

'No . . . ' he studied her intently again, 'I don't think you are. You have her beauty, but not her fragile character.' He fell into a muse again, staring out into the garden. Then, almost as an afterthought, he said, 'Richard Stacy has a horse he'll lend you, get you out a bit.'

When Richard Stacy, Philip's father visited

her father later that day, he agreed at once to lend her his wife's horse while she was away with her sick mother.

The horse was a grey, called Prima Donna, she had an intelligent face and a good character. Delphina was thrilled with her.

She rode most days, loving the pearly light of the early morning, the sharp yellow sun breaking through the cloud. It was spring now and the countryside was coming to life again. She rode over the fields of the farmer's land adjoining their few acres and up to Aurian Hall, the large, now empty property of the Ashburns. The family had died out; the only son had returned from the Great War a broken man and had shot himself, his aged parents dying soon after.

Lady Ashburn had often invited her over with her mother and had told her she could ride on their land whenever she wished.

She reached the wall surrounding the estate and looked in to the silent wood. No one rode there now. She'd heard that someone kept a vague eye on the property.

As she rode past the wall, she saw a part of it had crumbled. It was covered with ivy and undergrowth but it would not be difficult to pass through. She reined in Prima and sat looking at it. She longed to ride once more through those woods and along the path by the river. She'd do no harm; she couldn't resist going in to see how this once beautiful place fared now it was empty and deserted.

'Come on, Prima.' She persuaded her to go over the broken wall. They went through the woods, Prima's feet soft against the decaying leaves on the ground, there was the gleam of the river through the trees, then there was the house. It was white with sweeping steps and long pillars by the door. Its long windows looked out like dead eyes into the overgrown garden making her sad. Once the house had always been a hive of life, now everyone had gone.

She reached the river with its small stone bridge in full view of the house. The river curved sharply round, meandering on. She followed it, the silence of the deserted place creeping over her like a mist. The shrubberies, once pristine and cared for, now lay bedraggled and forgotten. Then, suddenly, up from the bank close to her came the figure of a man. Both surprised the other, Prima skitted about snorting down her nostrils; only Delphina's quick reaction to calm her, stopped her from taking to her heels.

As he approached her, she saw that it was Lorin Courtney, Cedric Hartford's nephew, her father's enemy.

She tensed, searching round for Cedric

36

Hartford who would surely appear at any moment.

'It's you, Miss Graveson,' Lorin said. 'What a beautiful mare.' He laid his hand on Prima's neck and she nuzzled her nose in the crook of his arm.

'Good morning.' She didn't look at him, waiting with coiled hatred for Cedric to appear.

'Do you often ride here?' His voice was pleasant and despite herself she felt herself softening towards him.

'No,' she answered shortly, still keeping a look-out for Cedric. Why were they still in the district? She was about to ask him this when he said, 'Do you know the property well, and the house?'

'Quite well. My mother and I, and my father if he was here, were often invited. The Ashburns loved to fill the house with people but now ... ' Her voice trailed off not wanting to give too much of herself away.

'It's so tragic, their only son dying like that.' He paused, watching her intently. 'I wonder, well, I suppose it's a dreadful imposition, if you could show me round the house, as you used to know it.'

She looked at him sharply. 'Show you round?'

'Yes.' He dangled a key in front of her. 'I've

permission from the estate agent to look round. My car's round the back, I was just looking at the river, to see if there were any fish.' He smiled. 'But seeing you here is a bonus. I really would appreciate it if you would bring it to life for me, tell me about the parties, the people who lived here.'

He looked so eager and there was such friendliness in his eyes she hesitated a moment before she said, 'No, I can't, I must get back to my father.' But the gleam of the key in his hand caught her curiosity, and she couldn't resist asking 'Why have you got the key? Surely you're not going to buy it?'

'I don't know, my uncle . . . '

Uncle — that unpleasant man. She wasn't going to show him around it. She drew up her reins and would have ridden off had he not stopped her.

'I was going to say my uncle is not here; he's in London. I stayed here to look at a couple of properties.' As she said nothing, he continued, 'I could see . . . that day we met at your house, that your father disliked him, and for that I'm sorry.'

'Don't be,' she blazed, 'we're not.'

'I'm also sorry my dog ruined your plants,' he went on, speaking through her anger. 'I've been meaning to contact you and ask what they were so I could replace them.'

38

'It's not so easy.' Her voice was hard. 'You can't just go to some nursery, or order them by post.'

'Tell me then where I can get them. You said they were not special, but I think they were. I will go anywhere to fetch them for you.' His grey eyes were soft as he regarded her and the concern in them intrigued her. It was so long since any man, except for Philip Stacy whom she hardly counted, had looked at her like that.

But she must not be side tracked; she cried out, 'And bring the feeling back to my father's limbs? No, you can never do that. They are gone for ever and so are the plants.' The words were wrenched from her with anguish.

'I will get them for you. I cannot cure your father, but I will get you the plants. Tell me their name and I will get them.' He leant close to her. The wind caught his hair blowing it over his face; impatiently he pushed it back smiling at her, his eyes shining.

The warmth of his look touched her, glowing through her, he was after all an attractive man. But suspicion soon followed. Cedric Hartford wanted to know where her father had found the peony. Her father had told her stories of Cedric being in league with a millionaire collector who paid well for new, rare species of plants for his gardens. Surely Lorin was in league with him too. To buy a property such as this would need money, not the sort of money an ordinary plant hunter earned. She must be on her guard; no doubt Lorin was trying to prize the information of her father's find from her.

'I don't wish to discuss it further,' she said coldly, moving to turn Prima round and leave.

Lorin laughed. 'I'm not trying to find out where they are and go and steal them, getting credit for finding them.'

'Maybe you wouldn't, but your uncle would; he would do anything to get what he wanted.'

He looked at her gravely. 'I wouldn't, nor would I tell him anything about them. I just want to replace them for you. It upset me to see how distressed you were.'

She wished she could hate him, kick him away with her boot and gallop away from him. 'I'll tell no one,' she said firmly, 'no one at all.'

'As you wish, but now,' — he smiled cheerfully at her — 'please, if you've time show me round the house. Don't let your father's feud with my uncle spoil a friendship between us.'

'We will not see each other enough for a friendship,' she retorted, though her voice was softer. She longed to see inside Aurian Hall again. It had been so beautiful once.

'If I buy this house we'll be near neighbours,' Lorin said, amusement playing in his eyes.

Dismay filled her. 'But would you live here alone, or with your wife? Or would your uncle live here too?' Having Cedric so close would surely kill her father.

'I have no wife, no family, apart from my sister and uncle.'

'He can't live here; it would kill my father; he can't . . . ' Her voice was panic-stricken.

Lorin looked puzzled at her anguish. Seeing his expression, she cried out childishly, 'I will not show you the house, you cannot buy it. It is not for you.'

'I have only spent time with my uncle recently so know little of his life. He is planning this trip to Tibet and I jumped at the chance to go with him. I have always been interested in plants, but please, tell me why does your father hate him so?' He frowned a little as he waited for her answer.

'Because he is a bad plant hunter. He steals from other people. He came upon my father on his last trip and in trying to take some plants from him caused his accident, making

41

him a cripple. A cripple, do you hear? You saw him, he will never walk again, never go back to his beloved Himalayas; never see the plants he loves growing in their natural habitat. Can you imagine what that means to him, a man who always loved to travel, now stuck in a chair forever?' Her eyes blazed at Lorin with such hatred that he recoiled. She whipped up the reins and would have ridden away, but his hand shot out and he caught the bridle, talking softly to Prima, to steady her.

'And you take that out on me?'

'Yes, and all of your accursed family.'

Lorin's mouth tightened. His eyes became darker.

'It is unjust of you to blame us all.'

She stared back at him; seeing the hurt and anger in his eyes. She said, 'What he has done will never be forgiven. You cannot live here, so close to us. It would kill my father.'

'Look,' Lorin said, his voice measured, 'I don't know if I'm going to buy this place or one of the others I have seen elsewhere. I just want to look over it. I would be grateful if you would come round the house with me, bring it to life for me. Forget my uncle; he is not here: it is only you and I.'

'I cannot forget him. I live every day with the tragedy he caused my father. But I admit' — her face relaxed — 'I am curious about the house so I will come with you. But I beg you' — her expression was stern — 'do not buy this house and let your uncle come here.'

'I don't live with my uncle. Besides, as I told you, we are soon to go away on a plant-hunting trip so I might not buy anything before I go. Besides . . . ' — there was a glint of bravado in his eyes — 'I've been told the trips are fraught with dangers and hardship. I might not come back at all, so the problem of me living here might not arise.'

3

The massive front door of Aurian Hall opened with a reluctant creak as if it was despondent in its loneliness and could not be bothered to open to the world again.

Delphina entered almost reverently as if it was a tomb and she must not disturb the dead. The vast hall stretched ahead, the staircase ending in two large curls of dark mahogany in front of her. The floors without their rich rugs, and the windows, naked without curtains, added to the desolation, the sound of their footsteps on the bare boards echoing in the emptiness. It was a house that needed people and the feeling of loss hung as thick as the matted cobwebs in the corners and laced through the banisters.

Lorin shivered. 'How sad and lost this house feels. Tell me what it was like before.'

She stood at the foot of the stairs. Either side of the staircase ran a wide passage with doors of gleaming wood that opened into other rooms.

'It was furnished with wonderful furniture collected over the centuries, yet each piece fitted here as if it had been made for it. There were rich-coloured curtains, faded rather, but,' she smiled, 'I think the Ashburns considered it bad taste to buy new ones, or perhaps they'd rather have spent the money on other things.'

'I've noticed that so many of the aristocracy are like that. They live surrounded by priceless furniture and pictures while the rest of the place is getting shabby.'

'It was like that, but you didn't really notice. There were flowers everywhere. The gardens were wonderful and there were huge bowls of roses there.' She pointed to the middle of the hall. 'There was a large table always with a vase of flowers on it, then two smaller tables just here by the stairs with more. There was always their fragrance and the scent of wood smoke and the cold, musty smell of stone.' She sniffed to see if it still lingered there. 'No, it is gone, though I can still smell the cold stone.'

She shivered and he said, 'Are you cold? It is very damp here.'

'Not really it's just, I feel the desolation of loss, of death here. It may sound strange, but it makes me feel how insignificant we are, and yet how hopeful. Houses like this are built, loved and worked at for generation after generation, and then a cruel trick of fate destroys it all. Henry, the heir, came back

45

from the war supposedly not wounded, but it killed him after all. Now it is all gone.' She turned to him as if she wanted an explanation.

He said, 'Life has always been like that, from the very start of it. Look how many empires are now dust.'

'So here we are at the collapse of a tiny empire, the end of the Ashburn line.' She tried to shake off the gloom that crept over her.

She went into the empty drawing-room, almost barrack like without its furniture and thick curtains. She went over to one of the windows and looked out into the garden. Once there had been a neat path with crisply cut grass either side, going down to a huge stone urn overflowing with plants. Now grass and weeds had eaten into the path and the urn stood empty.

'Tell me about the furniture in here,' Lorin said looking at the stained walls. The pale yellow silk on the walls was now streaked with damp.

Delphina thought a moment. 'It was a blue and yellow room, the colours of summer. With light furniture. There were two silk-covered sofas facing each other there, a long table behind.' As she continued her description she could see the life in the room, the women in their elegant clothes, the men in their tweed plus fours coming in from shooting, their faces red from the wind, rubbing their hands before the roaring fire. The women becoming animated at their entrance, looking up with bright faces from their tapestry, or their skimming through a magazine. The dogs creeping in before their coats were dry, hoping if they looked at no one, no one would see them.

As she spoke, bringing the room to life again, she didn't notice Lorin. He leant against the fireplace totally absorbed in her. He saw all traces of tension and anger slip from her face, saw the smiles in her eyes, her wide mouth laughing as she described the people who used to be here. He was captivated.

A wind whistled, shaking the glass in the windows, and abruptly she stopped. For a second she seemed disorientated as if not knowing where she was, where the people she had conjured up had gone. Then, seeing Lorin watching her with such attention, she laughed quickly, and said, 'So there it is, all I can remember. I must go now or my father will worry about me.'

Lorin regarded her as if he was etching her face forever in his mind.

'Goodbye then.' Why did she feel reluctant

to leave him? But it was not him, only the ghosts she had conjured up reluctant to go back to obscurity again.

'I'll come with you.' He didn't add the place would die without her and fill him with depression.

'But you haven't seen upstairs.' She suddenly wanted to be away from him. For a moment she had been lulled into forgetting who he was and she was in danger of being tempted into sharing confidences.

'I've seen enough. We will leave together. Thank you for your time.' He was strangely formal and his voice had a coldness about it that made her feel as if she had been doused in icy water.

'So, will you buy it?' she asked abruptly.

'I don't know, it may not be for me.' He followed her down the passage into the hall and outside into the early spring sun.

'Who is it for then?' Was it for his despicable uncle? Why had she been such a fool as to show him round? But it would cost a huge amount just to put right, let alone run, so how had Cedric got hold of so much money? Had that millionaire who paid him to find him plants offered him a fortune to find him more? To find him something special, her father's peony?

'Do you like it?' Lorin asked.

She squinted at him from under her lashes. That was it, it would be bought with blood money, money for finding that peony. She must guard herself against Lorin's charm.

'What does it matter what *I* think?' She turned from him, going towards Prima who was happily eating through the lawn.

He said quietly, 'You made it come alive for me; I might not be able to do it on my own.'

A whiplash of elation surged through her. He stood close to her, his hand on Prima's rein. His eyes seemed to draw her to him. It was a pleasant feeling, evoking sensations in her rarely felt, subdued under the caring routine of her days.

Prima lifted her head and snorted, dancing on her feet trying to pull away from her tether.

'May I see you again, Delphina?' His eyes lingered on her mouth. He bent forward a fraction, and for one mad moment she thought he would kiss her but the image of Cedric Hartford strutting over the lawn to her enraged father came to her and her hatred for him seeped back into her. She stepped back.

'No, I don't think so.'

'Is it because of my uncle?'

She looked at him squarely. 'Yes, and for that I tell you this house is not for you or for him. You asked me what I thought and I say you will not be happy here.'

'Delphina.' He took her hand, and though she tried to pull it away she did not try very hard and it lay a moment in his.

'I feel close to you and, if you are honest, I think you feel the same way. Your feelings for my uncle must not sour what might grow between us.' He spoke earnestly and a moment of happiness pierced her, but then, like a maggot in her flesh the picture of Cedric came to her again.

'It would not work. An uncle is too close a relative,' she said, almost adding 'an uncle such as yours.' She turned towards Prima, letting down the stirrup. 'Give me a leg up please.'

'Won't you give us a chance?' He stood so close to her she could feel the warmth of him. She closed her eyes, feeling a sudden dizziness.

'No,' she said firmly, keeping herself turned towards Prima. 'Now give me a leg up please, I must go home.'

'Are you to let the quarrel between two older men come between a friendship between us?'

She turned then her anger whipped up by his remark. 'The quarrel, as you call it, has changed my life, too. How do you think I feel seeing my father who was such a fine figure of a man, reduced to a cripple? Every day I see his pain, his frustration. His suffering is my suffering. Are you so insensitive as to imagine that we can see each other openly, ever be friends? We would have to meet in secret, as if we were engaging in some sordid affair. No, there is no point in us seeing each other again.'

Lorin stayed silent, studying her face with careful scrutiny, as if giving his whole attention to every curve of her face, every faceted colour in her eyes, each gleaming hair on her head. Then, when she turned back to mount Prima, he took her leg and pushed her up, feeling her spring away from him on to Prima's back.

'Goodbye,' she said, and dug her heels into Prima's side and cantered away.

As she rode, a hundred emotions chased themselves through her. Never before had she felt so attracted to a man as she had to Lorin. She tossed her head with the stupidity of her thoughts. She was being fanciful. It was going back into Aurian Hall with all its memories that had turned her wits. Cedric, having stolen the pressed peony the day of Randolph's accident, and having seen her anguish when his dog had destroyed the roots, had put the two incidents together and guessed it was a new species her father had somehow managed to bring back. Not daring to come back himself, he would use Lorin to seduce her, to discover where her father had found the peony.

It began to rain, the sun completely banished behind dark clouds. Delphina urged Prima homewards. She was soaked when she reached home and after seeing Prima was rubbed down she went into the house, half expecting her father to call her and ask why she had been so long. Instead all was quiet.

For a moment the change in the atmosphere filled her with a fear that her father had become ill again. To reassure herself she went to the door of his study and called.

'I'm wet through, Father, from the rain; I'll be down when I've changed.'

'Mmm, fine,' his voice sounded preoccupied and she popped her head round to door to see what he was doing. The special table on wheels that Carson had had made for him was pulled over his legs. Laid out on it were some papers. Carson sat beside him taking notes.

'What are you doing?' She came into the room surprised, yet pleased to see him so occupied.

'I'm busy, my dear, I'll speak to you later.'

'I can see that you are.' She went over to him and looked over his shoulder. The top paper was a map; she leant over it and read out Shen, Hsi, Lung Jo, Tibet. 'Papa,' she laughed, before almost crying. For a second she'd forgotten he was paralyzed. It was like the old days when he laid out maps while planning a trip. She kissed him sadly, her heart too full to say anymore.

If he guessed her thoughts he did not mention the maps but said, 'You feel wet, my dear, were you riding in the rain?'

'Yes.' She straightened. 'I'm just going to change. Then would you like me to help you?' She forced a brightness to her voice. Whatever game this was she would play it to her utmost. If he wanted to plan a trip, or to retrace his old ones she would enter into it with him. Once he showed interest in a trip, accepting that he would never make one again, surely he would be happier?

'Not just now.' His voice was far away. She remembered that from childhood, how he became totally absorbed in his plans as if he was already far from them, and they had ceased to exist. It made her feel excluded, just as it had when she was a child.

'As you wish. Let me know when you want me.'

She went upstairs, but instead of feeling

free, glad she could put the time to her own use, she felt lost.

Randolph and Carson spent many more days so occupied. At meal-times Randolph was distant, hardly speaking to her, his mind elsewhere, just as he used to be before his accident when he was working on a trip.

'What is he doing, Carson?' Delphina asked, when she caught him alone.

'I can't tell you, miss.' Carson smiled at her apologetically. 'He will tell you in his own time.'

'But, Carson — '

'Not now, miss, excuse me.' His old face was expressionless. She knew she'd get nothing out of him. He and Randolph had come back from the war together with a strong bond between them. She suspected one had saved the other's life. Carson would rather die than betray his master, even by so much as a hint.

The days passed and she continued riding. She would not admit to herself that she hoped to see Lorin again. She was annoyed with herself for making so much of him, but he had taken over her thoughts and visited her in dreams. She had met him by chance at Aurian Hall, but she was convinced Cedric had made him stay in the district to spy on her.

She was on her way upstairs one afternoon when Carson came out from her father's study.

'Miss, your father wants to see you directly.'

'Nothing is wrong is there?' Carson seemed unusually grave.

'No. He is impatient to see you.'

She went into the study. Randolph looked up and smiled at her.

'Delphina.' He gestured her to sit down. The maps were neatly folded on one side, a habit he had when his planning was finished.

'I have a proposition for you, a favour if you like.'

'What is it, Papa?'

'I want my peony; I want it here so I can watch it grow. I want you to go and get it for me.'

'Me,' she laughed. 'Oh, Papa, how can I go? I don't know the first thing about plant hunting. Who would I go with?' she humoured him.

'I have worked it all out. Of course you can't go alone. An old friend of mine, Arnold North is about to go on a trip to Tibet, where I found my peonies. He has agreed to take you with him.'

'But Papa I can't . . . I mean . . . ' He must have lost his mind.

Randolph smiled. 'Don't worry, my darling, it will all be above board. We thought it best if you both married, so your reputation — '

'Marry him, Papa? Are you mad? I will not . . . '

'Calm down. You won't . . . ' He looked awkward. 'It will be a marriage in name only. Arnold — ' He became acutely embarrassed. 'I won't go into details, but after an accident there is no way he will . . . bother you in that way. You will be perfectly safe with him. It is all arranged, my dear. I know you won't let me down.'

4

'I just don't believe it, Papa.' Delphina fought to control her raging feelings of panic and despair. Papa had gone mad, something must have snapped in his brain giving him these preposterous ideas.

'If you had been a boy I would have taken you plant hunting with me already.' A fire shone in his eyes. 'You can't believe it, Delphina, being up there under the eaves of the world. The beauty, the sensation of life, of nature, the flowers growing in such profusion, with such glowing, intense colours. How ever pretty a garden, how ever magnificent a bloom we see here, it is nothing compared to seeing them growing freely in their native soil.' His whole face was alight with vitality, certain that his excitement would chase her objections out of the way.

'I know all that, Papa, you've often told me about it. I might like to go, but not like this . . . ' — she frowned at him — 'without any warning, and your ridiculous idea of marrying an . . . ' she paused, not wanting to be offensive, but her temper got the better of her, 'an old man. It's out of the question. You know it is. Anyway, you can't fix a marriage just like that.'

Randolph seemed not to notice her anger. 'This will suffice for our purposes. I know I'll never go back, but I want you, I ask you, beg you, to go there for me. You are so much more like me than like your dear mother. I can see, feel the restlessness in you. You'll love it out there, become as keen on it as I am. It is right that *you* will bring back my peony. After all,' — he smiled at her proudly — 'you are the only person in all the world that I can trust.'

'But your friend, this . . . Arnold North, surely he will bring it back for you?'

'Arnold is a good man, one of the best. And don't think' — his voice became grave — 'that even in my determination to see my peony again I would entrust you to a scoundrel, but like all of us, Arnold works for his living, and precious little he gets for it. So if someone else offered him a large sum of money to get information from him, he might . . . ' He tailed off, fixing her with his piercing eyes. 'No, my darling, you must go. I will tell you where I saw it growing. You will bring it back to me.'

'I can't,' she said firmly, standing tall and defiant before him. 'I'm sorry, Papa, but I can't possibly go.'

'Are you afraid?' He had determined that she should go. He'd expected a little opposition from her, but nothing she could say would shift his plans.

'No . . . but — '

'I would like to have been the one to take you.' His voice cracked, angry that he could never take her now. Angry that he had to depend upon her to go for him. He'd been so used to setting off himself without a backward thought for anyone. 'As I cannot, will never go back,' — anger and pain bunched on his face — 'I must do the next best thing and send my child. If you were a boy,' he said, glaring at her, 'then you would go.'

'I do not wish to marry your friend, however it is done!' she said angrily.

'You cannot go without marrying him. What would your mother have said, and her smart relations?' There was a sneer to his voice. He knew Sophia's family had never approved of her marrying a humble plant hunter.

'I shouldn't care what they think. Besides you never have, so why start now?' Delphina retorted.

'I care what they think about you. If . . . ' he paused, 'When I die, you might have to be dependent on them. You and Arnold will be married. I promise you it will be just a legal formality, not a binding marriage. He is a kind man, a fascinating man. You could not find a better companion for the trip, and I promise you,' — his voice softened — 'he will not touch you. When you get back, the so called marriage will be annulled, he has agreed to that.'

'It is a ridiculous idea.'

'You will go for me, please, Delphina.' There was a catch in his throat and she saw his eyes were bright with tears. 'You cannot know what it was like when I saw those peonies; it was like a heavenly vision.' He paused. 'Scoff if you will, but until you have been there yourself, you cannot understand. I want to see those peonies again. That bastard Hartford, with his dog.' His face went dark. 'It is him you can blame for this. His dog killed my plants, and he all but killed me. Do it for me, Delphina, I beg of you.'

It was the first time in her life he had pleaded with her. The first time, even in the worst of his depression at his injury, he had shelved his pride and was begging her.

'You will go for me won't you, Delphina?' Randolph laughed hoarsely, as if to cover up his longing. 'I know you want to be free. First your mother kept you here with her illness,

60

then me. You need to be free, and this is your chance.'

'Maybe, Papa, but not this way, not this sort of freedom.'

'You will go, Delphina, you'll go for me,' he said firmly.

'I will think about it, tell you tomorrow.' She smiled to humour him, hoping to escape from the room, lie low until he had seen what a ridiculous idea it was.

'Not tomorrow. There isn't time. Arnold leaves next week. He's coming down tonight and bringing a lawyer. It's only a marriage to the outside world. I've persuaded someone I know in the Foreign Office to produce the right papers for travelling.'

'Tonight!' Her voice was shrill with panic. 'I won't do it, not just like that.'

'There is not much time. He must leave next week. It is good of him to spare the time to come here at all,' Randolph said calmly, as if he was suggesting a minor formality instead of her signing herself away in this bogus marriage to a man she'd never met.

'What's in this for him?' she cried out angrily.

Randolph said airily, 'He owes me a favour. That's all. Now my dear, think of it as an adventure. If only it was me going. My God, I'd give my life if it could be me.' He broke down, bent his head, tried to cover his face with his almost useless hands, but he could not hold them there, they kept falling back on his lap, revealing the humiliation of his tears running down his cheeks.

Delphina was appalled. Never, ever had she seen him cry before, not even at her mother's death. She put her arms round him. 'Papa, you're not well, let me get the doctor.' That was it, she thought, his attack had weakened his brain, made him have these ridiculous ideas. She must call Carson, tell him to put off this man, fetch the doctor.

Randolph took hold of himself, lifted up his head. He looked straight into her eyes. 'You will go,' he said, his voice hard, 'you will go for me and bring back the peony. You'll thank me for sending you to Tibet, for nowhere in the world is more beautiful, nowhere do you feel nearer to Heaven. You'll see that whatever man can create, however clever, however beautiful it is nothing compared to nature. It will touch your life as nothing else can, and it will be richer because of it. Take it, as the best gift I can give you.' His voice was quiet now, reverent, the fire gone from it. His face folded into the creases of an old man. Delphina saw as suddenly as if he had donned a mask and was impersonating old age, that he was indeed old. It frightened her.

'Papa, I will go, but I will not pretend to be your friend's wife. It is too risky, besides I'm sure,' she laughed weakly, 'he doesn't want to marry me.'

Randolph looked at her, lifting his lids as if they were a great weight, then he smiled. 'It will be nothing but a legal formality to protect your reputation. When you come back you can marry whoever you choose.' He laughed. 'I've seen that rascal Philip Stacy's eyes on you. I think he makes so many visits to me as an excuse to see you. I'll explain the situation to him, don't you worry. He'll wait for you, you'll see.'

'But I don't want to marry Philip, I want to . . . ' and in her mind there came an image of Lorin Courtney and she cringed at the thought of what her father would say if he could know of whom she thought. Then the doorbell rang, making her jump. She turned to Randolph with agonized eyes.

'Who is that?'

'It will be Arnold; run, my dear, and change out of your riding clothes.' He looked excited now, his face a little pink, a sparkle in his eyes.

'No I will not,' she said defiantly. 'There is no need for me to pretty myself for such a man.'

Randolph did not seem to hear her, his whole being was concentrated on the door. It opened and two men came in. One was thin, grey-haired with skin like tissue paper. He was soberly dressed in a dark suit. The other man was in his late forties, a tall, solid man with a shock of greying, dark hair and side burns on his cheeks. His complexion was ruddy, his eyes black, his nose too large, as was his mouth, and once again she found herself thinking of Lorin and the comparison of the two men made her shiver with revulsion. She could not possibly be alone with this man on such a journey. Yet even as she looked at him she saw that his ugliness gave his face character, it split open with a smile as he greeted Randolph.

'It's good to see you, Randolph.' His voice was rich and melodious. He clasped Randolph's hand, taking it up from where it lay almost useless and holding it in his own. 'I have brought Quentin Farrar.' The other man stepped forward and gave a small bow.

'Thank you for coming, Arnold,' Randolph said.

'I'm pleased I can help you.' He smiled down at him. 'Or I hope I can, you know how elusive these plants can be.'

'It will be there, I'm sure of it,' Randolph said; then in a louder voice, 'This is my daughter Delphina.'

He could not move round in his chair and she had gone to the window, as if it held some means of escape. But the instinct of good manners bade her come forward and hold out her hand.

Arnold hardly looked at her, he took her hand briefly, muttering, 'How do you do,' then introduced his companion.

Delphina wondered if the idea of this marriage was as repugnant to him as it was to her. If so, she might persuade him to oppose her father in that.

'Would you like to go to your rooms?' Randolph asked, making Delphina feel as if she was neglecting her duties as a hostess.

'No . . . thank you,' Arnold said, 'let us get straight down to the plans. I only have this evening.'

'Of course. Copies of the maps you already have. I shall tell Delphina where the peonies are. I'm sorry to be so secretive but . . . '

'Don't worry, my dear fellow; tell her where they are and she can find them, bring them back to you.' He still did not look at her and she began to feel awkward. Perhaps he hated women and was annoyed and bored to have to take her with him.

'Bring me those papers, Delphina.' He gestured to the desk with a slight inclination of his head. 'Perhaps you would like to look through these, Mr Farrar?'

Delphina could bear no more.

'Papa.' She stepped out of the shadows and stood over him. 'I'm sure I could go on this trip with Mr North without going to such lengths.'

Then Arnold North looked at her. He got up from his chair and came over to her where she stood at the window. His voice was very gentle. 'We must appear to be married. There will be no question of me claiming anything from you, but it will make it easier when we travel, and also,' he smiled now, kindly, 'if I should die on the trip then all the plants, including your father's peony will go to you.'

'It seems too far fetched to me,' she said, grumpily, but somehow his voice had calmed her, quenched the angry feeling of outrage in her, but determined not to give in so easily, she said, 'plants are not like jewels or money, they belong to no one.'

'Your father wants to protect his property. If I should die then you can say they belong to you and can keep everything. Otherwise unscrupulous people, other plant hunters whom we might meet, might take everything if I am dead.'

'They might anyway, or I might die. Is it so dangerous?' She was not convinced it would be so easy to pull this off.

'Nobody knows what will happen, but it is only sensible that we take every precaution,' Arnold said.

'These other plant hunters, is the place littered with them? How will they know what we have?'

Arnold said, 'I need not tell you there are people in the profession who would do anything to steal another plant hunter's finds.'

Then he turned to Randolph, 'You should have told her sooner, she can hardly be expected to accept all this at a moment's notice.'

'She's never here, always out on her horse,' Randolph said defiantly.

'You could have told me about it before.' Delphina was angry with him for his selfishness. He was using her, and he knew it. If he'd told her before it would have given her chance to get out of it, to escape.

'Randolph, I will not take her if she does not want to come. It is not fair on her. I may have misunderstood you, but I thought you said that she wanted to come. You must trust me to bring back your plant, myself.'

The room went very quiet. The light had gone from the day and the grey dusk filled the room giving it a sinister look. The lawyer stayed impassive, as if immune to such situations. Arnold stood still, staring at Randolph, the bulk and strength of him somehow diminishing Randolph.

But as she looked at Randolph, his eyes boring into her as if they were the only live thing about him, she felt again the fear of losing him. That old fear of displeasing him. All her life she'd worshipped him, waiting for his return, yearning to be noticed by him. If she refused his wish, his most fervent wish, his anger might seize him again and he might die. If he had been his old self, strong and healthy, a man built to withstand any amount of shocks and rebellion, she would have defied him. But now, in the face of his broken, twisted body, his never-ending struggle to hold on to what little power he had, she could not refuse him. With sickening clarity she knew there was no choice.

'I know I have no choice but to go,' she said sourly.

'Randolph, I cannot, will not take her unless she really wants to come. You know how arduous these trips are. I cannot be responsible for — '

'I know.' Randolph turned to Delphina, his eyes hard. 'You will go,' he said, 'and accept it with good will, or your indifference will put everyone's lives in danger. We have no time to lose as I've heard that monster Cedric has been seen around here. I've had Ely move the roots for no doubt he is trying to steal what is left of my peony. I know he'll try and track it down in Tibet. You cannot, Delphina,' — his restless eyes bored into her — 'let him get there first and take it from me.'

She knew she could not refuse him. She felt ashamed as she thought of how she had been attracted to Lorin. It was as well that she would now be taken away from temptation.

'As you wish, Papa.' She looked at Arnold. 'I will do my best on the trip and it only appears to be a marriage for form's sake.'

He nodded, but he did not look very happy about the arrangement and seemed as reluctant as her to go through the charade.

'Let's get on with it, we've lost too much time already,' Randolph said.

The legal papers were signed, various things were explained such as who owned what on death.

She was quiet through dinner and barely ate what was put before her. Arnold and Mr Farrar were polite to her, but no reference was made of the forms they had signed. Only at the end of dinner when she excused herself while they sat with their port did Arnold say, 'Will you please come to London the day after tomorrow to buy your clothes for the trip? You can be back here by the evening.'

'Yes, I can. When will we return from our trip?'

Arnold shrugged. 'It's hard to say, in about a year, a year and a half. No more than two.'

She knew the length of her father's trips so it was not a shock to her.

Randolph said, 'I have a list of requirements for you. I hope everything is in stock. You leave next Friday you know.'

'Next Friday!'

'You must set off quickly, get off before Cedric,' Randolph said. 'He is a lazy man and a slave to opium; that's probably why he is taking his nephew to do the hard work for him. Remember that, Delphina,' — his eyes were stern — 'no flirting with such a man; remember, he works with his uncle.'

'What do you take me for, Papa?' she said indignantly, trying to ignore the quick beating of her heart at the sound of his name.

'Just remember,' he said, 'it's lonely out there sometimes, so far away from home, feelings can get magnified out of all proportion.'

'You need not worry on that score,' she said, 'we may not meet up with them at all.'

The rest of the evening was spent in further talk of the trip and when Delphina got up the next morning she found that Arnold had already left. She had barely slept, yet the thought of the trip excited her. All her life she had listened spellbound to Randolph's descriptions of his travels, yet she was annoyed at the way she'd been forced into this charade with that ugly man and when she saw Randolph after breakfast she greeted him with impatience.

'What's up with you?' He too sounded irritable.

'What do you think? Marry me off to that old man like that. What if he acts on it?'

'I told you he won't, Delphina, there is no other way you can go with Arnold. Think of his reputation too, if you do not care for yours.'

'I am to enhance *his* reputation now.'

'Why are you so sour this morning? You should be glad you are to go on such a trip. I would give my life to go.' Bitterness dug into his face.

'I'm sorry you can't go, Papa, but I still think you could have told me more about it sooner. Asked me how I felt instead of throwing me in like that, catching me unawares.'

He had the grace to look ashamed, 'I'm sorry, my dear, but it was the only way. Look now how you are fighting against it? You

71

would never have agreed; it was better to push you into it. Now sit here beside me, I want to tell you as much as I can about what to expect, how to collect plant samples.'

'Surely Arnold will show me,' she said grudgingly.

'Of course he will, but I don't want you to be totally ignorant. I've my own reputation to keep up, too.'

'You men and your reputations. It's only your fear that Mummy's relations would blame you for letting me go off with Arnold unmarried that started this fiasco,' she retorted.

All day she worked with Randolph as he described the journey, the clothes she would wear, the illnesses she might get and what treatment to take. He told her of walking high in the hills, of altitude sickness, how to gather the plants, make a herbarium, and countless other things until her brain felt full to bursting with information.

'It is a pity we haven't longer for you to learn Tibetan, a little Chinese,' he said, 'though here are some books that I suggest you study.'

'That's your fault for not telling me earlier.'

Then she remembered something he had said last night.

'Is it true that Cedric came here and you

have asked Ely to move the peony root?' If Cedric was here, was Lorin, too?

'I heard he was seen hanging round Aurian Hall. If he hopes to buy such a place he must be in the money and the only way he can be is through dishonesty. Ely is nursing the root carefully out of sight. I do not trust it to be left in the ground where he can find it.'

His words were like sharp stones hitting her. So Lorin had lied to her, telling her he was interested in Aurian Hall and Cedric would not be living there. He was his spy and she had so nearly succumbed to him. Her body tingled thinking of how she had wanted him to kiss her. She must never allow herself to get so close to him again.

But it was easy to keep out of their way while she was here and for her father to hide the peony root, but what would happen if they met on those windswept mountains under the eaves of the world?

5

'Delphina! I haven't seen you for ages, how are you?' The plummy voice of Marsha Barker broke into her thoughts as she waited on the platform for the train to London.

'Marsha,' Delphina smiled, though inside her spirits dropped. Marsha, a statuesque, dark-haired girl dressed impeccably in the latest fashion, was a great gossip. She prided herself on being the first to know of people's misfortunes handing round her knowledge like trophies at her social gatherings.

'I've been meaning to have you round for a little lunch, or cocktails, but' — Marsha lifted her over-plucked eyebrows — 'you know what time is like, it simply flies.'

Delphina continued smiling. She knew Marsha only invited people who were useful to her, or considered the 'right' people to know.

The thought of having to put up with Marsha all the way to London depressed her, and she looked round hopefully for someone else whom Marsha would find a more amusing companion. Marsha seemed to be looking round too, but as no one else turned up she boarded the carriage with Delphina, and settled herself down by the window.

'It's too, too awful about your father,' she began, when she was settled. 'Is he completely paralyzed?'

Delphina was tempted to tell her to mind her own business, but said, more to dispel rumours that her father had become a total imbecile, than to discuss her father's condition, 'He has a little movement in his arms; his mind is quite unaffected.'

'So dreadful, and so soon after you having to nurse your mother, too. Quite ruined your social life, I should think. I haven't seen you about for ages.' She lit up a cigarette.

Delphina made no answer and stared out at the countryside. How, she wondered was she going to explain Arnold North meeting her at the station?

'Why are you going to London? A shopping trip?' Marsha asked her.

'I'm shopping for my father. One of his friends is meeting me, helping me to get the right things,' she said, appearing to be more interested in the passing scenery.

'I hope you'll be doing some shopping for yourself. London's the only place for decent clothes, apart from Paris, of course.' She gave a shrill laugh. 'I'm going shopping and meeting friends at Claridges for lunch.'

Delphina let her prattle on until at last they arrived at Victoria. Delphina said goodbye, hoping Marsha would rush off to meet her friends and not wait for her, but instead she lingered, obviously waiting for Delphina to leave the train with her.

Almost at once Delphina saw Arnold North standing by the ticket barrier. He was scanning the crowd for her, and she guessed that as they had only met one evening and that in the dusk, he might not recognize her.

'Don't let me hold you up, I'm waiting for my father's friend,' she said to Marsha, wishing her out of the way to avoid gossip back home.

'You won't hold me up. Look, there's a man waving at you. I must say he's quite the ugliest man I've ever seen,' she laughed. 'Just as well, or I might have suspected you of having an assignation. He's quite a bit younger than your father too.' She gave Delphina a sideways look.

Before Delphina could answer, Arnold hurried over to them. 'Glad you took the early train; we have a lot to fit in today. Buying your clothes will take up most of the morning, if my judge of women is correct.' He gave her a twinkling smile.

'Aha,' Marsha said, loudly, in her ear, 'sounds naughty.' Delphina turned her back on her knowing Marsha was longing to be introduced to him so she could go back to her little lunches and her cocktail parties and entertain her guests with how she'd seen Delphina Graveson, with 'quite the ugliest man', who'd met her off the train and who was going to buy her clothes in London.

Arnold didn't seem to notice her agitation. He took her arm and hustled her out of the station saying, 'The Army and Navy is only up the road, it's not far. We'll walk. You've got to get used to walking, you know.'

'I'm very fit,' she said, amused by the look of total shock on Marsha's face. What would she think when she disappeared with Arnold for a year or so? No doubt she'd beef up the story and tell her set that she'd actually been there, seen her elope with him.

'I do hope you will not find the trip too arduous, Delphina,' Arnold said suddenly, as they pounded up the pavement.

'I'm sure I shall manage it. I'm determined to enjoy it,' she answered. 'Ever since I was little, Papa has been telling me about his trips. The wonderful beauty of these far off places, the fascinating people and, of course, the plants.'

'Trust him to only tell about you the good bits,' Arnold said with a gruff laugh.

'I know it rains a lot, sometimes for days,

77

and there's danger of landfalls; the food is terrible, and leeches suck your blood.' She tried to sound light-hearted, but what she dreaded more than anything was being alone with Arnold, day after day in a tent miles up some remote mountain.

As if he guessed her fear he said, 'The worst thing can be your companions, I should warn you about that.'

'What do you mean?' She regarded him with apprehension. Was he now going to tell her he expected his conjugal rights? He'd better not even think there would be anything in that direction.

He laughed, his ugly face becoming almost pleasant. 'Don't worry, you will be quite safe with me, but even the best of friends get edgy stuck in a tent, with the rain pouring down for days.'

'I suppose they do.' It was the sort of thing that made her edgy after five minutes.

'Delphina.' His tone was serious now. 'I don't know how much your father told you, but I assure you I will treat you with respect at all times. You will have your own tent entirely to yourself.'

'Thank you,' she said, feeling suddenly reassured.

'I'd bring some books to read in the long hours,' he said briskly, as if he'd said enough on such an intimate subject. 'Here we are.' They had arrived at the Army and Navy Stores and he opened the door of the shop for her. 'We'll get the clothes first, I'll leave you to choose them. Suffice to say you need strong trousers, skiing ones are best, a good waterproof jacket, a shirt or two. Here I have made a list in case your father forgot anything.' He took one from his pocket and thrust it at her.

He sat in a corner of the department while she chose the clothes, taking no notice of her at all. Then he took her to buy strong boots and socks and lastly to buy a tent, it being advisable, he'd told her, to buy a new one each year.

She paid for this with the huge wad of money her father had given her. It was all so expensive and she had said to him, 'This is costing you a great deal of money, what if I don't find your peony?'

'You will.' Randolph's voice had been a command. 'But don't worry about the money: I've got Kew to help with the finances by promising you'll send them back some plants. I've made up a list for you to work from.'

She remembered his voice as he had read it out to her, 'Various primula, poppywort, anemone, caragana.' It was like a litany.

'You'll write a journal every day,' he'd insisted. 'Remember you are my eyes; I want to know everything.'

Arnold broke into her thoughts, 'I think it better if some of this is delivered to my flat here. It's pointless it going down in the train with you then coming back again.'

'Fine,' she agreed.

'You must get some food too, chocolate, tins of this and that. Things you like that will keep, of course.' He smiled. 'To my mind the two most important things to bring are whisky and jam. Apart from drinking it, whisky can be used as an antiseptic, and most things become palatable if you mix them with jam.'

'I'm glad there are porters to carry all this,' she said.

'May I have the address to where this is to be delivered?' the assistant interrupted them.

'Of course,' Arnold gave her the address, and she wrote it down carefully. Delphina saw she put Mrs North at the head of the delivery sheet.

'Arnold! And if I'm not mistaken Miss Graveson.' A male voice made her whirl round. Cedric Hartford came towards them, a look of sneering surprise on his face. 'What are you two doing here?'

'I need some things for my trip,' Arnold

said easily. 'Why are you here?'

'The same. Where and when are you going?' He made the question sound more like an interrogation.

Arnold said pleasantly, 'You'll know in good time, Cedric.'

'Who's sending you?'

'Kew. Are you still with Bees?'

'Maybe.' He eyed Delphina. At the same moment the assistant said pleasantly to her, 'Thank you, Mrs North, I'll see these are delivered today.'

'*Mrs* North?' Cedric's mouth fell open, then he laughed. 'Why, you're a sly one, Arnold. *You* married to Randolph's daughter? How did you manage that?' His mouth sneered with cruelty and derision. Delphina knew at once he was referring to Arnold's impotence. His accident must be common knowledge, but only someone like Cedric would mock him for such an injury.

She saw a flash of pain and embarrassment cross Arnold's face. In that moment she felt a wave of sympathy for him, and realized what a terrible thing it must be for a man to lose his manhood. There was sneering malice in Cedric's face, cruelty glittering in his eyes. He was enjoying Arnold's discomfort and unhappiness, enjoying the power he had, knowing of, and exposing his weakness.

Without thinking, but determined to hit back at Cedric's cruelty, Delphina flew to Arnold's side and slipped her arm through his. 'We are blissfully happy,' she said with a huge smile.

'My, she must be some woman. You lucky dog,' Cedric leered at her.

'We must be on our way,' Arnold said sharply, not looking at him.

'What a trip you'll have, if you're taking her with you. Not much time for plant hunting, I should say,' Cedric called after them.

'You are the most vile man I have ever met,' Delphina hissed at him, pulling her skirt close to her as she passed him as if she could not bear it to come into contact with him. Arnold had gone on; Cedric came close to her.

'You'll take that back one day, my dear,' his voice oozed into her. She could see the brutal hatred in his eyes producing a shaft of fear in her.

'Why, Delphina, what a surprise.' Lorin appeared from another department a pile of packages in his arms. His face glowed at the sight of her and she felt her heart soar.

'It certainly is a surprise and what's more she's married,' Cedric said with a laugh.

'Married?' Lorin almost dropped his parcels staring at her in shock.

'Yes, to a man old enough to be her father. There must be something going on there.' Cedric regarded her intensely. 'I'll get to the bottom of it, see if I don't.'

She tried not to look at Lorin, but her eyes would not obey her. He was studying her now with reproachful dismay. 'I did not know you were engaged to be married?' His voice was hard and she saw the anger dart into his eyes.

'She married Arnold North,' Cedric laughed, clapping his hand on Lorin's shoulder. 'We'll see how long that will last.'

She turned from them and hurried after Arnold, sick at heart.

Arnold seemed to have lost his ruddy glow of vitality. When they finished their shopping he took Delphina to lunch in a small, rather dull restaurant nearby. He barely looked at the menu, ordering soup followed by lamb cutlets. Delphina not sure how to deal with his obvious unhappiness, ordered the same.

At last he sighed, said heavily, 'I know you meant well, Delphina, pretending to Cedric that we have a . . . normal marriage, but please don't ever do it again.' He fiddled with the stem of his glass, keeping his eyes firmly on his fingers.

'I hope I'll never meet anyone as cruel and wicked as him again.' She expelled the words as if they were like acid on her tongue.

'I hope so, too. But you've met him before?'

Her eyes blazed at him across the table. 'He came to our house to gloat over my father. Then his monster of a dog killed off the last hope Papa had in his life, by savaging the roots of his new species of peony.'

Arnold looked thoughtful for a moment. His dark brows drawing over his eyes as if shuttering them from outside distraction, then he said quietly, 'So that's why Randolph cooked up this fantastic idea to send you out to bring back his plants.' He laughed shortly. 'He wouldn't trust me to do it. I hope he's given you precise instructions as to exactly where they are. There's a whole lot of space out there you know.'

'Yes he has.' He had drilled their position into her hour after hour until he was sure she knew it perfectly. 'Tell no one,' he had said, his voice harsh with desperation, 'not even Arnold, and certainly not that bastard Cedric and his nephew. You'd better know that Cedric is an opium addict so I'm sure I don't need you to promise me that you will have nothing to do with him or anyone in his accursed family?'

'Of course I won't, Papa.' She'd tried to reassure him but she felt the fear rise in her. 'But tell me,' she went on, 'why Cedric wants to know so much about your peony? Are there not countless new species of other plants to collect?'

Then his face changed, his voice was bitter.

'He is not a true plant hunter. He is in the pay of a rich eccentric who collects peonies and will pay a large price for them, not only in money either.'

His words had sent a chill through her and when she had asked him to explain further he had refused.

'Just tell no one, no one at all, where my plant is and bring it back to me.'

She looked now at Arnold sitting across the table from her. Perhaps he would tell her more, but instead she asked, 'Are you annoyed that I'm coming with you?' For the first time it crossed her mind what it must be like for him to have an inexperienced woman thrown at him, to take on his trip, and at such short notice too.

Arnold gave her a bashful smile. 'I admit I wasn't too pleased when Randolph first suggested it. It's going to be very hard you know, not a peaceful saunter through lovely hills looking for flowers.'

'I know that. Papa has always told me how hard it is, and I'm strong.'

'I owe him a favour, but I insisted I would only take you if you were tough. A feminine, fastidious little woman would be no good out there at all.'

'I'm not like that,' she retorted. 'I admit I've not had much chance to show my strengths being at home nursing my mother, or stuck in a dreary girl's boarding-school, but I've always wanted to travel.'

Arnold laughed. 'This is travelling in its real sense. No luxury cabins and comfortable hotels here.'

'I'll cope, you'll see.' Her meeting with Cedric and Lorin, especially Lorin, who turned her body to fire and she must resist at all costs, added to her determination to succeed. She would find and bring back that peony come what may.

'You'd better,' he said seriously, then called for the bill.

'What was the favour you owed my father?' she asked him.

Arnold's face went dark, his brows came over his eyes and he shifted uncomfortably in his chair. 'It's a private matter just between us,' he said, 'but don't worry I'll honour it in seeing you bring back his wretched plants.'

She sensed the bitter anger coiled inside him. He didn't speak again to her apart from suggesting that she come up to London the following Thursday. He would meet her at the station. She could stay at his flat and they would set off the following day.

She was about to protest at staying at his flat overnight, when she remembered that they were pretending to be married and they were to be alone miles from anyone up in the Himalayas. It was too late now to behave like a nervous maiden aunt.

Before he left her at the station, he thrust an envelope in her hand. 'I bought a wedding ring,' he said brusquely, 'you'd better wear it from next week.'

'Thank you,' she said, and put in her bag, thinking it was surely one of the least romantic and peculiar 'marriages' that had ever taken place.

6

The *City of Canterbury* nosed her way out of the docks into the open sea. Delphina stood on deck determined to stay there until the last trace of land had been swallowed up on the horizon. A waving, cheering crowd swarmed over the quay but there was no one waving her goodbye. A sharp, salty wind whipped round her and the gulls, stark white against the grey sky, circled and called out in their melancholy way.

Arnold had gone down to his cabin. He'd explained that he liked to settle himself in at once, then he could relax and enjoy the trip. But her mind felt so restless, her body so charged, after the new developments that had overtaken her, she wanted to put off being in the confines of her cabin for as long as possible.

It had been so hard saying goodbye to her father. She could not bear to think of him alone each day and she'd asked Philip Stacy if he and his father would visit him when they could.

'I have a dreadful feeling I may never see him again,' she confided in him.

'He seems healthy enough,' Philip said, 'but we'll visit and try to persuade him to ask over some of the neighbours. They'd come you know, if he'd let them.' He smiled down at her.

'Thank you, Philip. That will take a load off my mind. Carson is marvellous, but, he needs other . . . more mentally stimulating people.'

'Don't worry about it, we'll look after him. Enjoy your trip.' He'd smiled, touched her face with the back of his hand. 'You're a brave girl, Delphina, going all that way, camping out and so forth, not to mention being married to a man you've only met once. I must say,' he frowned, 'I thought that was going a bit too far.'

She was to tell no one that it was not really a marriage.

'I do too. But you know Papa and how he blackmails me with his conditions making me do what he wants. He knows how afraid I am to bring on another fit. He might not survive another one.'

He said more seriously, watching her closely, 'My father tells me it's a marriage in name only . . . owing to an accident.'

Despite knowing he was a doctor and used to such things she blushed. 'Yes, in name only,' she said firmly.

'I'm glad of that.' She'd seen the

admiration in his eyes but to deter any more remarks in that line she began to talk about Prima and how much she'd enjoyed riding her.

The sea wind nipped at her like a terrier. She could still see her father's gaunt face, his eyes burning as if with a fever, straining to catch a last glimpse of her, wishing with all his heart that he were going with her, tossing his bags in the car, walking with that jaunty way he had, like a boy unable to hide his excitement, the self-importance of being the one to be setting off to unknown dangers, while those left behind hid their fears for his safe return.

Arnold had met her at the station and, sensing her sadness, had left her alone. He'd barely talked to her as they ate the plain dinner in his dreary bachelor flat, cooked and served by his Scottish housekeeper. Now, here on the ship with the skyline fast receding, her journey had begun. She turned away from the diminishing sight of the teeming port and the smudge of land and looked out at the heaving, gelatinous sea and the new life that was to come.

Arnold kept her busy most days teaching her Tibetan and some words in Nepali and Urdu.

'There are so many dialects you can't learn

them all, but it's a start,' he said, making her write down and pronounce each word.

She was determined to learn. She must fill her mind with so many thoughts and puzzles that it would be unable to throw up pictures of her father waiting impatiently for her. Would hold off the fear of whether she would even find his plant at all, and what would happen if she met Cedric on the way. These endless anxieties jostled for attention in her mind like noisy, demanding children clamouring to be answered.

Arnold had reserved them two cabins on the ship so there was no embarrassment of her sharing one with him. Delphina hardly ever wore the wedding ring he'd thrust at her. She took it off to wash her hands and more often than not, forgot to put it on again, and Arnold, occupied with his maps and lists did not notice.

He did not mix readily with the other passengers. He was polite when he encountered them, and would listen idly at meal-times to their conversation. But apart from stating his profession, and answering their excited questions in as short and understated a way as possible, he kept to himself.

To her annoyance, Delphina found that she was the one left to be interrogated, especially by the older women.

'My dear,' said a Mrs Bowen, an over-made-up matron, 'is this your first trip with your . . . ' — and here her eyes flickered to Delphina's naked fingers and back to her face — 'husband?'

'It is my first trip so far afield. I've been to France and Italy that is all.' She smiled tightly, putting up a prickly wall between her and these inquisitive ladies.

'And did you go there to search for plants?' Mrs Smart asked.

'No. I went with my mother and my aunt on holiday.'

'Have you been married long?' They had seen their names, Mr and Mrs Arnold North, but, as they had informed each other, in loud, delightedly shocked whispers, 'She looks too young to have been married long, yet they have the air of a couple long bored with each other.'

Delphina disliked their hard, spiteful faces, the way they hung on to her words as if they were morsels of food that they could devour yet pass on greedily to other hard-faced women. She was tempted to say, 'We are involved in a dangerous, secret mission,' but she kept her words to herself.

There was a young man on board, somehow connected with them — a nephew, a godson, who watched her with covetous passion. His skin was pale, his hair blond, he had a moustache like a rim of Cornish cream over his top lip. He watched her from a distance, frank admiration for her in his eyes.

One afternoon she was on deck leaning over the rail staring out at the endless sea, watching its sinuous, muscular writhing when she sensed someone approach her.

'Don't you think all that sea gets tiring? Don't you long for green and brown earth, and buildings?'

She knew it was him with the lovesick eyes, but she kept her gaze on the dancing sea.

'I haven't thought, but I find it restful, the rhythmic moving of the water.'

'My name is Henry Orsin; what is yours?'

He had a pleasant voice and this time she turned and, with a slight smile, said, 'Delphina Graveson.'

'Delphina . . . ' He let the words run through his mouth as though it was fine wine. 'It's a beautiful name.' He was regarding her with such undiluted admiration that she recoiled from him, moving away.

'Thank you, now if you'll excuse me I must go; I've letters to write.'

'Wait just a while.'

'I can't . . . I have so many to do.' She tried to sound businesslike. She judged him to be not much older than her. How she longed for someone her own age with whom to laugh, joke about the spiteful ladies, for though he belonged in their party, she was sure he was not cast in the same mould as them.

'Delphina . . . oh there you are.' Arnold came towards her.

'Here is your father . . . ' Henry said. He obviously did not know of their supposed marriage.

Arnold nodded at him and took her arm. 'Come now,' he said, 'we have a lot of work to do.'

'I know, I was just coming. Goodbye.' She smiled at Henry, who with a sudden, impulsive movement seized her hand and held it, then as quickly dropped it, as if realizing he was going too far.

'Goodbye . . . Delphina, see you later,' he said, his eyes burning into her as if he would not see her again. They reminded her suddenly of her father, that look of desolation that he tried so vainly to hide as if he was saying goodbye forever.

The swift feeling of pain at this memory must have shown itself in her expression for Arnold pulled her away briskly, and marched her along the deck and down to their cabins.

'Now, Delphina,' he said sternly, 'we cannot have any shipboard romances. You're married, remember.' He glanced at her empty ring finger. 'You must wear your wedding ring at all times and not mislead besotted young men.' His voice and expression held no jealousy, it was more impatience. It made her feel at fault.

She said defiantly, 'It's hardly a romance.'

'It could become one. He's half in love with you already. There will be too much gossip, too many complications. Now, where is your ring?' He opened the door to her cabin, more like a father teaching his child the right way to behave than an angry husband.

'I keep forgetting to put it on. I'm sorry, I just don't feel married and I thought here it wouldn't matter,' she said, going over to her dressing-table and taking it out of her sponge bag and putting it on.

'It matters a great deal here. All those tiresome women with nothing better to do or think of than chase scandals. I don't like being the object of gossip,' he said, severely, as if she had stripped off her clothes and danced naked round the deck.

'I told Randolph taking a young, pretty woman would be a bad idea. I wish he'd trusted me enough to bring him back his plant by myself.' He sighed, then said, almost under his breath, as if he was thinking aloud,

'I can't understand why he trusted me to look after his daughter, but not to bring back his plant.'

His words hit her like a blow, knocking away her first thought that Arnold was bored at being landed with her, solely because she was a woman. It seemed that by his standards all women were frivolous people ever ready to complicate life with starting romances. But it was true her father had put his plants before her. But had she not always known it? Had not her mother wasted away and died, knowing that it was not other women who were her rivals but plants, travels, a way of life with which she could never hope to compete.

Seeing her face, Arnold said gently, 'I'm sorry, I shouldn't have said that.' He put out his hand, then withdrew it awkwardly, shuffling his feet and raking back his hair with his other hand. 'I'm sorry,' he said again.

'It's all right. I always knew Papa's work came first.'

'When you get there and see the savage beauty of the place, you might understand. It's like men and the sea; however much they love someone they can't stay away from it. It becomes their very reason for living.'

'I know.' She picked at the ring on her finger.

'I only agreed to take you because he can

never travel again. It would have been better for him if he'd been killed. This living death, stuck in that chair is hell for him.' He said it gently, as if trying to explain Randolph's behaviour.

'Don't you think I know that?' she burst out in despair.

'I know you do. I was just trying to explain why we must act out our parts. Why you must steer clear of young men like Henry Orsin,' he spoke calmly. 'We don't want any gossip to get back to Randolph, making him think you might prefer to stay with some young man instead of finding his plant.'

'As if I would. I don't care for that man. I want no shipboard romance, I promise you that,' she said sharply.

'I'd understand it if you did. He's an attractive man, and you . . . ' — he smiled — 'you are young and beautiful. It seems unfair of me to stand in the way of a genuine love story, but — '

'There is no genuine love story,' she retorted. 'I don't care for him, nor do I care for romance.' She jabbed at the ring on her finger. 'I want to hear no more of it. I want to work, arrive at our destination and start looking for the plants and Papa's peony. I will think of nothing else.'

'As you wish.' He seemed taken aback by

her vehemence. She marched into his cabin where the maps and books lay on the table and sat down and began to study, not looking up from her work until dinner.

At dinner she was aware of the whispers and glances from the tiresome women.

'Are you all right, *Mrs North*?' Mrs Bowen said, her voice cloying.

'Why shouldn't I be?' Delphina said.

'We . . . I . . . ' Her eyes, the lids crepey like a lizard's, shot to her friends and back again, 'heard raised voices; we wondered if you were all right.'

'I am fine, thank you. I'm sorry if we disturbed you.' Delphina's lip curled with contempt. She saw Henry come in and look her way, his face strained and reproachful. No doubt he now knew she was married. She saw the women had seen his reaction and felt the slight frisson of their malicious curiosity at what would happen next.

She walked away from them and went and stood by Arnold, realizing for the first time, why her father had insisted on their appearing to be married. There were too many people in the world like Mrs Bowen and Mrs Smart, ready to put themselves up as keepers of other people's morals. If too much attention was paid to her and Arnold, it might also get back to people like Cedric Hartford. Then, by following the stories left like pebbles in the moonlight, he could follow them to the peony. The thought stilled her anger. Nothing mattered but bringing back that ivory peony. She wanted it for her father, but also, she wanted to find it before Cedric Hartford, so she could hold it up triumphantly like a trophy in revenge for her father's broken life.

The next day she said to Arnold, 'Tell me everything you know about peonies. I want to know all the species that have been found. I want to know enough so as to be able to recognize any new ones, then I can bring them all back to my father.'

Arnold smiled at her shining face. 'I think I should I warn you, one is often mistaken when discovering a new species. Just because we have never seen it before, it doesn't mean no one else has.'

'So you mean that Papa's plant might have already been found by someone else?' The thought was too terrible to contemplate.

'It might. There was a rumour going round that it had been seen in flower, but when the plant hunter went back to find the seeds, he couldn't find it. But,' — he smiled sadly, went on slowly, as if probing a wound — 'one has to say, it might just be in his mind. Not until the root he brought back flowers will he know for sure.'

'You mean he might have built it up into something better? Something different?'

Arnold pursed his lips. 'It is possible. Sometimes the light makes a plant look different. Once I saw a rhododendron in glorious sunshine. It looked so bright, almost luminous. I saw it from afar and was certain it was a new species. The next morning when I set out to look for it, the weather had changed, it was grey with teeming rain. When I found it, it was just a common variety, but I had never seen it in the sun before, and it looked so different.'

'So we might be going on a wild goose chase?'

'Don't look so alarmed,' Arnold smiled, 'but yes, we, or rather you, as I have many reasons for my trip, may be disappointed. But until we go there and find it, we cannot be sure.'

'It *must* be there,' Delphina said fervently. She sat down at the desk, picking up a pen. 'Tell me all the species of peony you know, their colours, shapes, everything.'

He laughed. 'I'll tell you the ones I know, but it will be easier to point them out when we are there.'

'Just tell me the names so I can remember them,' she said, 'and tell me something else,

Arnold.' She fixed him with an intense gaze. 'Who is this man that Cedric Hartford collects for? You know the rich . . . my father calls him Hartford's benefactor?'

Suddenly Arnold became agitated. His tongue darted from his mouth moistening his lips as if they were cracking; his eyes stared glassily at her; he moved back and forth as if in a dance. 'I . . . well, I'm not sure, there are many . . . Kew, Bees . . . '

'I don't mean people like that.' She was amazed by the sudden change in him. It was like a deep fear, yet in a moment he had controlled himself. A line of sweat still beaded his forehead but he said briskly, 'It's nearly dinner-time. If you want to learn the names of these peonies we'd better start. Now there's *Paeonia delavayi*, it's yellow and grows in — '

'Arnold,' she said firmly, 'why is it no one will tell me who this demon is? Papa wouldn't, and now it seems to upset you. Why can't I know . . . just his name?'

'Because it is none of your business. It's nothing to do with this trip.' His voice was hard with authority. She should change the subject, yet some devil in her forced her to go on.

'It is to do with this trip, anyway with Papa's peony. Cedric Hartford would have killed him for it, to take to it to this person. It may be just for the money, though I can't help feeling there's a lot more to it than I've been told.'

Arnold looked so miserable she felt ashamed. 'I'm sorry,' she said, 'I won't ask anymore. I just can't understand what sort of hold he has over everyone. Why he is hated, feared so.'

'I hope you'll never have to know, Delphina. Now,' — his voice was weary — 'I must ask you not to ask about him again. I don't want to discuss him, or anyone to do with him. Is that quite understood?'

'If you really won't tell me, I won't ask again.' She sighed impatiently, determined to find out somehow.

'Good,' he said, and then as if they had never discussed it, he sat down beside her and began to reel off names of peonies until she had to beg him to slow down.

★　★　★

The day before they arrived at Calcutta, Henry Orsin approached Delphina again. Up until then she'd managed to keep her distance, pretending not to notice his resentful, smouldering glances whenever she passed him, or avoiding him altogether by staying in her cabin and studying with Arnold.

Henry had obviously been watching for her and he came up to her at once, saying, 'Delphina, I must talk with you,' with all the urgency of someone passing on some vital information.

'What about?' She held herself stiffly as if she had grown spikes around herself, warning him to keep his distance. He was a good-looking man, but there was a weakness in his face, which deterred her.

'I know it's hardly my place to mention it,' — rose pink flooded under his pale skin — 'but . . . well, it's about your marriage.'

'What about it?' She kept her voice brisk, her eyes on the sea.

'Well.' He gave a sharp laugh, shot a beseeching look at her as if to beg her to put him out of the misery of questioning her, but she ignored it. 'I wondered if you were happy, or if you'd been forced into it. I mean, your husband seems so much older and you don't exactly look . . . ' Henry stumbled over the words, 'well . . . in love.' He was quite flushed with embarrassment as if he had questioned her on the intimacies of their lovemaking.

Delphina stared out at the churning sea. He seized her hand and said breathlessly, 'If you want to escape, come with me. I am going up to Darjeeling; I will take you with me.' There was a look of such fervour in his eyes that Delphina felt quite sorry for him.

'Look,' she said, in a softer voice than she meant, 'it's kind of you to worry about me so much, but I'm perfectly happy . . . really I am.'

'You don't look it. I mean, you can't have been married long and there seems to be nothing between you, no feeling of anything, not even friendship, whereas if you were *my* wife . . . ' he finished in a rush.

'Arnold suits me perfectly.' She pulled her hand firmly from his grasp. 'Now, if you'll excuse me . . . ' She saw the figures of Mrs Bowen and Mrs Smart approaching. Their heads peering forward like chickens searching for food. They were searching for gossip and she, standing so close to Henry, with his face so red and his hands darting out to catch hers again, would surely feed them for a week.

Henry saw them too and withdrew, but not before he had taken a white square of card from his pocket and pressed it into her hand. 'If ever you need me, this is where to find me,' he said, giving her one more burning look before quickly walking away from her and the squawking approach of the two gossipmongers.

'My dear, have we interrupted something?'

Mrs Bowen greeted her. 'We should have gone the other way. I said that, Deirdre, didn't I?' she shrieked at Mrs Smart who shrieked back, 'So you did. Henry is so attractive, and quite taken with you. *Such* a pity you're married already.' She fixed Delphina with a probing look.

'If you'll excuse me,' Delphina felt her temper rising. What odious people these women were feeding on people's lives like carrion.

'Going back to your husband?' Mrs Bowen smiled.

Delphina turned her back on them and walked away. Their intrusion and indeed Henry's questions unsettled her. Although she didn't like them, had not found any real friends on board, there'd been other congenial people to pass the time of day with. From tomorrow she would, apart from the guides and porters hired to carry their equipment, be alone with Arnold and the thought depressed her.

He was pleasant, but having been with him for some time now, she realized that he was rather bored at having her with him. He was a loner, addicted to his plant hunting and the beauty of the country where he found them.

She thought of the loneliness ahead, the long days and nights spent in tents and poky bungalows, sometimes in teeming rain, with only Arnold, who would surely come to resent her presence more and more. She understood his feelings. She was a complete novice in the art of plant hunting and one of a different sex. He'd see her as a thorn to irritate him when he was content with his own company, wanting to endure and enjoy the experience of his travels alone.

She went back to the cabin determined to kill such negative thoughts with trying to master more Tibetan. To her surprise Arnold was not there, but she sat down and religiously opened her book and started to study. But the words jumped before her refusing to make sense. She found it impossible to get her mind to absorb anything. At last giving up, she put down the book and began wandering round the cabin, fiddling with this and that, trying to throw off the restlessness in herself.

There was a small pile of novels by Arnold's bed and she wandered over to look at his choice for the hours of solitude that lay ahead. *The Arrow of Gold* and *Lord Jim* by Conrad, *Hard Times* by Dickens and *The Way We Live Now* by Trollope. This she picked up. It was a favourite of her father's. She opened it idly, reading a few familiar passages, seeing how worn the pages were from much reading. These were the companions he chose to lighten his hours of solitude. He must think very highly of her father to allow her to intrude in his ordered life.

Arnold came in making her jump and she almost dropped the book.

'Do you want to borrow a book?' He looked at her with irritation as if annoyed that she was touching his belongings.

'Sorry.' She put the book down. 'I was working, but my attention was caught by your books. This is a favourite of my father's.'

He sat down. 'One needs a good solid book for these trips. I trust you have brought something to read too.'

'Yes.' She felt awkward now, felt that he wished to be alone. She moved to go but as if guessing her thoughts he said, 'I'm sorry if I've given you the impression that I find your presence a trial. It's true when that young man started sniffing round you I began to wonder what I had let myself in for, but you've dealt with the situation admirably. And I'm very pleased at the interest you're taking in learning the languages. You are certainly Randolph's daughter.' He smiled at her.

'Papa says I take more after him than my mother. She would never have gone on such a trip.'

'But you look so very like her,' he said suddenly, and then stopped, his skin took on a ruddy glow as if he was blushing.

'Did you know my mother well?'

Arnold didn't look at her, but walked to the books by the side of his bed and picked them up and pushed them into a bag on the chair.

'Yes,' he said, his face grave as if he was debating something then he turned to look at her. 'I shall tell you once, and we will not bring it up again. I was in love with her cousin Selena.'

'Oh Selena. Mummy often talked of her. She was an orphan and brought up by my grandparents; she was much younger than my mother, but she . . . died . . . didn't she?' she said gently.

'Yes.' Arnold's face went hard. 'Now, I want no more questions. I just wanted you to know that I knew your mother well, even before she married your father.'

Delphina tried to rake back to the snippets of information her mother had told her about Selena. She'd been very fond of her and her face would go still and sad when she spoke of her death. When Delphina had asked why she'd died, her mother had said vaguely, 'She was taken ill; the medicine they gave her was wrong,' and she would refuse to say any more. Delphina hadn't thought of Selena for years; after all, she'd never met her, she'd died before she was born.

'Are you ready for tomorrow?' Arnold asked her briskly, quite in command of himself again.

'I shall be.' Perhaps his impotence was caused by some accident involved with Selena and losing her had made him retreat into himself using his books and plants to forget her. She was aware that her questions would cause him pain so she would not probe any deeper, but how she longed to know the whole story.

7

From the moment the boat docked at Calcutta and their feet touched Indian soil Arnold seemed transformed. It seemed to Delphina that he grew in stature, that his face, before so pinched and creased, now filled out and glowed. He appeared younger, possessing a vitality she would not have believed before. Did her father undergo such a transformation? If so, she could understand why he was so addicted to this profession, it held the secret of eternal youth.

Terrified of losing him in the crowd yet determined not to show it, Delphina followed Arnold into the teeming mass of people. The hot air was heavy with the pungent smell of unwashed bodies, spices, and petrol. She felt a little fearful at the huge noisy crowd of brown-skinned people all jostling and calling yet at the same time she felt excitement at being in this fascinating, alien land.

She jumped, feeling a hand stroking her arm and looked into the merry face of a youth whose hands ran over her sleeve, then touched a strand of her bright hair, staring at her in wonder.

'Keep back.' Arnold cuffed him making Delphina cry out, 'Why did you do that? I'm sure he meant no harm.'

'Keep with me,' was all Arnold said, before diving back into the seething crowd.

She followed him, pushing through the mass of warm, excited people, desperately trying to keep Arnold in sight.

'Stay with me.' Henry Orsin suddenly appeared beside her. 'It is always pandemonium when you arrive here. Your skin is so fair, the people are fascinated by you, and want to touch you. They mean no harm.'

'I'm sure they don't, it's just . . . a little overwhelming. I'll get used to it.' She wondered if Henry had seen Arnold cuff the young man, and if he behaved in the same way. She was relieved Henry was here beside her, steering her through the jabbering throng. The people seemed so cheerful, yet some were barely dressed, half covered in dirty rags. She saw beggars, their limbs twisted and mutilated, and turned away feeling sick with sympathy and disgust. At the same time she was hit with guilt at her revulsion and these emotions chased through her as she struggled to find a balance in her mind.

'Where are you staying?' Henry said, bending close to her ear.

'With some friends of Arnold's for tonight. Then we go on to Saikhoa Ghat by train.'

'I see.' They had reached the edge of the crowd. Arnold was looking round for her anxiously and, Delphina thought, a little irritably.

'There you are at last,' he said. 'Come, here is the car. Goodbye.' He nodded dismissively towards Henry and with his hand on Delphina's back propelled her towards the car.

Henry let go of her arm and she felt instantly bereft as if she was losing someone else familiar and going into the unknown.

'Goodbye, and thank you so much, Henry,' she said warmly.

'Contact me if you need me,' he said sincerely, his eyes anguished as he left her.

Arnold stood between them, saying briskly, 'Come along, Delphina, let's get out of this mêlée. How glad I shall be to be out of it all, high away in the hills.' He got into the car after her and they drove through the crowd of people, the driver jabbing at the horn to clear the way.

The following day they took the train to Saikhoa Ghat.

'I've been thinking,' Arnold said, regarding her intently as they shuddered across the endless land. 'Perhaps it would be better if you dressed as a boy. Or at least put your hair up under a cap, and didn't look just so . . . ' he paused, looked away, 'so feminine. Women in Tibet have the same status as men, but, well, you are obviously a foreign woman.' He looked embarrassed.

Delphina tried not to smile. 'I'm meant to be your wife, so surely I'm safe on that count; besides, I look like a boy in these trousers.'

'It's just your hair; it might attract too much attention. It's so bright, that gold . . . copper colour, compared to the dark people here, it might be a nuisance for you if they keep touching it.'

'I'll see what I can do, but surely I needn't pretend to be a boy? That is too confusing.'

'They are probably expecting two men, or a battle-axe of a woman. Besides,' — his smile was wider, Delphina suspected he was enjoying himself — 'the Tibetans never bathe, so there will be no difficulties about keeping your clothes on.'

'I can think of others,' she said drily, not knowing if he was teasing her. 'Better let me know when I am to be a girl and when a boy.'

He smiled. 'Perhaps I am exaggerating the situation, but I suggest you put your hair up.' He dropped his hand on hers for a moment. It was an unexpected gesture and she did not know how to respond. As if guessing her thoughts, he removed his hand immediately and went on, 'There are three valleys that lead to Tibet, but there's only one we can take safely.'

'Which one?' She played his game, determined to smooth over that moment of intimacy.

'The Lohit Valley, here.' He took out a map and showed her. 'There are two clans who mostly inhabit this part. The Digaru and the Miju. We mostly use them as porters to carry our stuff. They don't get on well with each other, a little like the Scottish clans,' he said, smiling. 'There's often quite a bit of squabbling among them.'

'I remember Papa telling me about that. On one of his trips one of them killed another.' Delphina turned back to the window suddenly hit by a surge of panic. Her father had told her so often of his adventures but now she was really here, wild thoughts and fears crowded in on her. She dared not voice them to Arnold as it would only irritate him, make him regret he had given in to Randolph's request and taken her with him. She stayed silent, drinking in the landscape until they arrived at Saikhoa Ghat.

'We have to cross the bridge to the road to Sadiya,' Arnold said, carelessly, marching forward. She followed him expecting to see a wooden bridge, but to her horror she saw that it was a rope bridge swinging high above the river. Arnold did not seem to notice. With the help of a guide he pushed the porters across first, then he turned to her.

'Your turn now, Delphina. Hold the rope each side and walk straight on; don't look down. I'll be behind you.' He barely looked at her, obviously expecting her to use it as if it was a simple path on the ground. She took a deep breath and stepped out keeping her eyes firmly on the bank ahead. The further she went across the bridge the more it swung as if it was alive and would pitch her off into the raging river below at any second. Vomit surged into her mouth; she swallowed it and pressed on, clinging on to the ropes either side of her, willing herself to reach the end. At last, nauseous and dizzy she stepped on to firm land and was promptly sick.

'Poor you,' Arnold said, matter-of-factly. 'Have a mouthful of water then sit in the shade for a while. You'll soon be fine.'

She lay back on the ground her body still swinging and swooping.

He glanced at her, then in a voice of a teacher giving a lecture said, 'You know on the Mekong the Tibetans use the rope bridge as a way of measuring time. They measure the distance of the sun as to the length of the bridge, I've never known them out by more than half an hour.'

'Fascinating,' she said drily, still feeling sick, but seeing him pacing back and forth in impatience to be off, she struggled back on to her feet and insisted she was well enough to go on.

The next few days were spent in buying rations and dividing everything into loads to be carried by the porters, a motley crowd from various tribes. There were some women among them in coarse trousers as baggy as skirts.

'They carry loads just as well as the men,' Arnold said, in a tone that Delphina felt implied that she could not use her sex as an excuse for weakness.

Three Tibetan men came to join their party. Tewang, a guide, was a tall, wiry man with a hard face and a scrappy pigtail. His height was emphasized by his extreme thinness. He bullied the porters, standing no nonsense when they complained of sickness. Pasang was a man of all work, his hair like a thick black mop and Mano, short and sturdy with spindly legs, was the cook. They all had high cheekbones and slanting eyes. They wore long cloaks that they wore looped up like a kilt, or tied round their waists in the heat. They wrapped themselves in them for sleeping and kept all manner of things hidden in the folds, producing, like conjurors, their possessions, a knife, a chicken, a *tsamba* bowl. Mano and Tewang smoked long pipes. Arnold had warned her that the Tibetans' way of greeting was to stick out their tongues, and for the servants to take a curious intake of breath, which he explained was a sign of respect in taking in the polluted air so that the guest would not breathe it.

'Most of them are illiterate, but they speak enough languages between them to be of use to us. They are Buddhist, which means they don't suffer from any religious fads,' Arnold told her.

'They look rather terrifying, especially Tewang with his glaring eyes,' she said.

Arnold laughed. 'He's one of the gentlest men I know. I think he knew your father; we must ask him. They're a hard, tough race, but you'll come to like them.'

Arnold found a lorry to take them on the next leg of the journey. It was so packed with luggage and porters that Delphina wondered how they could possibly fit themselves in. A further fifty or so porters had been sent on in advance in charge of a *gam*, or headman.

'You sit by the driver, Delphina,' Arnold ordered, as he checked again that everything they would need for the trip was there.

If only she were not sitting in the front seeing so clearly each hairpin bend whipping round the narrow roads. The driver behaved as if his was the only vehicle on the dusty road and swept round the corners as if there was no possibility of meeting someone else tucked into the bend. Delphina tortured herself with the thought that there would be no hope for them if someone did come round the corner. She tried not to imagine herself lying broken and deserted on the rocks below.

The first few times the driver nearly ran down a bullock cart or a stray cow, she almost screamed and once she held on to his arm. Then she realized that he was indifferent to any hazards that might be, or her fear. What if they were all killed here before she had time to get anywhere near her father's peony? Arnold told her more than once not to distract the driver. She grumbled at him and closed her eyes to shut out the terrifying sight of the landscape swinging away from them each time they went round a bend.

'Look, Delphina,' Arnold said, after what seemed like a lifetime of twisting and turning, her being thrown first against the driver, then against Arnold until she felt quite sick. She opened her eyes gingerly, and saw a breathtaking view before her.

There were gentle hills clad in trees acting

as a softer frame to the background of snow-capped peaks that towered behind them. The sun caught the snow and touched it with apricot, pink and violet. The sky was an intense delphinium blue. A river surged downwards dancing and breaking on the rock, cutting through it as if it was as soft as marzipan.

'It's so wonderful,' she said, and forgot her sickness and her fear of the precarious driving as her eyes devoured the scene. They passed through tiny villages, the huts shabby with corrugated-iron roofs, the people looking up as they passed, the children running after them, calling out to them. They passed a government resin-collecting station, the smell sharp on the clear air. Then on up, the road getting steeper and steeper, until the lorry mildly protesting now, climbed over a high ridge.

'Look at those magnificent rhododendrons,' Arnold said.

'They're wild,' she said stupidly, looking at the sea of pinks, purples and reds. She laughed. 'I can't believe it to see them as they really are, as they should be. When you think of the fuss we make of them at home, when here they are so magnificent, looking after themselves like weeds.'

'We're not far now,' he said.

'Good, it's so cramped.' Arnold's words of her father trusting his only child to his care but not the location of the peony came back to her. Now she was here, Randolph seemed in another world, another life. It seemed so stupid not to tell Arnold where the peony was. How could she go tramping over these hills alone, looking for something that might not even be there? She was about to say something about it, when the lorry jerked to a halt. They had arrived.

It was the smell that hit her first as she eased her cramped limbs from the cab. She almost clamped her hand over her nose to avoid it, but seeing that Arnold took no notice forced herself to ignore it. It was of petrol and oil mixed with a stink of bad drains and unwashed bodies. In the dirt close by her was a pile of what looked like entrails swarming with flies. A motley collection of beggars, their eyes sunk in their gaunt faces, approached them, and in hideous irony like the overture to a play, a dreary tune rasped out from an unseen gramophone.

Arnold seemed more concerned in supervising the unloading of the lorry than his surroundings. Package after package came out and he organized it into loads for the porters to carry.

A beggar, one eye-socket empty and

running with pus, nudged Delphina's arm. His fingers curled round an empty tin, which he thrust at her. His remaining eye glared at her malevolently.

She moved away in disgust, in pity. She had no money and went over to Arnold and whispered, 'Can I have some money for the beggars? They look so desperate.'

Arnold paused for a second from his task. 'No,' he said, 'there are beggars everywhere; you have to get used to it.'

'But they need food, medical treatment . . . '

Arnold let out a huge guffaw of laughter. 'My dear Delphina, this is not some leafy village in dear old England. Their lives, their expectations are quite, quite different than ours. A little money will not put their world to rights.'

'But — '

'Keep your energy for the march ahead. Stay beside me. Keep away from those devils.'

She kept quiet, but she felt the misery of these people settle like lead upon her. She had never seen such dirt, such degradation. From the corner of her eye she saw the beggars watching them, warily like a pack of hungry wolves ready to dart in at any sign of weakness. They disgusted her, made her afraid, and yet she was filled with such an overwhelming feeling of pity that she wondered if she should not stay and try and bring some help to them.

They slept the night in a small hut. Delphina was too dispirited to do more than curl up in her sleeping bag. Dinner, if it could be called that, had been terrible. Whatever it was, Mano had forgotten to cook it before serving it. He had shrugged off Arnold's complaints as if to say, 'Your tastes are not mine, that is all there is to it.'

Arnold woke her early, it was dull with rain, but he thrust a steaming bowl of tea at her and said cheerfully, 'Get up, we must move on.'

How she longed for a few more precious hours in the oblivion of sleep. But she dared not let Arnold down, and she forced her aching limbs back into her clothes. As they left this dreary village, something made her turn back and she saw Arnold throw a handful of coins in the dust, and the beggars rushing and scrabbling after them.

It was muddy underfoot as the rain had washed down the topsoil from the Mishmi hills that surrounded them.

'This mud can cause terrible floods as it clogs up escape routes for the water. It collects in huge pools then overflows into landslides,' Arnold said, catching up with her.

'I've never seen such rain,' she said. 'When will we meet the leeches and sand flies, and goodness knows what else Papa used to enjoy boasting about?' She grinned wryly and Arnold responded by giving her the warmest smile she'd yet seen from him.

'That's my girl,' he laughed, and moved away from her. He had shown her how to dress to try and avoid the leeches, wearing two pairs of socks, her skin well covered with a mixture of areca nut. She carried salt in her pocket to put on any attacking leeches to make them drop off. He'd warned her that it was painful pulling them off once they were sucking.

The path zigzagged up the mountain. It was lined with thick jungle, so dense and enclosed that Delphina could only get a glimpse of the mud flats below.

The walking became harder. It was hot and wet. The porters poured with sweat under their loads. Delphina wondered how they could possibly carry so much and in such heat. Their *gam*, a thin individual called Jagum, was far too independent to take any notice of Arnold's orders. But Arnold pushed them on. She felt nauseous and had a headache, but she dared not complain. She forced herself on, putting one foot in front of the other, thinking of nothing else, just keeping going.

It irritated her that Arnold's step was so jaunty, his head held high. He didn't talk to her. It was as if he was alone and he was hugging his enjoyment to him like a secret pleasure.

Delphina's feet ached up to her armpits. She tried to take in their surroundings to keep her mind off her pain. How she longed to stop, to throw herself down on the moist earth, but she knew if she did she would never get up again. Besides she would more than likely get covered with leeches and other horrors. Bending down to pick a flower she was just in time to snatch back her hand to avoid a couple of leeches edging their slimy way towards her fingers. The sight of them, attracted by the smell of her blood, filled her with revulsion. There were some on her boot. She tried to kick them off with her other boot, but they stuck fast. Arnold glanced back at her from time to time, but, as he said nothing, she assumed he was thinking what a fool he was to bring her on this trip, so she kept on doggedly, determined not to give him the satisfaction of thinking her weak.

Up and up they climbed until she felt her legs might disjoint themselves from her body. They reached the end of the forest and came on to the ridge and there, to her undisguised joy, she saw the bungalow where they were to stop.

The sight of the bungalow nearly made her collapse with relief, like a small child bursting into tears at the comforting sight of its mother after an absence. Her courage and determination wavered, tears of exhaustion rose in her throat, which she hastily dashed away before Arnold caught sight of them.

It was with unbelievable exhaustion that she fell upon a camp-bed, hastily put up for her by Pasang, in one of the small rooms.

Arnold followed her and took off her boots, and then, taking her hot and throbbing feet in his hands, rubbed them briskly with spirit. With a cigarette he burnt off the few leeches that had found their way through her clothing. They itched terribly and, when she scratched them, her hand came away covered in blood.

'Try to leave them alone, Delphina. The blood won't stop for a while; the dratted beasts leave some chemical behind which stops the blood coagulating.'

Delphina moaned in disgust.

'You've done very well,' Arnold said admiringly, 'for a first climb, and it's beastly wet and hot today.'

Delphina was conscious only of the aching in her body, the swimming tiredness in her head, and maddening itching of the bites on her skin.

'I'll leave you to rest, dinner won't be long,' she heard Arnold say, before she sank into sleep.

He woke her early the next morning and they set off again. She felt in a daze now, unable to take in much of her surroundings, keeping her energy for just going on. The ground was carpeted in flowers, dazzling white and pink. She picked some to press, but Arnold laughed at her.

'Don't bother with them yet. There'll be many more further on. Besides, these low lying plants don't do well back home. We need to get them from a higher altitude.'

At the next village Arnold had to change porters. Narbu, the new *gam* was a surly man, who insisted that unless they were given 'presents' there would be no new porters. Arnold refused his request walking away to see to setting up their camp near the river.

Delphina was relieved at this disruption. She didn't care if they never moved again. It was too hot to lie in the tent, so she threw herself down on a mattress outside her tent, and closed her eyes, her spirits sinking.

What was the point of all this? Even if she found the peony would it be worth it? Would it even grow in England?

Then she thought of Cedric Hartford. She saw his cruel smile, his taunting pity at her father's broken body. She must get to the plant before he did. She must be the one to take it back. But she had to find it. It might be, as Arnold had more than once suggested, a freak of nature, never to be repeated. She groaned aloud, exhausted at the very thought of the idea that all this excruciating effort might be for nothing.

'You're bearing up well so far,' Arnold said, hearing her cry of despair. He was stretched out on his camp-bed reading a book.

'What if I don't find the peony?' she said, finding each word an enormous effort to say, making it difficult to catch her breath.

'Then you don't find it. Randolph knows the score. Some plants can be there one time and quite disappeared the next.'

'But it will kill him if I don't find it.'

'I doubt it. But, Delphina, now that we are here I do think it would be sensible if you told me exactly where he saw it. I don't know what Randolph meant you to do, but you're hardly experienced enough to set off on your own on a wild goose chase after it. It's easy to get lost if the mist comes down, or to fall over a rock, or into a river. It's too risky for you to go alone.'

'Let's see when we get there,' Delphina

said, as firmly as she could.

'Where is 'there'? I haven't a clue even which district it is in.'

'You must just tell me the name of every place we pass. He has drawn me a plan of where it is.' She didn't tell him that the plan lay under her clothes, next to her heart.

'Then I will know, seeing you disappear to look for it,' he laughed. 'Really, it's too absurd; you'd much better tell me now, then I can help you. Make sure we do go to the place where he saw it.'

'I promised Papa that I wouldn't tell anyone.'

'The whole plan was a nonsense right from the start,' Arnold said with impatience. 'I was a fool to go along with it, but I let my sympathy for poor Randolph get in the way of my common sense.'

The exhaustion of the travelling, the altitude, the overpowering pressure of the damp heat whirled through her.

'I don't need your help; I know where it is and I shall find it on my own.'

'Suit yourself, but don't expect me to risk the life of the men, or myself, for you if you get into difficulties. We're not in Hyde Park you know.' Arnold dug his nose firmly back into his book.

'I can rely on myself.' She sprung up and

marched away from him, down to the river. The heat pressed down on her and she felt the niggle of a headache. She tossed her head to shake it off. She had never felt so alone in her life.

In the evening there was a storm. Delphina sat alone in her cramped tent. She ate the dinner Tewang brought her, a sort of stew, and some biscuits. She thought it wiser not to ask what was in the stew, and tried to lose herself in *Pride and Prejudice*, but all the time pictures of Lorin and Henry came to her and she thought how much more amusing companions they would be for her than this grumpy old man.

She sat there miserably as the rain poured down outside and the thunder cracked open the sky. She might as well be the only person left in the world in this shadowy tent smelling of kerosene and damp clothes. Arnold was not far away, nor were the other men, but each was huddled in their tiny cocoon of shelter and would not venture out again that night.

To her surprise she slept soundly. Arnold woke her before five with a bowl of Tibetan tea. She grimaced as she tasted it and he laughed.

'They put yak butter in it, and that's well flavoured with yak skin and hair. You'll soon get used to it.' Then he said gruffly, as if steeling himself for an unpleasant chore, 'I'm sorry about yesterday. We were both on a short fuse.'

Delphina nodded, too drugged with sleep to elaborate further. During those long hours closeted in the tent she had come to terms painfully with the fact that she was on her own. There was no one else out there whom she could trust. She must find and bring back the peony alone.

Arnold had succeeded in persuading Narbu to make the porters work and they set off again walking through a forest which seemed to trap the muggy heat, climbing ever upwards. Delphina found her breath becoming more laboured, nausea rising in her. It was like trudging through a hot, steaming bath.

Narbu sidled up to her, 'Cigarettes, sugar. Please, miss.'

'What?' she looked into his sly face.

'Walk ahead, Narbu, those men look to be flagging,' Arnold said curtly, catching them up. Narbu scowled, muttered something, but did not go forward.

'Hurry on,' Arnold said, his voice stern.

Cursing, Narbu slowly obeyed him.

'Give him nothing,' Arnold said to her, 'he's a greedy beggar.'

After two more days travelling, one spent

chasing lost loads, they arrived at another rope bridge that led to the first village in Tibet. Strings of Tibetan prayer flags fluttered in the breeze. There was a smell of juniper branches being burnt by the villagers in welcome. It was very clear and beautiful. The snow-clad mountains soared ahead of them gleaming like stained-glass windows in the rays of the sun. The silver ribbon of the river wound below them with the jungle on the other side. The ground rose in narrow terraces covered with pine forest. The air was sharp with the smell of resin. For the first time since they had set out on this march Delphina felt her heart surge and her spirits lift. She forgot the pain of the climb, the itching of the leeches, the constant dull headache caused by the altitude. At last she saw what magic led her father to this country again and again, the place that had stolen his heart and left him ever restless without it.

Tewang came and stood beside her and she said, 'Did you know my father, Randolph Graveson?'

'I did. He was a good man. I am sorry for his accident.'

'Were you there then?' She found she was holding her breath as if afraid of the description he might give of it.

'No. If I had been there, he would not have

accident,' Tewang said, fiercely.

'I'm sure he wouldn't have,' she said sadly, then feeling she might have somehow insulted him she said, 'What are those mountains over there?'

'That's Zayal.'

The blood rushed to her face and she ducked her head so that he wouldn't see. Zayal. Somewhere, between this village and those mountains was Randolph's peony; she could not believe she was really near to it at last.

Please be there, oh, please be there, she begged silently, and let me get there first.

8

The layout of the village where they set up their camp was zigzagged with muddy paths and on each sortie they encountered perilous meetings with pigs, goats and small children.

Arnold showed Delphina how to collect and catalogue the plants. She began to feel better, thrilled by the shimmering clouds of delphiniums, primula of every colour, blue and white anemones, and pink rock jasmine. She learnt the name and habitat of each one, drawing them in her journal.

While they marched on to the next site, Arnold took great pains to point things out to her, explaining the customs of the place, how the land had fallen this way. He showed her clumps of the opium poppy carefully hidden among pea plants or planted in discreet places behind rocks.

'It's used here for medicine, or smoked with leaves, but also it's sold off and smuggled into Assam. The soldiers often split open every bag of grain in a passing load, searching for it.'

'Papa told me that Cedric Hartford brings opium back to his benefactor,' she said.

At her careless remark Arnold's face seemed to shrink with pain. '*He* breaks every decent code of behaviour there is.' He clamped his mouth shut in a hard, tight line and refused to answer any more of her questions, awakening her curiosity again. If only she had asked Randolph more about him and found out about this secret before she had left.

Their day was spent looking for plants, noting where they were for their return later to gather the seeds. For the herbarium collection every species had to include a plant in flower and the same when in fruit. Each day after pressing the plants the ones already done had to be opened to the air. Notes had to be taken, plants listed and numbered. Each find was signed with the finder's initials and the date. Delphina became so absorbed in her task she forgot the nagging pain of her tired muscles.

'Look at this,' she said, pulling Arnold over to a tiny chocolate-coloured slipper orchid.

'Clever you,' he cried out joyfully, bending closer to it, as if he would kiss it. 'I saw this once before but my specimen got lost. I always hoped to find it again; we'll number it as your find.'

'It's yours really,' she said, 'if you found it once before.' She experienced a sudden glow of happiness at his delight, exaggeratedly pleased with herself.

'But you found it this time. So often you never find things again,' he said, noting it down.

Her glow faded at his words. What if she didn't find the peony, all this would be in vain? What if Cedric got there first?

As they neared the town of Rima, Arnold sent word to the governor and when they arrived at the town on the edge of the plain they found the street lined with people all curious to see them. Donkeys waited to carry them to the headman's house. Delphina had forgotten to put her hair up. It lay like a sheaf of gold wheat on her shoulders causing a stir among the people. Arnold told her sharply to push it under her hat.

The headman had a flowing beard and a close-cropped head. He welcomed them to his house laying before them bowls of dried persimmons and walnuts. There was the by now familiar buttered tea and a fiery rice spirit. His wife, a square, cheerful woman dressed in a shirt-waister and a fur-lined cap with silver jewellery hanging profusely from her, hovered round them.

Delphina sat cross-legged on the floor like the others, drinking in this hospitality greedily. This, compared to her tiny, kerosene-scented tent, and Mono's attempts at cooking, was indeed a treat.

The headman explained that the governor of Zayul was there in his winter palace but he would not be seeing them that day.

They were shown to a building built of timber raised on wooden piles capped by flat stones, the dividing walls of which did not meet the ceiling, leaving a gap of a few inches above each room.

'The house is raised to keep out the rats,' Arnold whispered to Delphina, with a mischievous smile.

'I know you are enjoying my discomfort, but I shall take no notice,' she said archly.

He laughed. 'I must say you've coped far better than I thought you would.'

'I'm doing this for Papa and to get back at that fiend Hartford who put him in that chair. Never forget that.' She pushed past him into the large room that was being proudly shown them by a misshapen youth, who, despite the curious curve to his body, seemed cheerful enough.

'I would prefer two rooms,' she smiled sweetly at the youth. 'My husband snores most dreadfully and I cannot share with him.'

The youth, not understanding her words went on smiling.

'As good an excuse as any,' Arnold said to Delphina, 'but he won't understand. Don't worry I'll cope with it.' He said something to the youth in Tibetan.

'Well I shall stay in here,' Delphina said. 'Tell them to bring in my baggage so I can go through my clothes. How nice it will be to get them dry.'

'We don't want to be held up too long in case Cedric catches us up,' Arnold said, more preoccupied in sorting out some presents to be sent to the governor. He laid out the usual ceremonial white scarf given as a gift of welcome and then passed on an alarm clock and a torch.

Fear grabbed at her. 'Is he close by? Have you had word of him?' Was he expected here at any moment? And Lorin, what would she feel if she saw him again? If they had to live closely together in the same camp? She quickly banished him from her mind, why did she keep thinking of him, wanting to see him again? Why did she not dream of Philip Stacy or even poor Henry on the boat? Lorin was her father's enemy, she must never forget that.

'I haven't heard anything, but we must remember that he is on his way and we must not become tempted to stay anywhere too long. It is for that reason you should tell me where the peony is, Delphina.' He regarded her gravely. 'After all, Cedric was with Randolph when he had his accident and that was caused by him knowing he had found something special. He may not know the exact spot but he won't be far off.'

'I never thought of that,' she said with horror. 'We must get on, we cannot wait for the governor to see us.'

'We must wait, for without his permission we cannot move anywhere.'

'But while we are sitting here he might be taking the peony as his own.' She could not bear it.

Arnold smiled. 'Stay calm; remember he too must get the governor's permission to travel in his territory and he has not passed here yet. We still have time.'

Vainly she tried to curb her impatience, tried to show interest in the presents that were brought to them. A sack of flour, another of rice and some walnuts. To her relief, the following day the governor came to tea. He was curious to drink tea the British way with sugar and condensed milk. He was a round, plump man with a warm twinkle in his eyes. He stared at Delphina with her pale skin and golden hair with delight like a curious child. He seemed surprised to see them in his town and could not believe that they had walked so far.

'Only beggars walk in Tibet,' he said disapprovingly before asking them why they were here.

Arnold explained that he was a plant hunter, and was here with his wife. 'May I have your permission to travel in your territory?' he asked respectfully.

'Of course,' the governor smiled and nodded at him, 'I will sign the necessary papers.' He drank more of his tea and ate another of their biscuits. How impatient she was for him to sign it, now afraid that it might be some days before the governor got round to it. When he had gone she asked Arnold how he could hurry things along.

'He's a useful friend to us. We'll stay here a few days to cultivate our relationship.'

'We must stay ahead of Cedric.'

'Without a pass we cannot go anywhere and nor indeed can he. We must be patient and anyway I don't know where the peony is so I don't know if we are near to it or not, or if Cedric can reach it without passing here.' There was a slight irritation in his voice and in his expression.

She had promised her father not to tell even Arnold where it was. She must not give in. 'It is ahead of here; we have not reached the place yet.'

'Then nor has Cedric,' he said, and left her to write up his notes.

The following day a religious troop came to Rima. They showed the crowd how to rid a man possessed of devils. They led out a man who hid behind a paper mask, dancing in a frenzy round him until even the spectators became quite dizzy watching.

The air was filled with the fragrance of burning offerings given daily to the shrines. Every day the men and women marched round the square incanting their prayers, twirling prayer drums.

Each night there was a curfew, and a man was employed to go round every night telling the people to go to bed and put off their lights.

'Reminds me of my hideous boarding-school,' Delphina said.

'It's as a fire precaution. These butter lamps can be dreadfully dangerous,' Arnold smiled at her.

In the evenings they had taken to sitting together. Sometimes Arnold played music on his gramophone. This amazed the Tibetans who crept as near as they dared, listening with awe and excitement to this strange, singing box. Some evenings Arnold would talk to her about his other trips as if nothing else held any importance to him. She listened politely, but how she longed to ask him about his love for her mother's cousin Selena. This led her to wonder about his impotence, and if it had been that that had come between him and his love for her.

But despite the semblance of comfort after the other camps, she became more and more impatient to leave.

'The governor has invited us to dinner,' Arnold said, 'we cannot refuse him.'

'Well afterwards then,' she begged. 'I am so afraid that Cedric and his nephew . . . ' She felt her skin flush as she thought of him and hoped that Arnold would not notice.

'Patience.' He did not look up from his work. 'Remember he too must get a pass to go there. He has not come here yet.'

She tried to curb her impatience. At the dinner they ate from bowls of chicken liver, spinach, pork and a curious and a rather heavy dumpling made of maize. They drank the buttered tea or the rice spirit, which Delphina found too harsh for her taste. The room was lit only by butter lamps, which threw shadows on to the wall like dancing spirits. Rifles, wooden saddles and leather whips hung from wooden pegs on the walls.

'If you've any letters give them to me; the governor will send them with his dispatches to Sadiya,' Arnold had said earlier, and later that night she finished a long missive to her father, trying to sound happy, hopeful that soon she would be near his peony.

'When will we get letters back?' she asked

him, as he handed them over to a man on a shaggy pony, a rifle over his back.

'I hope in a few weeks; they'll be brought to us by messenger,' Arnold said, his mind occupied on seeing that the baggage was being properly loaded up for the journey.

They crossed the river from Rima by the familiar rope bridge. The river gushed from a deep gash in the rock spraying the air with a thin white mist. The sky was cobalt blue and its intensity of colour washed the hills ahead in a violet hue. The mountains scattered with pine forests were high around them. Below, there were deep glens and cool north-facing slopes. There were oak and maple trees, rhododendrons and magnolias, some still in bloom. There were huge cherry trees, their branches weighed down with pink blossoms. The air was cooler and fresher here. Delphina gazed round her with almost reverent awe at her surroundings.

'It's . . . breathtaking.' She turned to Arnold, her face and eyes shining with delight.

'Now you see why we go through so much torture to get here,' he said. 'How everything else in the world seems so paltry compared to this.'

'I do see.' She filled her eyes again with the magnificent colours, the texture of the rock, the water and the sky. Then a pang of sadness hit her, her father would never see this again, never stand in these hills under the eaves of the world.

She walked on, head down, not wanting Arnold to see her distress.

The days went on, they passed paddy fields and woods blue with iris, and tiny villages. Everywhere was rich with plants, primulas, rhododendrons, and anemone. The people were a mixture of indigenous pygmies and tall, swarthy people. The women were handsome with black eyes and raven hair; they were covered in jewellery, large silver earrings, bangles and beaded collars.

Two of their loads went missing and they were held up again. Arnold sent Pasang to find out what had happened to their mail. They waited for him at a small village scattered in a valley. For the first time since their arrival, Delphina felt a feeling of hostility towards them. Some round-headed monks stared at them with suspicion.

'Why don't they like us?' she asked Arnold quietly.

'They distrust us as they think we are after the gold in the mountains. It belongs to the monks and they don't believe we have come here solely to look for plants. Besides,' — he lowered his voice as a monk looked their way

143

— 'they think we will disturb the spirits, bring down rock falls and bad weather to ruin their crops.'

'Can't Tewang tell them that we're not going to?'

'It's not as easy as that. There may only be two of us, but they are afraid we will bring other people, people with guns to hurt them.'

They were sitting by a fire in a guesthouse. Delphina stretched out her legs towards the fire. The ripple of animosity that went through the Tibetans sitting with them could have been ladled out with a spoon.

Arnold put his hand on her legs and said quietly, 'Move your legs, you are disturbing the hearth spirit.'

She jerked her legs back, tucking them under her. 'Arnold, I don't feel happy here; we haven't come across this kind of feeling before.'

'Only some of them are as bad as this. It's probably the fault of the monks here; they look a surly lot.'

Delphina hardly slept that night fearful of offending one of the spirits. She was relieved when Arnold suggested they go on to Zayul and leave word for Pasang to follow on.

They had barely settled in Zayul, before news was brought to them that a messenger carrying mail and some silver ingots belonging to the governor had been found murdered and the mail stolen.

Arnold swore when he heard the news. 'I hope there was nothing important in his mailbag for us. With any luck it will be found discarded somewhere, after all the silver must have been the reason the poor fellow was murdered.'

'Does this often happen?' Surely they were *her* letters that had gone astray she thought sulkily, like a child.

'Yes, or they get lost, or forget to bring them. But it's a bloody nuisance,' Arnold grumbled.

'Will they find out who did it?'

'I don't know. A lot of drifters come to this part of Tibet. It's well away from the main road to Lhasa and people who need to disappear can do so easily here.'

Pasang returned with an urgent message for Arnold from the governor in Rima who was furious that his silver had been stolen and his messenger murdered. He was holding various suspects and he wanted Arnold to return at once to help with the judgement.

'I suppose I must go as he has requested it, and we need to stay on the right side of him,' Arnold sighed heavily. 'I just want to be left in peace to collect my plants but one's always called upon to act as a judge, or a doctor on the way.'

'Go back?' Delphina cried with dismay. Cedric would surely overtake them at this rate and get to the peony before her.

'It won't take me long; you stay here, you'll be quite safe.'

'No,' she said. 'I want to come back with you.' She was not going to be left alone here in this wild and savage place with just the baggage carriers.

He looked at her gravely. 'It's a long way back, and you'll be quite safe here. Besides there's quite a bit of work to do.'

'I won't hold you up. Mono can see to the flower presses. He'll do exactly what you tell him.'

From his expression she knew he didn't want to take her back. She thought quickly of some way she could persuade him without sounding as if she was whining when, to her extreme relief he said with a sigh, 'All right, but we've got to move fast; I can't waste much more time.'

It nearly killed Delphina to keep up the pace, but she was determined not to hold him up. She did not speak during the journey back, but conserved all her energy for just getting there. They arrived at Rima late in the afternoon and early the next morning Arnold

146

was summoned to the governor's presence.

'Can I come?' Delphina asked, thinking it would be interesting to see a Tibetan trial.

'I don't think you should; their justice is quite different to ours,' Arnold said firmly and left to go to the governor. But curiosity got the better of her and she followed him, thinking that if she didn't like it she could leave.

The governor was in his study going through a pile of statements. He seemed pleased to see Arnold, but took no notice of Delphina who kept herself in the shadows.

'We have some suspects,' the governor told Arnold, 'we will see which one is guilty.'

Various officials hovered round them. The first suspect was pushed into the room. Arnold, who did not hide his annoyance at Delphina's presence, reluctantly explained to her that he was a headman from a local village. He was smartly questioned, then dismissed. The next man was from the Mishmi tribe who scuffed his feet in the dust, his eyes never meeting anyone's gaze. His voice, when he answered the questions was squeaky with anxiety. Next was a lama dressed in a red robe, a purple sash wrapped round his body. He too was questioned and dismissed.

'What's happening?' Delphina whispered to Tewang.

'They're being asked if they knew the messenger and what they were doing on the day he was murdered, but the governor's not pleased with their answers.' His voice tailed off as another man came in.

He was Tibetan, a tall, swarthy man who seemed to dwarf the room. His slanting cheekbones gave him a sinister look, and his eyes, bright as a snake's, stared defiantly at the governor. He too was dismissed. Then another man entered and went over to the governor and whispered something in his ear.

The governor nodded and said to Arnold, 'Let's go outside.'

Delphina thinking the trial was finished followed them to the square. It was crowded, many of the headmen from the neighbouring villages had been called. A long, low veranda ran along three sides of the square. A limp prayer flag drooped from a pole in the centre. A wooden bench was brought out and the governor sat on it motioning Arnold and Delphina to sit down too. Tewang stood behind them. Various other men took their places round her, hemming Delphina in. The atmosphere was of subdued excitement as if they were scenting blood. She wished now that she had listened to Arnold and stayed in the guesthouse.

Looking up she saw the circle of mountain

peaks, glistening white against the rich, blue sky, savage in its beauty. The heavy, sinister silence hanging over the crowd began to eat into her as if it was she who was on trial. Her stomach contracted when she noticed a coil of rope and two whips lying in the dust.

The headman they had seen inside was brought before them. He knelt down before the governor. Again he was questioned, but the governor seemed unimpressed. He made a gesture to a couple of men who seized him and pushed him to the ground on his stomach. An old man picked up the rope, deftly tied him up and dragged him like a dead tree to the centre of the square. Another man pulled the suspect's clothes back from his buttocks, then squatted down in the dirt and took the suspect's head into his lap, holding him fast by his neck. Two men picked up the whips and stood either side of the squirming body. The crowd pressed forward; a dog began to bark. Delphina closed her eyes.

Arnold whispered, 'I warned you their kind of justice is different to ours. He has been questioned, but they don't believe what he says.'

The men with the whips lifted them and brought them down alternately on the suspect's skin, counting as they lashed. She could not bear it, the sound of the swish of the whip and his screams as it cut his flesh. On it went, the rhythmic thwack of the whip, the intoning call of the count, the suspect screaming and sobbing. If only she could get away, drown out the sound, escape the taut, excited atmosphere that hung over the crowd. After twenty lashes the man was questioned again. It seemed he was still not believed, for again he was beaten, then again questioned. Not until a hundred lashes were inflicted, was the man allowed to crawl away. Delphina opening her eyes in sickening curiosity to see if he was dead, saw another man pour something on to his wounds.

Then it was the Mishmi's turn. Delphina tried to get up, to escape before the second whipping, but the men around her with their pungent smell, with heavy overtones of yak, pressed forward and she could not move.

'Arnold,' she said weakly, grabbing his hand and holding it tightly, feeling sick at the sound of the whip swishing through the air and the cries of the suspect renting the air.

She made another attempt to struggle up and leave.

Arnold pulled her down. 'It's too late; you might offend the governor. Remember these are their customs, we cannot criticize them.'

She sat beside him, hands over her ears, her eyes tight closed, but still she felt the torturous atmosphere and heard the screams.

Then she felt a wave of even more hostility and opened her eyes. It was the turn of the sinister Tibetan. He knelt down in the dust in his bright clothes, his silver earrings and his long boots, almost mocking them all. His face held a look of sly ruthlessness, as if he was the judge not the suspect. Even as he was pushed to the ground and trussed up like the others he seemed not to lose one ounce of his malevolent dignity. The man who tied him with the rope, did so reluctantly, as if by touching him his life would be at risk. Delphina screwed her eyes shut bracing herself for the screams to penetrate her ears even with her fingers pushed deep into them, but there was no cry. She loosened her fingers from her ears, thinking he had confessed already and it was over. The whistle of the whips cracked again, but the man uttered not a single sound.

When it was over, the Tibetan got up shook himself as if he had not been touched and stalked away, throwing a contemptuous glance at the governor.

Arnold leant over her. 'Remember, they are not like us. They are a tough race of people and these are their ways. You have to accept

151

what you see, not judge it by our ways back home.'

The governor spoke.

'One of these men has murdered a messenger and stolen the money he was carrying.' Arnold translated the governor's words for her. 'If they had confessed they could have escaped a beating, but every day they will be beaten until one confesses. Come, Delphina,' Arnold said when he had finished. 'Let us congratulate the governor on his justice.'

She wanted to shout, 'Justice! It's more like barbarism!' but Arnold's expression warned her to hold her tongue and she nodded mutely, though inside she burned with anger.

She went to her room in the guesthouse and threw herself down on her camp-bed. Arnold followed her.

'Delphina,' he said, 'if we don't appear to agree with the governor's way of meting out justice, he may turn against us and stop us resuming our trip.'

'But what he did was so . . . barbaric. Beating people that he seems to have so little evidence against.'

'I know, but remember they don't have detectives and fingerprints and forensic labs.'

'You're laughing at me; you enjoy seeing me suffer. You hope I'll collapse, beg to be allowed to go home, don't you?' She blazed at him like an angry child overcome with fury of the sickening scene she'd just witnessed.

'On the contrary, Delphina, I think you're wonderful.' He put his hand on her shoulder. 'Really wonderful.' His expression was warm with admiration as he looked at her.

For a moment she thought she saw desire burning in his eyes. The sight of it brought her up with a jolt, made her hold back, move away from him.

'I hate to be teased,' she said vehemently.

'I'm not teasing you,' he said, giving her a long, intense look as if he hadn't really seen her before. Then he got up briskly and said cheerfully, 'You see, if we don't agree with the governor he can stop our trip dead in its tracks, and you won't even have a chance to find the peony.'

She swallowed her anger with difficulty. 'I'll keep quiet, but I hope I don't have to sit through that torture again tomorrow.'

'No, we must leave tomorrow. The governor has given us another pass that will be invaluable for us to travel in his jurisdiction and get fresh supplies. Believe me, that's gold dust out here. You can be held up for months while various officials decide where or where not you can go.'

'So you think witnessing this barbarity was

worth it?' she said sourly. 'I'm certain it was that sinister-looking Tibetan, don't you?'

Arnold shrugged. 'I don't know. Tewang knows him. His name is Wunju. He's not liked but he was the only one in command of himself.'

'He's probably had a lot of practice.' Delphina shivered, thinking of him. 'I wish you hadn't told me his name as it makes him more real. I hope they execute him; though nothing will make me watch that.'

'We won't have to,' Arnold said. 'Besides they don't go in much for execution, blinding is more their line.'

Delphina shuddered. 'I've had enough horrors for today. But that man really made me feel afraid, as if he was a snake about to crawl over me. Silly really, as whatever the outcome I won't see him again, will I?'

'I doubt it,' Arnold said. 'Now let's go and eat; are you hungry?'

'No,' she said, 'I'm going for a walk. I need to drink in some of that wonderful nature to chase away the ugly cruelty of man.'

She walked through the town looking up at the ring of faraway mountains dazzling in the evening sun, the warm apricot colour tipped with the fiery red of the sun glowing deeper and deeper red as the sun slipped away. She willed the beauty to wipe out the sight and sounds of the whippings.

But she could not. Strangely, it was not the beatings that stuck so fast in her mind, but the cruel, sinister face of Wunju that hovered like a ghastly apparition in her thoughts leaving her feeling threatened and afraid.

9

The days merged into weeks. Delphina began to feel that she'd known no other life than this precarious living in a kerosene-smelling tent, or in a damp cabin, in the savage beauty of Tibet.

The days, when the weather permitted, were spent in careful plant hunting. Arnold had taught her so much that now she went alone or at least with only Pasang or Tewang as a companion. She became totally absorbed in her work, coming back to Arnold delighted with some find, a new, to her anyway, species of impatiens or salvia. But more often that not, Arnold would smile kindly and say, 'This is well known,' or 'yes, this is new, I found it too where I was working. But the rhodos, there are many species I haven't seen before. Look at this orange one, I must get the seed of that.'

'There are more rhododendrons than anything else, I'm almost sick of them,' she teased, knowing they were one of his passions.

But as she worked methodically, noting and collecting, her mind buzzed with the thought of Randolph's peony and whether they would reach it before Cedric and Lorin. Just the thought of Lorin made her body quicken and she despised herself. It was just the trap Cedric hoped she would fall into and she must guard against it.

They were not far from the peony now; the next camp should be close to it. Close enough, she hoped for her to find it with Pasang without having to involve Arnold.

Pasang was malleable like a child. He was fascinated by her bright hair and would happily follow her about, doing exactly what she told him, collecting the plants she wanted, helping her press them, or packing them up to send back to England.

With her newly acquired freedom, Delphina kept religiously to Arnold's rules. She only went in the direction he suggested, and if there was any hint of a sudden change in the weather she made her way back to camp at once. Each week he became more relaxed about her movements. They no longer talked about the peony. There were so many other plants to interest him she felt he had almost forgotten about it. When they came to the place, she would be able to collect it and keep it hidden from him among her other plants.

For two days she was ill with a stomach upset, only managing to do a little easy work.

Arnold dosed her with some of his medicines and took much of the work from her. Then, before she'd recovered properly, he went down with a recurrence of a fever he had caught on a previous trip. As she sat by him reading to him, she was seized with the most appalling homesickness. She could see her father imprisoned in his chair staring out of the window, watching the days crawl by without her. She thought of her bedroom with the pretty blue and cream-flowered chintz, the soft, smooth sheets on her bed, the smell of newly ironed laundry and baking that travelled up the back stairs from the kitchen.

They were mad lying here both so ill when they could be in good health at home with proper food, warmth and comfort. She would die, she thought, if she woke up one more morning to the dun colour of her tent, to the buttery tea that tasted of yak. Not that everything in this godforsaken place didn't taste or smell of yak, or have yak hair in it. What wouldn't she give for a hot scented bath. She wanted new clothes instead of these endless, nearly always damp, trousers and jerseys. She wanted to wear a long, silky and frivolous dress and drip with jewellery, coil her hair up with satin ribbons, wear an outrageous hat, anything to get away from this filth, this wet, these disgusting meals.

'Have you been caught by the black dog, Delphina?' Arnold said quietly.

'I don't know what you mean, I just want to go home. I've had enough, Arnold. You being so ill, me feeling weak and sick.'

Arnold smiled sympathetically. 'I call it the black dog. It hits us all from time to time. A terrible isolation, a loneliness beyond description. But it goes. Tomorrow, or the next day it will have left you.'

'I don't think it will ever leave me. I feel completely devastated by it. I want to go home, Arnold . . . ' She looked at him imploringly. 'I want to go home.'

'Well, you can't, my dear. You'll have to accept that,' he said firmly. 'Now, help me up, I must try my legs, see how far they'll take me.' Weakly he edged himself up in his bed.

Delphina wanted to howl. She wanted more sympathy from him, but she bit back her misery and helped him up. He tottered over to a chair and sank down on it heavily.

'Do you feel dizzy?'

'A little, it will pass. I'm used to this damn fever. I got it badly some years back, I had to abort the trip and be carried back on a stretcher. Damn thing never quite leaves you.'

'But still you come out here instead of staying in England to get over it completely?'

she said irritably, as if he should have stayed at home, then she would not be here either.

'I can't bear to stay at home for long. I understand exactly how you're feeling, Delphina, but you know I've often felt worse back home surrounded by so-called comforts and people of one's own race. You can be terribly isolated by social conventions, just not fitting in with the right set, whatever that is.'

His words touched Delphina and made her think of Marsha Barker and their journey together on the train. She certainly made her feel excluded.

She said, 'I haven't been around much socially, what with Papa and before his accident Mummy being so ill and dying.'

'I don't fit easily into conventional life. I suppose it's not surprising if I've been away so much, but Randolph was the same, though he did have a family. An explorer, for that is what we are as well as plant hunters, is like a nomad, always wanting to travel some more, to move on, to experience things that the . . . more saner, perhaps, among us, only like to speculate about.'

'Will you ever come to rest? Find a haven? Or are you always looking for the impossible, or even . . . ' She paused, wondering if that was one of the reasons her father went away so often. 'Are you running away from something?' Seeing a look of discomfort cross his face, she realized that she'd hit home. He was escaping from his impotence and the strain it must put on him. 'I mean,' she said hastily, 'I always thought Papa was escaping from Mummy's cloying, possessive love. She adored him and if only she was alive now she'd be in her element.'

'So she would, poor Laura,' Arnold said, his eyes taking on a faraway look. He was thinking of Selena and she was about to ask him about her, when he continued, 'Perhaps you're right, Randolph was escaping the confines of a suffocating love. He never could abide being possessed. But you must agree that these mountains, the wonderful surroundings so remote from the hurly burly of life, are addictive. The mundane life of nine to five work, social gatherings and all, are nothing compared to this.'

'Perhaps not. But just now I'd give anything for a hot bath, a clean room, a comfy bed and a meal cooked by Mrs Crane,' Delphina said, longingly.

'I know,' he said gently, 'but ride with it, Delphina; these feelings will pass.' He took up his book and began to read and she felt suddenly close to him as if he understood her, cared for her struggle with depression, so she went on sitting there beside him in silence, drawing comfort from his presence.

The next day Arnold was well enough to continue with his plant collecting and the day after that they moved camp and travelled on up the valley. They stopped after a couple of hours' march to rest, Arnold not wanting to tax their strength too far. Ahead of them above the rocks, Delphina saw a crowd of dark birds circling, then darting down and flying away again, something dripping in their beaks.

'Look at all those birds, they must have found a feast,' she said idly to Arnold.

He glanced to where she pointed, then looked away. 'It's probably a sky burial.'

'A what?'

He grimaced. 'It will probably upset you if I tell you. It's another of their ways, which is understandable here, but wouldn't go down well at home.'

'Tell me about it,' she said.

He glanced at her apprehensively. 'They don't have enough earth around to bury their dead, so . . . ' he paused.

'Go on.'

'When someone dies here, after certain ceremonies at home, the body is taken to a special place where it is dismembered and fed to the vultures.'

'How horrible.' A nightmare image of their sharp beaks tearing at human flesh made her flinch.

Arnold put his arm round her. 'I shouldn't have told you. I know it's the sort of gruesome thing that upsets you,' he said, gently.

She leant against him trying to force the pictures of bleeding bodies being hacked to pieces and thrown to the birds crowding into her mind. The bodies held the face of her mother and her father. How could the grieving relatives support this?

Arnold tightened his hold on her and laid his head against hers for a moment. 'The Tibetans don't value the body as we do. When the spirit has gone, the body is nothing. The Buddhist belief is one of compassion, the dead body is of no value, but it can feed the birds.'

'It is too terrible,' Delphina said, pushing herself closer to his warm, living body. 'We're not going to pass the place, are we? I couldn't bear it.'

'No. Stop drawing pictures of it in your mind. Strangely, it does become acceptable after a while. After all, worms eat us.'

'Why can't they burn their dead?'

'Not enough wood.' He squeezed her shoulder. 'Come on, forget it.'

'But vultures.' She shuddered, looking up despite herself and seeing the black cloud of birds still circling. The rest of their party seemed to take no notice of them at all.

'The Tibetans think highly of vultures. They don't hurt anything living. They only feed on what is already dead. Come, Delphina, don't dwell on it.' He released her and got up. 'We must push on. But don't worry, we'll steer well clear of the burial site.'

Almost as soon as they arrived at the village where they were to camp, the headman came to ask for Arnold's help. A child was sick and was getting worse. Did he have any medicine that would work?

Arnold had often been called upon to administer medicine, advice, or justice. The people were delighted to try out new things. When one person came to consult Arnold, others, all clamouring round with strange and mostly unconvincing ailments, crowded him out.

'I'll come with you,' she said, following him.

They entered the hut. When she'd accustomed herself to the darkness, Delphina could distinguish the body of a child lying in a corner, a woman sitting by him. The place smelt strongly of yak, and the sourness she'd become accustomed to.

The child lay very still, his eyes closed. There was a curious knotted sort of mat over his forehead, but when Arnold sat down beside him and put his hand there, Delphina saw that it was a tight cluster of flies.

She gasped, and the woman gave her a look of despair as if to say, 'What can I do? The more I chase them off the more they come.'

Arnold questioned the woman in Tibetan, sometimes turning to Tewang to interpret a word. He switched on his torch, shining it over the child's head and Delphina saw a huge bloody gash, which apart from the flies looked filled with dirt.

'We must clean it; he'll be poisoned,' she said at once, swallowing her revulsion.

Arnold asked for water. 'You see,' he said, as he began to wash the wound, the child wincing as the disinfectant touched him, 'they pack wounds with manure out here, and, surprisingly, they often heal.'

'Manure!' She was horrified. This child looked so weak, so near death they had surely contributed to it by filling his wound with manure. No wonder the flies had been so prevalent.

Arnold grinned at her. 'Their ways, my dear. We're not at a nice, clean, country hospital now. Where will they get Dettol from? There are no chemists here.'

'There must be a plant or a herb,' she retorted, watching him deftly clean the wound, pack it with a pad soaked in antiseptic cream.

'I've done my best. I'll dress it again tomorrow and leave them with some cream and hope he survives.' He said something to the woman, and she nodded. He crushed two aspirins and told her to put it in water and make the child drink it.

But when they got outside the tent they found the *gam* waiting for them, his face grave. The porters were on strike and would not walk another step unless their wages were increased.

It was not the first time they had been difficult. At one place they had refused to march more than half a day, at another the weather had been wrong. Delphina was hit with agitation; not another delay, would they ever reach the peony? Arnold seeing her distress smiled.

'We'll get there,' he said, going off to deal with it.

Some time later, Arnold returned and told her they would leave in the morning as planned.

'Well done. I must say they are a surly lot,' she said, 'and you manage to deal with them very well.' She was sure that they were about two days away from the peony though the thought made her edgy with fear that after all their hardships it would not be there.

After more complications they set off the following day. Delphina had visited the sick child and had thought he looked a little better.

'They'll probably fill his wound with manure again as soon as we've left,' Arnold said, 'but our antiseptic might have given him a chance.'

After a few hours' march they came to a river but they found that the bridge had been swept away. After some discussion with Tewang and Pasang, Arnold said, 'We'll have to wade across. Don't be alarmed, we just hold hands firmly in a line and go across slowly.'

The water was surging and bubbling as it rushed past them filling her with panic. What if they couldn't cross the river, or, worse still, be washed away?

Arnold was busy securing the loads on the backs of the porters and the mules and urging them into the swirling waters.

'It all right, don't worry,' Tewang said to her, seeing her face, 'hold on, you won't fall.'

The porters waded into the water, first one, then another holding on to the person in front of them, until a line of people formed.

Tewang took his place and Arnold pushed Delphina in next, taking up the rear and holding her hand. The water was icy, it swirled round her body and for a moment she thought she would lose her footing and fall, but Arnold held her firm.

'Go on,' he said, 'each step brings the bank nearer.'

'Or the other one further away,' she remarked, with an attempt at a laugh. She moved on, being pulled by the line in front of her, urged by Arnold behind. One of the porters stumbled and the movement went down the whole line. Delphina bit back a scream. Arnold squeezed her hand.

'Don't stop here. We're nearly there.'

At last Tewang reached the bank and pulled her out after him. Her wet clothes clung to her.

'The sun looks as if it's coming out, we'll soon be dry,' Arnold said cheerfully and went back to help with the mules.

After an hour or two, the weather suddenly closed in. Snow began to fall and a swirling mist came down. They were in the middle of a ridge and after a quick consultation with Tewang, Arnold said, 'If we keep straight on for a little while longer we'll reach shelter. But move as quickly as you can.'

'If I don't freeze to death first,' Delphina

grumbled. Fear of being lost in a blizzard high on this rock face added to her discomfort. Arnold again walked behind her and she pushed herself on, her breath hurting in her chest, parts of her body sore from the chafing of her wet clothes, her whole body crying out for rest. At last, Tewang stopped and she could dimly see the outline of a building.

It was a deserted Buddhist temple. They all crowded in away from the weather, and before long a fire was burning merrily in the centre of the room and tea was being brewed. Delphina cupped her hands round the bowl of steaming tea with its aroma of yak and drank it gratefully. Her body felt heavy with fatigue. As the fire began to warm her, she almost cried out with the pain of her thawing limbs. Arnold rubbed her feet and hands until the pain subsided.

Exhaustion and the bliss of being warm and dry took over and it was not until the next morning that Delphina took notice of her surroundings. When she woke the next morning, the sight of the sun and the clear, dazzling blue sky seen through the slits in the wall, lifted her spirits. She sprang up and pulled out her father's map from her clothes.

They had passed countless ruins on their journey, but surely this was the deserted temple her father had marked on his map. He too had got stuck in bad weather and had stayed here. He had marked it with its steep path behind used by pilgrims on their way to the monastery. A few miles up, this path forked with a choice of roads going either way. Randolph had marked the left route up some way along a path until he'd crossed a spur of rock. This he had drawn and marked, 'Looks like a profile of Punch, with his huge nose.' Then he had gone down a path, 'that did not look like a path', until he'd reached a large round boulder with a mass of primulas growing round it. A hundred or so paces on, led down to a shrubby patch hidden by rocks where he'd seen the peony.

Her heart beat faster as she read his careful instructions in his scrawling hand. She forced herself to read them slowly, take them in. It seemed unbelievable that after all these painful weeks of travelling, all the plans and dreams, she was near to it at last. Maybe tomorrow or the next day she would hold the peony in her hand. She wished with all her heart that she could share her joy with Arnold. She was also filled with a grim satisfaction that she was here, so close to it before Cedric Hartford had come. If all continued to go as planned she would find it before he got anywhere near here — if he was

170

coming this way at all.

She dressed quickly and went to look around her. The place had an eerie deadness to it. The courtyard was overgrown with weeds; the heavy doors of the temple hung crookedly on their hinges. Going on, she saw round the crumbling walls rows of leather prayer drums, their stuffing bursting through their rotting skins. She heard the chatter coming from the porters and the smell of the fire being lit to cook breakfast and, craving human contact, she went out to join them.

'Will this weather hold?' she asked Arnold, hoping her voice did not betray her excitement.

'You never can tell, but we might make the most of it. I found a very pretty species of saxifrages and a new, I think, strain of begonia.'

'We must collect as many plants as we can. I'll take Pasang and go and explore,' she said, spreading a biscuit with some tinned butter.

'Stay close, there are plenty of plants around here,' Arnold said.

Hugging her secret excitement to herself, she didn't notice he was watching her. He ate as gustily as she did, but all the time he kept glancing at her thoughtfully.

She packed some provisions for lunch, put Randolph's map in her pocket and set out with Pasang. Arnold had gone off happily after his saxifrages, so it was easy for her to take the pilgrim's path without him seeing. Pasang however began grumbling at once.

'It not safe, spirits are there.' His eyes showed white in his ruddy face.

'What spirits?' Delphina said crossly. It would take a lot more than spirits to deter her now.

'Bad spirits,' he said, backing away.

Delphina was about to scold him for his stupidity when she remembered Arnold's way of dealing with them. She came over to him and pulled out a locket from round her neck. It held a small picture of Randolph; he had given it to her before she'd left.

'At least my picture will be there, if not me,' he'd said, looking ashamed at his sentiment.

'Look,' she said smiling, 'this will protect us from the spirits.'

He still looked alarmed so she opened it and showed him the picture of her father. 'Look, this is the picture of a very powerful god who lives in my country. It will protect me and whoever comes with me, from all bad spirits.' She smiled again and held out her hand. 'Come,' she said, 'this is magic and will protect us.'

Pasang did not look much happier but he

followed her. Every so often he would stop and look fearfully round as if a spirit was about to challenge them. Then Delphina would take out her locket and wave it and he would go on.

They went on for about two hours. Pasang grew more and more agitated. At last, when Delphina thought he might turn tail and leave her, she saw the large spur of rock, which indeed looked so like the old pictures of Punch's profile that she burst out laughing.

'We're nearly there now,' she said, smiling encouragingly at him, 'close to the special plant I'm looking for, then we can go back.'

On she went searching now for 'the path that was not a path', near the boulder and the primulas. If only Arnold was here with her to share this or better still Papa, whole and well again. There were primulas everywhere and rocks, but then at last she saw a boulder, bigger and rounder than the rest and the ground sloping downwards, away from it. Surely this was it. A tiny ribbon made by the melting snow, running through the scree marked the place.

'It's just here. Soon we will go back,' she said, her breath coming fast. In a moment she would surely see the peony, just as Papa had described it, dancing in the wind. She was too impatient now to wait for Pasang and she ran down the path that was not a path counting her steps as she went, Randolph's instructions in her hand. Her eyes scoured the landscape for a dash of white that would herald it, but the only white came from tiny flowers creeping from the rocks.

A hundred paces, or so, Randolph had said. Did he mean more or less? She went on, still she could not see it. She counted another hundred, went back, then forward. She reached a huge wall of boulders that cut off any further passage.

She turned round again. She must keep calm, take more time to look more carefully. She must have missed it in her agitation. She went slowly up to the top again, first to one side then to the other. Pasang scuttled after her.

'Where is plant? Which one do you want? These are pretty. Hurry, we must go.'

'Don't fuss me,' she said sharply, adding more kindly, 'I look for a white flower, a peony. Big white flowers. It should be here.' She thought almost as soon as she'd said it that she shouldn't have told him or he would tell Arnold, or far worse, Cedric, should he come. But he might know where it was, and when they'd found it she'd beg him not to tell anyone. Threaten him with the bad spirits if he did.

For over an hour they searched. There were so many paths it was confusing, but there was nothing. Delphina tried not to think of Arnold's many warnings that it might not be there. Villagers picked plants to decorate their shrines, or possibly animals ate them, or they'd died or had not seeded. She knew all these things were possible but still she could not bear to admit defeat.

The sky became darker and Pasang began to panic.

'Snow comes, storm,' he said, pulling at her arm. 'We must go.'

He was right but her heart felt as if it would break. She had been so sure she would find it, would bring it back in triumph to Randolph. But it was not there. She felt dead inside, her limbs leaden. She took one last look round that sea of pink and purple flowers and reluctantly followed Pasang. All the way back, even when they were far from the place her father had marked, she kept searching for it. Sometimes running down another path, just in case she had mistaken the instructions, but there was no sign of the peony.

They trudged back along the pilgrims' path to the temple. She felt as if the whole path was indeed inhabited by spirits, evil spirits with faces like Cedric Hartford that mocked her as she went.

Pasang as if guessing her thoughts said mournfully, 'The bad spirits are angry with us.'

'Let them,' she said, and marched on. He ran after her calling for her to wait, to be careful.

They reached the temple. How could she bear the pain of her disappointment, the feeling that she had let her father down? Was it there all the time and she had missed it? She went to the small room she slept in, without looking to see if Arnold was back. She threw herself down on her bed and gave way to wild weeping. The whole trip had been a failure. The hardships, the torturous marching, the mean diet, the cold and wet, the leeches and the flies, all had been in vain. But, far worse than all of these, would be Randolph's disappointment.

She tortured herself with seeing him waiting for her return. The light in his eyes at seeing her, the agony when he realized she had not found it.

If he had been well he would have understood. He knew the precariousness of plants better than she did. His disappointment would be tempered with the discovery of another plant, or the thought that on the next trip, or the next, he would find it. But for her to return without the peony would be like stabbing him to death.

She lay there a long time overwhelmed by the pain of her disappointment. Then, deep inside her, she felt the faint nudge of determination. She'd go there again tomorrow. Maybe she'd chosen the wrong boulder, or maybe that wall of rocks cut off the way to the peony and she could somehow get round it. She could not rest until every part beyond and around 'Punch's nose' was combed and double combed. She must have slept, for when she woke, the room was in complete darkness. She did not care, the darkness hid her, she would stay here until the morning, then go, alone, without Pasang and his fear of spirits, to search again.

'Delphina?' Arnold had come into the room but she could not speak to him, could not voice the agony of her disappointment. A light flickered across the walls and she burrowed her head further into her sleeping bag.

'Here's a lamp, and I will light this one. Why are you in the dark, are you not well?'

'Go away. I want to be alone.' Her voice was muffled in the pillow.

'As you like, but first I have something for you.'

'I don't want anything. Please, Arnold, leave me alone.'

'Just sit up and look at this, then I'll leave you. Not before. Please, Delphina,' he insisted.

'Oh, all right.' She struggled up, her swollen eyes hurt against the light, dim though it was. Arnold was standing a few feet away, a lamp in his hand.

'What is it then?' she said, with ill grace.

Slowly he drew his other hand from behind his back and held out an ivory peony. The light from the lamp in his other hand infused its pale petals as if it was illuminated.

10

For a moment Delphina was unable to believe it. She stared at the peony as if it was indeed the Holy Grail. Surely it must be some other plant, or a hallucination to her troubled mind.

'I think this is the one that Randolph found,' Arnold said gently.

'But . . . ' She put her hand out gingerly as if by touching it, it would disappear. 'I looked for it everywhere, exactly where Papa told me it was on his map. Where did you find it?'

Arnold put down the lamp and, taking her hand, pulled her up and led her over to a ledge where they could sit down. It was dark and he went back for the lamp and put it on the floor between them. It threw up shadows, lighting only their faces and the peony.

He put it in her hand and said, 'I found it quite by chance, the other side to where you were.'

'But how did you know where . . . oh, I suppose Pasang told you.' She held the stem in her hand, gently stroking the pale petals with the tips of her fingers.

'I knew more or less where Randolph had seen it . . . '

'You didn't look at my map he gave me?' she cried out.

'No, but you are not the only one who's after it. And there were rumours of one being seen before, I told you about it. Besides,' — he smiled at her — 'this morning you were different. You may have tried to keep your excitement hidden, but seeing your face, your shining eyes, I guessed that we had reached the place. Quite simply I followed you.'

'I never saw you, and you didn't take the last path with me. I would have seen you then.'

'That was the luck of it. I didn't follow you down that path. I took another path the opposite side. I was planning to stay near you, in case you got into any difficulties. There were lots of plants there; I got quite mesmerized by them. Then I saw the peony, just as Randolph described it, with the sun reflected in the petals, so it looked as if it glowed.'

'How I wish I had found it; I wish I'd known you were there, I wanted to share the moment with you.' She felt such a warmth for him. 'Dear Arnold, thank you for giving it to me. You could have hidden it, kept the knowledge for yourself. Will you show me where it is tomorrow?'

'If you're not too tired, you've had a stiff day today.'

'I must see it.' She could not keep her eyes off it. Happiness began to seep through her dead misery. She put her arm round Arnold's neck and kissed him, holding her cheek against his for a moment. 'Thank you,' she said, 'I really thought I would die not finding it.'

Even in the dim light she could see her gesture had moved him. He said gruffly, 'It was only luck on my part. I just felt I should be near you in case you got into trouble.'

'There is no one in the world kinder than you,' she smiled. 'But you say you knew where it was?'

'Cedric Hartford always boasts about his finds. I saw him at the Geographical club. He was with a group of chaps and describing the time he'd found your father before his fall.' He smiled grimly. 'He made it sound as if he had saved his life but . . . ' He held up a hand as she protested. 'He mentioned the pilgrims' path, and the deserted temple, and seeing your excitement this morning . . . '

'Is he here?' she broke in, unconsciously clutching the peony to her.

'Not that I know of, though there are rumours that a group has been seen on the other side of the valley. It may not be him. I'm not sure when he set off, or which route he will be taking, but no doubt he will come this way.'

'We should take the whole plant,' she said.

'You want the seeds, remember that. They won't be ripe for another few months. You must leave the plant alone until then.'

'I'd forgotten.' Her heart sank. 'Papa told me however tempted I was, not to take the seeds too soon, as they just shrivel up.' Her impatience was like a physical pain. If Arnold had found it just by chance why shouldn't Cedric find it too?

'I cannot bear him of all people to have it,' she said with passion.

'I know, my dear.' He took her hand, lacing his fingers between her fingers and the stem of the flower. 'He is a disgrace to our profession, a man whom no reputable company or collector wants to employ.'

'But he is employed, and so is . . . his nephew.' She dropped the words into the darkness, seeing Lorin again in her mind.

'Yes, Lorin.' Arnold glanced quickly at her. 'Do you know him?'

'I've met him.' She explained the scene in the park of Aurian Hall.

'You found him attractive?'

'He is very good-looking, but I won't forget

182

that he is the nephew of Papa's most hated enemy.'

'He's only related to Cedric by marriage,' Arnold said, watching her carefully. 'He shouldn't carry any of the bad genes of his uncle in him.'

'But even that is too much, and no doubt Cedric has great influence over him. I hope they don't come here.'

'Do you think if you see him you will fall in love with him?' he asked lightly. 'He's sure to be attracted to you as that young man was on the boat.'

'No . . . not with Cedric as his uncle.'

'But if he came alone?'

In this strange semi-darkness with the peony between them, their fingers entwined, Delphina felt as if he was asking her something deeper. She looked at him curiously, seeing the shadows on his face, his burning eyes on her. He looked away, gave a short bark of a laugh;

'Forgive an old fool, my dear. I just meant it would be difficult if you were attracted to him. It would not be surprising; he is after all an attractive man and you are young.'

'I will not be attracted to him,' she said firmly, wondering if he was asking questions more to examine his own feelings on the matter than her own.

'It would be a difficult relationship to square with your father.'

'It is not a relationship I will have.' How irritating it was that he should assume that she was just another giddy female interested only in the charms of attractive men.

Arnold let go her hand. 'It is natural that you should care for a young man. Lorin, Henry, they are both good-looking, both no doubt a little in love with you. It is unfortunate for you that you are trapped in this so called marriage of convenience, done really for Randolph's benefit and your mother's smart relations.' He laughed.

'Arnold, let us not talk of it any more. My only fear is that Lorin and Cedric will come here and take the seeds of the peony before we do.'

Arnold moved into the shadow away from the lamp so that she could not see his face. 'Let us hope they will not. Cedric has many problems; he drinks and takes opium and, like me, he's plagued with the recurrence of a fever. He may never get this far.'

'We *must* get there first.'

'We will try, Delphina.' His voice held a tinge of sadness that touched her deeply. The thought suddenly hit her that Arnold deserved to be loved. She supposed his impotence was a barrier to it. She understood why he preferred to escape from it all and come out here. If only she could think of a way without causing offence to say, 'I care very deeply for you, but I don't want any physical relationship.' But she dared not say it, afraid of being misunderstood.

The atmosphere seemed loaded with intimacy; surely, if ever, this was the time to say it, but she could not. Instead, she said tritely to cover her confusion, 'I'm hungry. Have we any food left?'

'Not much. I hope to get more stores when we move on. There's a few tins and some biscuits Mono made from the last of the *tsambi*.' He sounded relieved now, almost cheerful. Lots of their conversations had been about food, describing meals they'd eaten back home, ways of cooking various things, food they'd die for now.

'I won't open a new tin unless you share it with me. I'll have biscuits.'

'There's rice pudding.'

'I'll have that too, and some tea I suppose. You know I think I might miss that tea when I get home. All that yak.'

He laughed and got up. 'Press that peony before it loses its freshness, and tomorrow . . . if it is fine, I'll show you where it is.'

'I'll never be able to thank you enough, dear Arnold. It must be called after you and numbered for you, for you found it.'

'No, it's yours. I will call it after you,' he insisted.

'You let me have the slipper orchid.'

'We'll swap then. The peony is for Randolph and for you.' His beautiful voice curled into her. What it would be like if he recited words of love? she thought fancifully.

'I could fall in love with your voice,' she said impulsively.

'But not with me?'

'I meant . . . ' She felt his unhappiness as if it was solid there in the room with them. If only she could claw back that feeling of intimacy they had shared minutes before, but it had gone like the dousing of a light. 'There is so much to love about you.' She was overcome with sadness, sympathy for him, for herself at being unable to talk of love without the spectre of his impotence standing in their way.

'Bless you for that,' he said. Then, briskly, as if afraid too that his lack of manhood would be mentioned, he said, 'let's have dinner, such as it is. See you in a minute in the dining-room.' There was a ghost of a smile on his lips at his joke. It was that little flag of courage that nearly made her cry.

The next day the weather closed in and Arnold could not take her to the peony. There

186

was much to do with pressing plants, airing them, making lists, but she was restless, feeling that every moment spent away from the plant would make it more vulnerable to being stolen by Cedric. She felt, too, that Arnold had withdrawn into himself and she could not reach the intimacy they'd shared the evening before.

The following morning was clear and they set off early. When they arrived at the rock shaped like Punch's nose, Arnold went on up the rock face then across the other side.

'I think Randolph may have been confused,' he said, looking at the map. 'Remember, he had his accident not far from here. He may have forgotten his bearings when he came to draw that map. If he'd been here himself, there's no doubt he would have found it.'

'Thank heavens you were here and found it.' Delphina looked warily at the jagged rock face. 'Where did he fall? Do you know?'

'No. The only person who knows for sure is Cedric, and I hope we won't find him here.'

A cold shiver of fear ran through her. They must move off before they came.

'So we go on up a bit then over and down,' Arnold said, 'and there' — he pointed ahead — 'are the two boulders your father marked.'

'I see. Yes, they are as he described. But he

didn't make it clear to go higher first, or the other way.' Breathless with excitement she started to run through the boulders.

'Wait,' Arnold called, 'you won't see them unless you're careful.'

She stopped and waited with mounting impatience as he caught up with her. He was smiling. 'Come on, down a bit more.'

She followed him for what seemed like forever.

'He said a hundred steps,' she said.

'That is way out, more like five hundred.'

They walked on over some more boulders and down again and there it was, nestling near some rocks. It shone ivory in the clear light, the blooms bobbing slightly in the breeze. There was no sun so the whiteness shone out on its own.

She walked forward as if approaching a shrine and stood staring at the peony for some minutes in silence. It was so pure, so beautiful in its simplicity. It was terrible to believe that it had caused so much pain and hatred.

'To think Papa is crippled for this,' she said, in a small voice.

Arnold put his arm round her shoulders. 'Don't think of it like that, my dear. He was injured doing the job he loved best. Any of us could fall, as you can see from the terrain.'

'But it was because of this plant that he fell, escaping from Cedric who was so determined to have it. Do you think it's unlucky?'

'Of course not! What foolish things you think. This whole country is filled with plants unseen in Europe, any one would be a valuable find to take back. Why should this one, beautiful as it is, be any different?'

'Cedric's evil benefactor wants it for a start,' she said, and put out her hand to stroke the petals. 'I shall pick one flower and take it, and leave the others to seed, so I can come back and get them later.'

Arnold stayed silent. Sneaking a look at him, she saw his face had taken on that pinched, tense look.

'He hurt you, didn't he, Cedric's benefactor?' she said, looking back at the peony.

'He hurt someone I loved,' he said, curtly.

Delphina slipped her hand through his arm and leant her head against him. 'Selena?'

'I don't want to talk about it.' His voice was thick.

'Wouldn't it help?'

'It wouldn't be fair to her,' he said, 'but suffice to say Cedric introduced her to opium and she died.'

'Mummy never said anything about that.' She was shocked.

'She never knew. It was kept from everyone but your father and me.' Arnold's face was tortured.

She put her arms round him and held him a second. She felt his body stiffen and she released him. Not wanting to hurt him further but curious to know, she asked, 'So somehow that ties in with the favour you owe my father?'

'Yes. He had just appeared in your mother's life. I met him with her and . . . Selena. He . . . ' His voice was laboured. 'She got into this . . . this devil's clutches. He rescued her, but it was too late.' He turned to her, with such agonized hatred on his face that she recoiled. 'I don't want you to ask about him anymore. It has blighted my life and I don't want to discuss it ever again. Do you understand me, Delphina?'

'I do. Thank you, Arnold, for telling me.' She longed to hold him again, offer him love to take away his pain, but the look of anguish in his eyes forestalled her and she said with forced cheerfulness, 'I'll pick one flower, and hope the rest will form good seeds.'

Arnold struggled with his emotions then said in a controlled voice, 'Like a good plant hunter you had better make a map of exactly how to find it again. In few months' time you might forget where it was.'

'I'll do that, but you'll be here to help me,' she said, but she looked round carefully, trying to fix forever in her mind, the exact pattern of the rocks.

'I might not come with you,' he said. 'There are so many seeds to collect and label at that time, we could be in different places.' He said it nonchalantly, but a sudden coldness went through her. She looked back at the peony to watch the wind ruffle through the petals that had brought the sudden chill but the flowers were still.

The next days were busy collecting plants and looking after the ones they had. Arnold threw himself into it, barely stopping to rest. She guessed he was afraid to give himself time to think and tried with gentle words to talk of other things, to urge him to stop to eat, but he seemed indifferent to her care.

They moved on to another camp and then another, staying in tiny villages, once a small town, where the monks, in their bright robes and head-dresses, woke them in the mornings with their strange call on their long horns. They managed to pick up a few stores, chickens, a goat and some eggs. But when they neared the lower reaches of Assam, Arnold sent Tewang and some porters into India to stock up fully on more supplies before their journey back into Tibet again to collect the seeds in the autumn.

Delphina felt content settled in the camp and saw too that Arnold was more cheerful. It was milder down here and each day she enjoyed pottering round collecting plants, drawing them, and pressing them. One evening, when they were working companionably together, Arnold said, 'I'd like to climb right up into the mountains for a couple of days. I would take you, but I think it would be too much for you. You'll be quite safe here with Pasang, and I'll leave Mano to cook for you, and some of the servants. Tewang is a good mountaineer so just he and I will go. I'll only be gone four or five days.'

'I'll be fine,' she lied, hoping to hide her shock of Arnold leaving her. She had her back to him as she wound tapes round a flower press. She was annoyed with herself for being unreasonable. Why shouldn't Arnold go off without her for a few days? She knew he loved mountaineering, and would enjoy savouring the experience alone.

'You would not enjoy it. It can get so cold, and if a blizzard comes down, you just have to sit it out,' Arnold said, as if he guessed her feelings.

'I should hate it, and it's really quite civilized here.' She turned and gave him a smile. 'But will you be safe?'

'Of course,' he grinned, then, looking serious, said, 'if I should not, you must go on down to Darjeeling. I'll give Pasang instructions to take you there. Then you take a train back to Calcutta and a boat home. I'm going to leave plenty of money with you, so you'll be all right.'

'Don't say such things, of course you'll come back,' she said, sharply, to hide her fear.

'I will, but still, as my mother used to say, better to make a plan in case of emergency.' He got up and called for Tewang. 'I'll get myself ready; I want to leave at first light. You've plenty of food, and there are masses of plants still to collect. You've quite got the hang of it now. I don't think I'll even bother to check them when I get back.'

Delphina lay awake most of the night. She was afraid to be alone, yet she would not let Arnold know that. He had been excessively kind in bringing her here with him, putting up with her slowness, her tiredness, and above all finding the peony for her. She would not be the slightest bit ungrateful by showing him her fear.

He'd said good night after their dinner, holding her close to him a second, before going to his tent, throwing back over his shoulder his farewell, 'See you in four or five days then.'

'Have fun,' she called back, as gaily as she could.

Pasang woke her with tea. She'd fallen asleep, exhausted by her fears in the early hours.

'Have they gone yet?' She hoped he'd say they had not, so she could say goodbye to Arnold once again, but he smiled.

'Yes. It is a good day for a climb.'

She busied herself with the plants all day. Every time she felt the cold snake of fear in her belly, she turned to another plant, or made herself draw one, or wrote another list. She had time to write to her father, and she wrote telling him everything about the peony, but leaving out where it was, afraid, even now, that her letter would somehow be intercepted and Cedric would hear of it.

In the dark watches of the night, she kept waking suddenly thinking Cedric had come. In the day she sometimes found herself looking for him, certain he would suddenly appear while Arnold was away.

The new supplies Arnold had sent for arrived. There was also a bundle of letters, mostly for Arnold, but one from her father. She tore it open eagerly:

My Darling Delphina,

It is very quiet without you, but your letters go some way to comfort me. I think of you all the time, and imagine you in the places I have loved.

It went on for some time, describing his own travels and opinions, asking after Arnold and if she had found the peony. It ended:

Cedric Hartford and his nephew set out for India and Tibet two months after you. They had planned to leave about the same time as you, but Cedric became ill. No doubt his evil lifestyle has weakened him. It is a great pity he did not die. I pray you do not meet him on the route. Stay clear of him, my darling, he is an evil man. Do not put yourself in danger. You are more important to me than any plant; abandon the search for it and come home if there should be any fear of him trying to stop you getting it. His boasting of the peony he has never seen growing, has made his benefactor offer him an enormous sum to bring it back.

I pray that you get this letter. I have also written to Arnold to warn him, hoping that at least one letter will get through.

She could hear his voice warning her. She glanced round their peaceful camp as if expecting to see Cedric appearing over the brow of the hill, his cruel smile creasing his face. If only Arnold was here, he would reassure her, but he would not be back for at least three more days.

Then her mind snapped into action. She called back the messenger and, taking back the letter for her father that she'd given him to send on, she opened it and wrote inside:

I have just got your letter. How good it is to hear from you. Do not worry about Cedric, now you have warned me I will be safe.

She re-sealed it and returned it to the messenger. Through her fear came a slow anger. She, or rather Arnold, had found the peony. They would bring it home, the seed and all. She didn't know which route Cedric would take, but they were two months in advance and if Cedric was not well there was a good chance he might not reach the peony at all.

She reread Randolph's letter, picturing him sitting in his wheelchair at his table, writing to her. Every so often he would lift his head and look out at the garden, and his spirit would be with her somewhere in these hills. An overwhelming longing to be with him surged through her, making her almost cry out with pain.

'Are you all right?' Pasang had come up to her silently in his soft boots. He looked at her seriously. 'A sad letter?'

She smiled. 'No, it's from my father. I miss him so much.'

'He was a good man. Is it true he will never walk again?'

'Yes. Did you know him too?' She wanted suddenly to talk of him, to bring him nearer to her.

'I went with him seven years ago, through Burma and Tibet. He was a brave man, a good man.'

'I wish he could come out here again.'

'You have come for him. You will be his eyes and his spirit.'

'Yes. That I must be.' She glanced back at her letter and the words, '*and his nephew*', jumped out at her. She thought of Arnold's words and wondered how she would she feel if she met Lorin out here?

'Pasang, do you know Cedric Hartford?'

Pasang looked puzzled for a moment. 'I don't know. There is a man, a bad man who smuggles opium and steals from our temples. I won't touch him. Bad man.'

197

'Have you met him?'

'No. But we hear. We hear of foreign travellers. Your father, Mr North, other people. Some are good; others come here to steal. Take the treasures from our shrines, make the spirits angry with us so they throw rocks down, stop the food growing.'

'He is one of those. He may be coming soon. He wants to find . . . one of the plants we have. Someone in England will pay him a lot of money for it,' she explained.

'You do not want him to have this plant?'

'No.'

'Then we hope he will not find it. Mr North will know what to do.' He smiled, guilelessly as a child, perplexed at these strange people travelling so far and in such conditions to look for plants you could neither eat nor weave into anything.

Delphina did not sleep well that night. The wind tugged at the tent as if it would tear it away. She imagined she could hear footsteps, the scrape of boots against the rocks to herald Cedric's arrival. How could she wait three more days for Arnold's return?

She struggled through the morning forcing herself into a routine: airing the plants, collecting more, checking the herbarium. But as she worked she found her attention wandering to thoughts of Arnold. She missed his calm, even presence, missed the evenings when they sat together and read or listened to his music.

One evening she put on The 'Moonlight' Sonata and, as the music pulled at the very core of her emotions, she felt she could not bear to be apart from him. She wondered if she did love him or if she just craved the reassurance of his presence, needed him in the same role as her father. But he had loved Selena. She remembered the anguish in his eyes as he had talked about her; perhaps he could never love another woman.

She realized with a sudden shock that he did not repulse her; if he should attempt to kiss her she would welcome him. This thought produced a new yearning for him. Apart from a few burning kisses and hasty fumbles, she was innocent in love and it was her innocence that held her back, and fear that he would think she taunted his impotence if she should make the first move.

She thought of the young men she knew: Philip Stacy, Henry Orsin and Lorin. With each of them she had felt their desire, knew she could be swept up into their arms and into the throes of love-making should she want it. But, she thought with irritation, she'd felt no passion for any them, except for Lorin. And with Arnold there was none of that fire, none of that dangerous excitement lurking so close to the surface when she'd been at Aurian Hall with Lorin. If they loved it would be a chaste kind; she would have to accept that. And yet could she? She had enjoyed the stirring in her body when she was with Lorin, but it was no good, he was the nephew of her father's enemy and she must ignore it. Perhaps, she told herself wryly, she yearned for love, the comfort of the warmth of another human being and was imagining these emotions for Arnold just because he was there.

She lay on her bed letting the music seep into her, filling her with such a melancholy that she felt the tears run down her face. It seemed to encompass all the bitter-sweet love stories in the world.

It was so still and it seemed airless as if the surrounding hills and countryside were keyed up waiting for something, hardly daring to move in case they missed it. She fell into an uneasy sleep, wondering if it was her imagination that was transferring her yearning for love, love for someone she could not have, to Arnold.

11

The following morning the breakfast was just tepid tea and a few biscuits. When Delphina complained, Mano mumbled something and sloped off.

'I expect a better lunch,' she called after him sternly, getting down to her work all the while trying to ignore a feeling of rejection and the question as to whether they resented their duties towards her now that Arnold was not here.

At lunchtime she went over to the place they'd nicknamed the 'dining-room', where the fire and cooking utensils were. It was deserted and there was no sign of a meal. Exasperated, she called out and two of the servants appeared looking rather sulky. One grudgingly lit the fire, but when she asked for Mano he looked the other way, pretending not to understand her, although she knew she had used the correct Tibetan words.

'Where is he?' she demanded. Still they did not answer. Her fear rose and her temper with it. She went over to one of the servants, a small, wary-looking man and grabbed his arm.

'Where is Mano?'

His eyes slid away from her in fear. She shook him, demanded again. Reluctantly, creeping like a beetle, cowering from her as if she would hit him, he led her over to some rocks. Behind them lay Mano, an empty bottle of rice spirit beside him, dead to the world.

Fear and anger chased through her. Apart from Pasang she was alone with half-witted servants and porters and a drunken cook. There was nothing she could do but wait until he had slept it off.

She went back to the fire, found a tin of meat, the inevitable *tsambi* and some chocolate in the stores and prepared them herself. When Pasang appeared, having gone off on some device of his own, she greeted him angrily.

'The minute Mr North's back is turned, Mano takes to the drink. What am I meant to do with him?'

Pasang's face jerked with alarm. Delphina, thinking he was afraid of her anger and fearing to turn him against her, said more gently, 'I'm sorry, Pasang, but it is the limit.'

'He is dangerous when he drinks,' Pasang said, 'he takes up knives.'

'What? Does he do this often?'

'He thinks we are evil. He tries to kill us.'

Pasang hung his head as though it was his responsibility.

'But he's dead to the world now,' she said, trying to reason away her fear.

'When he wakes up he has bad thoughts.'

She fought to ignore the panic that threatened to engulf her. She said firmly, 'You will tie him up and move all the knives and any other dangerous weapons into my tent. Do it at once.'

'But when he wakes he is very strong,' Pasang said, as if her idea was as hopeless as stopping a landslide with one hand.

'Do it now, get someone to help you, but do it.'

Reluctantly, Pasang called over a couple of men and, taking some rope with him, he did as she asked. Delphina collected up all the knives she could see and hid them in her tent. She then put on Mozart's 'Jupiter' symphony on Arnold's gramophone, turned up the volume and tried to lose herself in the music and her book.

Early in the evening she was disturbed by shrill screams. She ran outside, terrified that Mano had got free and was now killing them all. Pasang, sitting by the fire, looked up and grinned at her. He said proudly, 'He is awake but he cannot move. He is very angry but soon he will be better.'

'I hope so.' She went back to her tent but Mano's curses and screams continued to disturb her so she ordered Pasang to move him further away.

She waited until the next morning to see Mano. His skin was puffy and sweaty and he could barely open his eyes or hold up his head. Pasang had untied him, assuring her that the fire had gone out of him and he was now as weak as a baby.

'When Mr North is back you go. Job finished,' she said sternly, standing over him and getting a small twinge of satisfaction as he winced at the sharpness of her voice.

'No, please. No drink, never drink,' he moaned.

'We will see what he says.' She suddenly had the fear that if she was too cross with him he might leave now and encourage the others to go with him. Once he started on about bad spirits he might convince them that she was responsible for them and they would only be safe if they left her.

'Come now,' she said, 'I need help packing up the plants. Come and help us.' He struggled up, swayed, almost fell before following her to where she was packing up the plants to send back home, but in his condition he was useless and she soon sent him away.

To her great relief, Arnold returned that afternoon. He strode into the camp surprising Delphina who was occupied with the herbariums.

'Oh, Arnold, you're back,' she said with relief. She half rose to go to him, but something about his manner stopped her.

'All well?' he said abruptly. 'Now we must move. Pack up everything and we move off tomorrow at first light.' He began at once to give orders to the porters almost ignoring Delphina making her feel uneasy.

'Is anything wrong? Why must we go so soon? Is it the weather?'

'I've heard that Cedric Hartford is on his way. We need to get ahead of him before he starts crashing about ruining all our finds.' His voice was curt, cutting into her relief at his return, flooding her with fear. Arnold called to Mano to look sharp and to fix a meal before helping to pack everything up.

The tension coiled tight in the pit of her stomach. 'I know,' she said, still following behind him like an eager puppy, 'I had a letter from Papa. There's one for you too, but how did you know?'

He turned to her a moment, his face softening. 'News travels, my dear. He's up to his old tricks, sowing bad feeling wherever he goes. Pack up your things; we'll have time to talk later.'

'I don't know if Mano is up to it, he got drunk yesterday and — '

'Bloody fool, did he hurt you?' His face was creased in sudden anger. He called out sharply for Mano.

'No, I got Pasang to tie him up.' Briefly she told him about the incident.

His face relaxed, he smiled, admiration in his eyes. 'Well done, you've got pluck as well as sense. He can be the devil when he's drunk, I've warned him about it before now. I shouldn't take him, but . . . ' He shrugged. 'I'm used to him and he hasn't touched it for ages. If I'd thought you were in danger I wouldn't have left you with him.'

'I managed.'

'Well done,' he repeated, calling for Mano again. Delphina left him to punish him.

It was so good to have Arnold back, but she felt agitated at his news. Was tomorrow too late? How close was Cedric? Was he in danger of coming upon them at any moment? All this she wanted to ask him during the long hours of the evening, but to her intense disappointment Arnold excused himself and went to bed early saying they must leave before dawn.

'Just tell me if we are in any danger,' she begged, before he left to go to his tent. 'How near is Cedric to us?'

He smiled. 'Don't worry about it; he's a lazy sod. Now sleep, we have a long day tomorrow.'

They were up before dawn walking first through the lush fields then on up to a pinewood pass. The pewter-coloured sky leant down on them leaching the life from the mountains ahead. They walked down the long slopes edged by the tangle of roses and barberry. Above them like a huge bee's nest, a Tibetan village clung to the side of the mountain.

Arnold seemed to be isolated from her, almost curt when he spoke to her as if he wished she were not there. Perhaps, she thought sadly, he has so enjoyed his few days without her, climbing alone with just Tewang for company, that now he found her a nuisance and wished he could just go on alone. But it was too bad, she had to get the seeds of Randolph's peony, for without them the whole trip would be pointless.

She followed him doggedly on up and down the slants and slopes of pathways above the raging river that bounced its way over the rocks. Up they went through the mud and slime to a village, the main street thick with oozing mud. Here they stopped for the night, making their camp in a deserted cloister.

Mano, now very subdued, knowing that one more fall from grace, however small, would mean his instant dismissal, began to make some mess to eat. Delphina sat quietly watching Arnold, wondering how to cope with his indifference. That night when he had given her the peony there had been an intimacy between them that she had felt was a new and pleasing shift in their relationship. Now they were like strangers. He was polite, handing her food, enquiring after her feet, but showing no more intimacy to her than if she had been one of the porters.

'Are you worried about Cedric?' she burst out, unable to keep it to herself any more.

He looked up startled. 'Not particularly, we must just keep ahead.'

'Have you heard where he is? Is he alone?'

'His nephew is with him.' He looked away into the distance, then, taking a tin opener from his pocket, began to open a tin of rice pudding savagely.

Something about his voice, his stance made her wary. There was more to it than he was prepared to tell her. She thought of her father's warning; how much danger was she in? Arnold got up abruptly, calling irritably to Tewang, leaving her feeling lost and afraid.

She wandered alone among the little walled yards of the forecourts of the dwellings, the children watching her with their coal-black eyes. She went into the ruined church. The towers had collapsed on to the floor. Broken, rotten planks stuck out from the veranda like huge teeth. It was dark, grimy with ancient decay. Scrolls hung like tattered curtains from the walls and on the floor were scattered mumming masks and piles of dusty sacred books. Delphina went forward cautiously, fascinated yet fearful in the gloom of this ruined place of worship. The only sign that it was still used by living people was the glimpse of tiny brass pans filled with holy water. She heard a step and a shape loomed from the darkness. She paused, looked around for escape, prickling with fear that Cedric had come.

She was quickly relieved by Arnold's voice.

'Don't be alarmed, it's only me.'

'Oh, Arnold . . . for a moment I thought . . . ' Her voice tailed off. 'This place is so neglected,' she added lamely, yearning to get back into his favour.

'Yes, it is a sad place.' He came and stood beside her in the gloom. She longed to reach out and touch him, but, afraid of his rejection, she did not.

'These mumming masks are very fine,' he said, stooping to pick one up and show it to her. 'They depict the characters in their plays, remember the one we saw in Rima?'

'Yes.' She touched it and the dust was as thick as felt.

'This must be the saddest place I have ever been in,' she said, shivering, looking up to the gallery that swooped down in ruin, the scarlet pillars slanting dangerously as if at any moment the whole place would collapse for ever, lost in a sea of filth and rot.

'They prefer to make new places of worship and let the old ones just fall into neglect,' Arnold said, telling her of the religion. His rich voice echoed round the leaning, rotting columns and the grim wall hangings, seeping into her, making her clutch greedily at every word searching for warmth in it, like a child once ostracized now back in the fold again.

Suddenly, as if aware of her rapt attention, he paused, gave a self-depreciating laugh and said, 'That's enough from me. I must go and write some letters.'

'Don't go,' she heard herself saying. 'I missed you,' she added lamely.

He cleared his throat awkwardly and said, 'You coped well without me, but I expect the evenings were long.'

'They were and . . . well, I like you being there.'

He paused as if to say something to her

and, in the gloom, she could see his face softening, but then with an effort he seemed to wipe this from his features and he said brusquely, 'I expect we'll have company before long and you will have Cedric's nephew to entertain you.'

'I don't want them to come.' She put out her hand to him.

For a second his hand closed over hers and she felt the warm weight of it before he removed it. He said, 'We will see. Now I must go, I've work to do.' She listened to his steps receding into the dusty gloom then she followed him hurriedly, feeling the ghosts of the place creeping round her adding to her fear.

12

At the end of the week they moved on to a more inaccessible place where Arnold wanted to catalogue some rock plants. He fell with joy on some pink Daphne, the flowers shining from tight, flat mats between the stones.

Delphina could not understand the change in him. She tried to share his pleasure, but she found it difficult as, apart from polite conversation, there had been none of the warmth she craved from him. Once or twice she caught him looking at her and saw a sadness in his eyes she could not comprehend.

That evening they sat together in the rough shelter of a derelict temple. Their tents were set near the walls and they sat, more because of the lack of space and light than for any intimacy, side by side, reading silently by the lamp. At last, Arnold looked up from his book, stared into the distance.

'What is it?' Delphina had not been able to concentrate on her book, reading and rereading each paragraph and remembering none of it.

'I love John Clare.' He waved his book in

her direction. 'Such a simple poet and yet so deep.'

'I can't remember him. I'm sure I did some at school but read me some, remind me.'

'Oh . . . you can borrow the book.'

'Poetry is so much better read aloud, don't you think? Please Arnold, read just one to me.'

'All right,' he agreed reluctantly. 'These were written to his wife Mary.' His voice was resonant with passion and he dropped the words into the air until they melted into her filling her with a melancholy so tangent so poignant that she could hardly bear it.

Mary, or sweet spirit of thee,
As the bright sun shines to-morrow,
Thy dark eyes these flowers shall see,
Gathered by me in sorrow,
In the still hour when my mind was free
To walk alone — yet wish I walk'd with thee.

'There,' he said, abruptly closing the book, 'that is enough.'

She could not look at him and yet she had this foolish feeling that Arnold had written the poem exclusively for her. It was the way he had read it, reluctant at first, then more resolute as if he wanted her to know that he loved her and could not say anything. She sat there still and silent hearing the echoes of the lines still in the air. *To walk alone — yet wish I walk'd with thee.*

He broke the silence. 'Your turn to read now, Delphina.'

'That was so beautiful,' she said slowly. 'The words seem to mean so much.'

'He was a wonderful poet and it is difficult to write well of love.'

'Love should be spoken of,' she said quietly, not looking at him. 'There are all kinds and none should be belittled.'

'But some fall like seeds on a dry rock and are quite pointless,' he said briskly.

'Your Daphne found a little scrap of earth on the rock to flower in,' she said, looking at him.

His face was grave and he kept his eyes from her. Then he said, 'When one is far from home one imagines things that would not work in the real world. Also, there are not many choices on to whom to pin one's emotions.'

'This is a real world, for the Tibetans anyway, why not us?'

'My dear, you must hurry back to Randolph with his peony seeds and then settle back into your life there. No doubt you will marry, have children, and forget all this . . .'

'I will never forget it,' she protested.

'Of course you won't forget the things you have seen, the things you have done, but feelings ebb and fade once one is back in the life one is used to. They are dulled round the edges and one is left wondering what was real and what was imagined.'

'I don't like to think like that,' she said.

He got up and, touching her briefly on the shoulder as he passed, he said, 'Enough has been spoken of love tonight, my dear. It is time we slept. I want to be up early in the morning. Good night.' He moved away before she could stop him and went into the darkness.

She could not sleep, hearing his voice, the words of the poem running in her head. The loneliness of being without him was like a hollow pain within her. Did he love her, or did they just imagine they loved each other? She fell into a troubled sleep then woke suddenly. There was an immense silence and stillness about her as if she was in a tomb.

Then she felt a movement as if the floor had shifted under her camp-bed. The floor moved again. She reached for her torch; it was so dark. Then she heard Arnold calling her.

'Delphina, pull on some clothes, quickly.'

She got out of bed and immediately the

whole floor shook. She could feel the vibrations in the structure of the temple behind her. She pulled on a jersey and trousers. There was a terrible noise as if the earth was being rent in half by some massive hammer. The ground heaved, bucked like a wild horse and the sound of rock thudding past in the darkness ricocheted round her.

Arnold pushed his way into the tent and, grabbing her, pulled her out. The noise was deafening. The ground lurched again. She clung to him, hearing his voice in her ear.

'It's an earthquake. We've got to get away from this temple in case it collapses.' He pulled her along, his torch a feeble light to guide them.

There was a rush of air filled with dust, making them cough. Above the thudding, screeching fall of the rocks, she heard the shouts of other men, a scream, then again the wrenching movement of the earth. Arnold pulled her to the ground, holding her closely against the earth, his body tight against hers.

Any moment, she thought, the earth would break open and devour them. All around them was the crack of rocks falling, bouncing off into the valley. There was a pounding on the ground like the relentless beating of a drum. There was nowhere they could go to escape the wrath of the earth.

She was terrified; she clung to Arnold, getting comfort from the bulk of his body, his arms around her. Sometimes above this unending noise and confusion she could hear his voice in her ear, comforting her. How weak they were against the massive might of the earth.

It was so dark she couldn't see his features. But the scent of him, the feel of him, even though they were wrapped in thick clothes, comforted her, gave her courage.

The ground rocked violently again. Delphina clung tighter to Arnold wondering if this was the end and they would be sucked into the bowels of the earth, or stoned to death by the falling rocks.

His arms tightened round her and she heard his voice firm and steadfast in her ear,

'Hold tight, it will soon be over. We will be safe, hold on.'

She felt his lips against her ear then on her face. One hand seemed to caress her hair. Surely she did feel this, it was not the wind? She moved so that her lips touched his cheek and then his own lips. The sudden ardour of his kiss overwhelmed her, and she kissed him back, drowning in the delicious intensity of it, holding on to him as if she would never let him go. The heaving of the ground and the thudding of the rocks seemed to be part of their passion, then, just as abruptly, he stopped kissing her, let her go and turned away from her.

'Oh, Arnold,' she said, 'I love you.' But he did not move. Perhaps he had not heard her in the din. He sat up as the tremors lessened their hold on the earth. On they came but slower like the shuddering sobs of a child after a tantrum. The sound of the falling rocks echoed round them. There was a sudden explosion, followed by another, then another, like giant fireworks in the sky. It made them jump and Delphina clung to him again. He loosened her fingers, said calmly, 'It is over now, let's go and see what damage has been done.' He got up, brushing himself down then helped her up.

'Arnold . . . '

He snapped on his torch, its light was dim in the searing darkness. She heard voices and the men came out of the shadows. Tewang asked them if they were all right.

'Fine. Is anyone hurt?'

'No.'

'That's a mercy. Now let's see what's happened to the tents. We'd better move them. We won't know until daylight exactly what damage has been done.' He went on giving orders, giving her things to do as well. She obeyed him bleakly still feeling the heat of his kisses, but also bewildered by his now apparent rejection of them.

Later, she lay miserably alone in her tent. She was not going to demean herself by going to him and have him reject her. She was exhausted, her ears ringing from all the noise. Then it began to rain, but the drops sounded heavier than mere water falling. She put on her torch and saw that the air was so thick with dust that it turned the rain to mud that splattered down leaving dark stains against the tent. She stayed huddled in the dark wishing Arnold would come to her. Were his kisses only a sort of reaction against the fear of death in the earth fall, and now that they had survived he was ashamed of his action and would not mention it again?

13

The night crawled by on leaden feet, the earth still sending out little tremors, some no more than hiccups. The rain stopped, and after a moment's freshness the dust swept in everywhere, clogging their mouths and eyes, making them cough, only to draw more dust into their lungs. In the morning light a sea of devastation greeted them.

Looking out from her tent, Delphina was horrified to see that the dust had clogged up the fresh spring so the water was the colour of coffee. There were huge wounds in the surrounding hills where the earth had been pulled away by force. Soil and rocks were piled high where yesterday it had been flat. The dust hung black like a funeral pall over everything. Far away she heard a bird call, then the shout of a child. Slowly life was stirring, feeling its way cautiously again.

Tewang came to her. 'We must go, the spirits are angry. There is no water.' He gestured to the oozing mud where yesterday fresh water ran. 'Maybe the earth will fall again,' he added darkly, his face grim. He was streaked with mud and dust.

'Where is Mr North?' she said, not wanting to listen to his theories of bad spirits.

'He says get ready.' He nodded and walked away.

She wondered why he hadn't come himself, but dressed and packed up quickly shaking away the dirt as best she could. She went to find him, wondering how he would treat her after his passionate kisses last night. She found him with a group of porters supervising the packing up of their equipment. He barely looked at her,

'We must move at once, this place is dangerous.' He gestured above them where she saw that even the shape of the rocks seemed different. 'They could all come down on us. Besides now we have no fresh water.'

'The spirits will punish us,' Tewang said again, ominously. 'There are bad people coming. Where strangers come, bad ones follow.' Some of the others nodded and muttered.

His words chilled her. He must mean that Cedric was coming; would he arrive today? If only she could laugh at these foolish omens, but who was she to question the beliefs of these people? They were not the first to believe that the gods or spirits showed their anger through the elements.

But Arnold said calmly, 'Then we must

make haste and leave.' He continued giving everyone things to do to speed their departure. He came over to her and said briskly, 'Hurry, Delphina, we must leave as soon as we can. The weather might change again and we could be trapped here.'

She looked into his face to see if there was any hint of last night's passion, but he would not meet her eyes, and strode away calling for the others to hurry.

It soon became apparent that the route back would not be easy. Boulders and debris blocked the way; trees had been pulled up by their roots and lay spreadeagled over the path. Yet among this devastation life seemed to go on. A group of goats tended by a young boy skipped past them. The boy grinned and waved when he saw them, gabbling something to the *gam*, his eyes large with delighted horror. Arnold went to hear what he was saying. He looked grave, swore, and muttered with annoyance.

'He says the bridge has gone and we will have to find another way to cross the river.'

After walking for an hour, they found the way blocked again. They stopped and consulted. The *gam* began arguing and Arnold shouted at him. Delphina, tired from the night's events, sat down and closed her eyes letting them get on with it. At last

Arnold came to her.

'As you can see the way is blocked. I am going to send most of the party with Pasang on a long and difficult way round that Pasang is sure they will make. It will take them some days, but they will make it. We will cross here, by the gorge. It is difficult, but we have no choice, so must do it.'

'How difficult?' Delphina asked wearily.

'You must do it, Delphina,' Arnold said. 'We have no other way.'

'We can go with the others, even if it takes a few extra days.'

'That is more arduous. This way will last a few minutes, the other many days. I don't think you could stand it. Besides, they have mules and large packages and will never be able to cross the gorge and I certainly don't want to lose all our work.'

'All right then.' She looked into his face and saw a moment's softness in his eyes. She did not really mind where they went as long as they reached somewhere green and clean, away from all the mud and hurling rocks. She imagined a gorge as a pleasant place with perhaps a running stream.

With much fierce talking from Arnold the other group turned round and set off again and she, Arnold, Tewang and Mono were left to cross the gorge.

They came to a scrub forest and the way through seemed easy enough. Every so often Delphina caught a glimpse of the river far below them. She was just thinking that Arnold had exaggerated the difficulties of the route when they came out of the forest and ahead was a sheer drop, a vast precipice.

'We can't cross here unless we fly,' Delphina said facetiously, staring aghast at the towering wall of rock beneath her.

'We can, Delphina, look.' Arnold put a hand on her shoulder and pointed down to a long, narrow tree trunk with notched steps like a ladder running down the length of it.

'I can't go down there.' Delphina let out a manic laugh. He must be joking, the earthquake had turned his head. Just looking down at that sheer, smooth drop was terrifying. But to climb down, holding on to that skimpy-looking ladder would mean certain death.

'There is no other way,' Arnold said firmly.

'Then we will go back, catch up with the others.' She half turned to go, unable to look any more at that endless drop.

'No. You will not go back.' His voice was icy calm, his hand still on her shoulder. 'You'll manage it, I promise you. Be strong, Delphina.'

'Why can't we go back?' Her fear made her

angry. 'It will be safer. I don't want to throw myself down there.'

'It will not be safer. Now, Mano and Tewang will go first, then you, and I will go last. Go slowly, keep your eyes firmly on the rock face before you. Do not look down.' He leant his head close to hers, said in her ear, 'If you show your fear, Mano might play up and we will all be in danger. Breathe deeply and go carefully. You will be safe.'

'I can't.' How she longed to cling to him, to beg him to let her go another way, but as if he guessed her wish he said firmly, strongly, 'I know you can do it, my darling.' He kissed her quickly on her cheek then released her, ordering a shaking Mano then Tewang to go down.

Before she could protest again, Mano had disappeared over the edge, quickly followed by Tewang. The huge pack on his back was the last part she saw of him. Wildly she looked round for some other route, but the only way back was through the forest. If she went back alone, then where would she go? She looked down and saw the top of Tewang's head below her. The rock was sheer, smooth as polished marble. If any of them slipped there was absolutely nothing to stop them. No shrubs, no convenient points of rock, nothing. They would fall on and on over the next sickening precipice far below into the river.

'Come on,' Tewang said, his black eyes commanding her. He stayed still on the ladder, willing her down with his eyes.

She was almost crying now. Arnold pushed her firmly but surely to the edge. 'Come on, you can do it: you *must* do it,' he commanded.

Still she hesitated. This was certain death, and such a death. She thought of Papa waiting for her to return with his peony seeds and how he would wait in vain.

'He cannot hold on for too long and wait for you. You must go now,' Arnold said. 'He will guide your feet, but you cannot expect him to wait forever. You do not want to be responsible for his death, do you?'

She wished she could die, but Arnold pushed her on firmly. 'Hurry, Delphina, it will soon be over. The longer you wait the worse it is.'

She took a deep breath and crept forward to the edge. The pack on her back was cumbersome and for a second she thought it would overbalance her and topple her over the edge.

'Turn round with your back to it.' Arnold pushed her to face him. 'Now, don't stop, just go.'

As if she was hypnotized she obeyed him. Turning round with her back to the void she edged her foot down, there was nothing there. She panicked, drew it up again.

'Put it to the right,' Tewang called to her.

With sobbing breath she tried again. She felt the ladder. Then Tewang came up again; she could hear his laboured breath, gasping with the effort. He took her foot and guided it into the notch, then, gently pulling her, made her go down one. Before she knew it she was over the edge on the ladder, clinging like a lizard to the narrow notches, her only lifeline between getting down and certain death.

'Good. Just look at the rock and keep on going down.' Tewang's voice was reduced to a whisper by his effort. She realized with dizzy horror that he must have been holding on only by his feet to have guided her so. She must go on down by her own efforts, or she would make him fall.

'I'm all right,' she squeaked, wondering if she would die of fear before she fell.

Arnold started down. She saw the soles of his boots and the large bulk of the pack on his back above her. She dared not stop now in case he crushed her. She became mesmerized by the rock and the tree trunk, going on and on down. There was no other life, this was all there was. Once she inadvertently glanced away and saw nothing but the river far below them. The sight so frightened her that she stopped, frozen in the middle of the precipice.

'Come on. We are nearly there,' Tewang urged her. Slowly she started down again and when she was completely numb with terror and certain that there would never be any escape from this perilous climb, she felt Tewang's arms round her and her feet on solid ground. She must have swooned, for a few minutes later she found herself lying on the ground, Arnold sitting beside her.

'Are we dead?' she said, her voice barely audible.

He smiled. 'No you are very brave, my dear. We are all safe. Have a drink.' He handed her a bowl of tea. When she refused, he put it to her lips. 'You must drink. It will make you feel better.'

Reluctantly she obeyed him. Then, feeling stronger, she looked about her. They were on a wide ledge. The blue sky stretched forever ahead.

'Where are we?'

'We have one more place to cross then we are safe.'

'Not another place like that?'

'No. It is not so bad. Rest a while. Then we will go.'

'I cannot go on,' she whimpered.

'You can. Think of Randolph. How proud he would be of you, as I am.'

'The price is too great.'

'It has been great, but you cannot throw it away now. Come, Delphina, it is the last thing I ask of you. It will not take long.'

She felt so tired, so helpless. But she knew she had no choice but to go on. It was dangerous waiting here, exposed to the coming night.

'Come. Don't think about it. Empty your mind,' Arnold said. He let her go and began to gather up his bags. Wearily, yet knowing she had no other choice but to die here, she obeyed him.

The sight of the next hazard pulverized her strength. There was a deep cleft in the mountains as if some giant had cleaved them in two with a mighty axe. The only way across was to crawl along a bridge of two logs, lashed together by creepers. It sloped sharply downwards to a flat piece on the rock below.

'Look,' Arnold pointed. 'When we are there it is easy. Trees, plants, a path. We will stop for the night. Just climb across there. It will take five minutes.'

'I can't.' She opened her mouth again but no words came.

'In five minutes' time we will be eating dinner,' he said. 'Let us be quick. Mano, you go, then Tewang as before.'

Mano looked nervous, but Tewang said something to him sharply and they set off. Delphina watched them in dazed horror.

Holding on to the thick creepers they crawled along like monkeys. Arnold pushed her forward and Delphina, now too tired to care, indeed she wished it was all over and she was dead, squatted down and, as if in the dream took hold of the creeper. She pulled herself on to it and started across. On either side of her was just a sheer drop to jagged rocks below. It did not seem like five minutes, more like five hours. She grasped each piece of creeper and edged forward, lying straddled over it, not daring to look anywhere but at the next handhold of creeper. Behind her, Arnold came, urging her on, telling her how brave she was.

Tewang was waiting for her, encouraging her for just one more effort, then another, until at last he could reach her and lift her off on to the ground.

'You are safe,' he said to her, but she barely heard him. Supporting her he led her on a few yards to where there was an enclosure of rock, like a small cave. He put her down. 'We will camp here. I will light a fire, soon we will eat.'

Delphina lay on the ground too shocked to care. Arnold came and sat by her. 'Well done,' he said. 'You have been so brave today.' She did not answer him but lay there with her eyes closed. She felt him touch her arm then get up and leave. She was too exhausted to call him back.

A long while later, when the dark was creeping round them, she managed to eat what Tewang had cooked. It was not good, a mess of vegetables, and a wedge of rice, but it brought her a little strength.

Arnold seemed completely at ease after their ordeal. They sat side by side by the small fire Mano had managed to make. He praised her again and promised that from now on the way would be easier. He ate heartily urging her to eat more. She shook her head, huddled close to the fire. The other two moved away into the night to sleep.

'Do you think that earthquake slowed up Cedric? Might we have time to get the peony seeds and move on before he comes?' she asked him.

'I don't know. I heard he is close behind us. He has Wunji with him?'

'Wunji?'

'You remember the Tibetan who was beaten at Rima? The one who seemed not to feel it?'

The image of him tall and unflinching while he was being beaten came back to her. 'He is with them? So he wasn't found guilty of the murder?'

'Apparently not. Unfortunately Tewang and Pasang are afraid of him. He will stop at nothing for money. He and Cedric will make a good pair.'

'And his nephew?' The words slipped out involuntarily.

'I do not know about his nephew.'

'Is he as bad as his uncle?'

There was a silence then he said, 'It is time to sleep.'

'Answer me first.'

There was a long silence then he said heavily, 'From all I hear his nephew is a good man. He is young and attractive and so, my dear, are you.'

'That doesn't mean anything,' she said. The exhaustion in her mind making her slow to understand his words.

'It might do if we were all together.'

'What do you mean?'

'I told you the other day that emotions run wild out here. It is a strange world, an unreal world. Relationships that could not possibly happen back home . . . ' His voice petered out, he shrugged and said, 'Enough. It is bedtime.'

'Do you mean you do not really care for me as I care for you?' she said, brave now after the terrors of the day. 'You kissed me that night as if — '

'Forget that night,' he said sharply. 'We could so easily have been killed and — '

'You did not think we would die. Why are you afraid to say you love me?' she challenged him, her eyes wild in the light of the fire. She put her hand on his arm and shook it. 'Why are you afraid to say you love me?'

His face was ghastly. He would not look at her, and then in a broken voice he said, 'You are young and beautiful, you cannot be with me. Not only am I too old but . . . ' and his voice broke and he bent his head in shame.

'Age is nothing, and as for your . . . impotence,' — she struggled over the word fearing it would wound him further — 'that does not signify.'

'Of course it does,' he rounded on her angrily. 'How can I cheat a young, full-blooded woman like you from a normal relationship? Do you not see how this pains me? Do you not realize how much worse it is that I love you, that I cannot bear to think of young, normal men, like Cedric's cursed nephew, giving you the love you desire?'

'I do not want it,' she said. 'It is you I want, you I love, Arnold, can you not see? What is that one thing when we have so much else?'

'You do not know because perhaps you have never had it,' he said. 'But believe me it will not work between us. I was wrong to kiss you, to hold you, but I could not help it when we were at those moments of danger. But I know even more firmly now, that there must be no more of it, and that it would be better if we part when we get off this mountain.'

'We cannot; and the seeds, we have not got the peony seeds.'

'I can send you with Tewang or Pasang and make sure you get on the boat to home safely.'

'Why are you doing this, Arnold? Is not every kind of love good? Can we not enjoy what we have, and not ask for any more. I do not mind, so — '

'I do,' he said sharply, 'and I do not wish to speak of it. I had got used to living with it until you came, now I see it as the curse it is. It was wrong to bring you with me. We will not talk of it again.' He got up and left her, walking into the night alone.

14

The next morning Delphina dressed and went outside to find Arnold. Her body felt sluggish and tired and she hoped that they would not have far to travel today. She found him sitting by the fire eating breakfast. She wanted to say something about loving him, but he was busy with his notes and giving orders to the porters.

'Have your breakfast. We must get on.' He handed her some biscuits and tea and told her the plans for the day as if they had never spoken of love.

After a couple of hours' walking they reached a pine forest. Seeing she was tired, Arnold suggested that they stop for a while. He sat down beside her under a pine tree. They were startled by a crack of twigs and a huge bear trundled into the clearing in front of them. It began grubbing for something in the earth. Her first instinct was to run, but Arnold gestured for her to stay quiet. They sat there together watching it feed. It seemed not to notice they were there and then it lumbered off, its soft, flat paws padding through the undergrowth.

'Oh, Arnold,' she whispered, when it had gone, 'how can we ever go back to the dull drawing-rooms of England with its petty gossip and social mores when we have this? The sheer magic and beauty of nature far surpasses all that.'

He smiled but did not answer her.

'Come,' he said, getting up from the ground, 'we must go on.'

'If only life would stop now,' she said, wanting so much to talk of their feelings for each other but not knowing where to start.

'Life never stops. Ever turning, there is no beginning and no end just a never-ending thread passing on,' he said. 'Accept that and you will feel easier.'

'It is so hard. I don't want to accept it,' she said, feeling angry like an unreasonable child, as she struggled under the huge weight of the truth of it and the knowledge that she could do nothing to change it. She felt helpless again as she had during the earthquake. There was nothing you could do with so much of life, but only enjoy the good things and keep their memory with you as a staff to go on.

'Don't make it harder on yourself. You should watch the people here more, see that so many of them do not suffer the pain of wanting to change things, or wanting things that are impossible. Some people may think them apathetic to just accept what life throws at them, but we complicate it too much with worrying about what might happen and how we could change it.' His face was tender as he looked at her.

'I know, I just — '

'Don't. Guard each good moment we have now. Don't spoil it by twisting it out of shape with your anxieties.' He patted her arm as if enough had been said and strode away to call the porters to pick up their loads.

They came out of the wood on to a flat plain. A few black felt tents were slung low on the ground. Yak and goats grazed nearby. A woman with a tawny-faced child with rosy cheeks, baked flat cakes over a fire. She greeted them, sticking out her tongue and motioned them to sit down.

Arnold greeted her warmly but moved away to talk to Tewang and Mano. Delphina sat down gratefully.

The woman passed her a cake, which she ate with pleasure. It was better than the lumps of rice and dry biscuits they were left with now. The child watched her, his dark eyes bright as beads. He detached himself from his mother and came and sat by her, touching her jacket with his fat little fingers.

Delphina smiled at him, spoke to him in

her own language laced with some words of Tibetan, which made him pucker up his face and turn to his mother. She said something to him and he stared at Delphina gravely as if trying to understand who this strange person was. She opened her rucksack and took her compass and torch and showed it to him.

The torch fascinated him. He clicked it on, laughing with joy at the light, then he clicked it off again. She heard a laugh and two more children appeared, chattering like little birds. They squatted down beside the baby and watched him playing with the torch. They made no attempt to snatch it or squabble over it, but sat and watched, commenting on it with great excitement.

She wished she had three torches to give them one each and she looked for Arnold to ask him if they had any to spare. The expression on his face as he watched her with the children smote her to her heart. Seeing her looking at him he turned away, but the whole stance of his body betrayed him and she knew he thought of the children he could not give her. She got up at once and went to him.

'Arnold.' She put out her hand to him.

'We must get on,' he said briskly, 'if you are ready.'

'You must not be so affected by these

things,' she started, not knowing how to relieve his agony, to say just because she found these children enchanting did not mean she wanted children of her own.

'There is nothing to say. Come, we must go on.' He picked up her rucksack for her, fastened it and put it on her back. He left the torch with the children, reassuring the woman when she tried to give it back that she could keep it. They set off again, Arnold striding ahead with Tewang while Delphina was left straggling behind with Mano.

As she walked she wondered at her feelings. Did she love him as a lover, or as a child loves a father? She was so inexperienced about love. She did love him, but her body did not soar with excitement as it had when she had been with Lorin that day. Was she trying to love Arnold so that she would be safe from Lorin if they met? Cedric would surely have schooled Lorin to try and seduce the secret of the peony from her. She must stop thinking of love. She must not forget she was here to bring back the seeds of Randolph's peony. Nothing else must get in the way of that.

She understood now what Arnold already saw, that problems could not be contained and, in insidious ways, seeped out into life. Like this morning just the sight of her playing with a child brought home to him the bitter truth that if she stayed with him, she would be denied them.

They arrived at a tiny village and after leaving her to rest awhile Arnold appeared with two rather scraggy mules.

'Here,' he said, 'you can travel in style, I'll use the other for the packs.'

Delphina only protested mildly, but being so tired she accepted his offer and rode it. It was a simple animal and rather lazy, but Arnold found a stick and tapped it sharply on the rump whenever it slowed down.

Soon they reached a river. The bridge had been smashed in the earthquake. Portions of it hung down while the water rushed through the gaps pushing more out of its way impatiently as it swept along.

'We must find a boat,' Arnold said. 'Tewang thinks there will be one further up. Soon we will stop for the night.' His face was concerned as he looked at her. 'You look tired. You need a long rest.'

'I'm fine. I'm thinking of those seeds and getting there before Cedric,' she said, determined now to talk no more of love.

The boat they found was small and rocked dangerously on the troubled water. Delphina wondered if the line being thrown across the river to take the mules across might be steadier than this craft. But Arnold urged her in before she could voice her fears and sat down beside her. The boat wobbled madly and she clung to the sides keeping her eyes away from the icy, dun-coloured water.

The boat lurched and rocked like a bucking horse, completely at the mercy of the swirling water while the boatman struggled to master it. Delphina closed her eyes, her body taut waiting to be catapulted into the water, certain they would be drowned at any moment.

Somehow the boatman managed to get the wayward craft which longed to go its own way with the bubbling water, under control. Swirling and rocking most alarmingly, they finally reached the other side.

Delphina, feeling by now sick and dizzy, stumbled ashore.

'Look,' Arnold said, to distract her from her sickness, 'here comes your mule.'

The unfortunate animal was being pulled through the water by Tewang and two other men who had appeared with the boatman. Suddenly there was a cry from one of the men; her mule was in a state of panic, kicking out at the man who led it, as he fought vainly to calm it. Delphina ran to the bank. The mule's eyes were white with fear. It lurched itself into the water, pulling on the line, almost knocking Tewang into the water. The other mule weighed down with packs began to feel its fear, tossing its head and rolling its eyes.

'Let it go,' Arnold called, as the mule struggled to buck and rear to escape from the teeming water, lashing out at the men beside it.

'No, don't!' Delphina cried, but in a moment one of the men cut its rope and the mule, struggling madly to keep its head above water, was swept away.

Delphina was horrified. 'How could you, Arnold? That poor animal.' She turned to him in horror, unable to believe that he had done such a thing.

'I had to,' he said shortly. 'It would have pulled down the lot otherwise.'

'No it wouldn't, it was almost across,' she said.

'Only halfway. Believe me, Delphina, I had to do it. Better to lose one mule than a man, or the whole lot of them.'

'You could surely have saved it, even stunned it a little, or covered its head, then led it on,' she said. 'You were too hasty letting it go to such a terrible death.'

'One has to make quick decisions when men's lives are at stake,' he said, and went to help the men and the other mule out of the river.

Her exhaustion peeled away all her rational feelings making her angry and sad. If only she was at home with Papa in a comfortable, warm house, eating a nourishing meal. An unbearable yearning for that life swept over her. She could almost smell the meal being prepared in the warm kitchen, feel the comfort of a carpet under her feet, her soft mattress under her body. And a bath! A deep, scalding bath, with huge towels to cocoon herself in afterwards.

'You are tired, and now your mule has gone.' Tewang came to her, he was dripping wet, but smiling all the same.

'Yes, I am,' she said. 'You must dry yourself. Shall we make a fire?'

'You must go home,' he said, as if he guessed her thoughts. 'It is there you will find peace. When you are back in your own life again, you will not be so worried.'

'I don't think I will ever fit back into my life again,' she said, 'despite all the discomfort and pain part of me will always be wanting to come back here.'

Arnold strode towards them, saying the boatman had directed them to a village just half an hour away and they would stop there for the night.

Delphina was still angry with Arnold over his treatment of the mule, but when at last they reached a shabby bungalow where they could sleep, it was such a welcome sight to Delphina, she forgot everything and fell at once upon the bed and into a deep sleep.

When she woke it was evening and the room was grey in the dusk. She lay a moment letting her gaze run round the room, trying to piece together her thoughts, get her bearings.

'How do you feel?' Arnold spoke from the shadows. She saw him sitting reading on a chair beside her.

'I . . . I don't know. How long have I been here?'

'A couple of days.'

'So long?' She felt too muzzy to care.

'You needed to sleep. You've been through far too much lately. Most men couldn't have survived what you have. I don't know how you did it.'

'Now you say it,' she said, with a wry smile. 'You seemed determined that I could do it.'

'You had to, or we would have died,' he said simply. 'No food, no fresh water. Anyway, it is as well that we have arrived here. It is quite a decent village as villages here go. We will rest awhile then we can go seed hunting. Your peony is only a days march away, you know.'

'We must get it, I almost forgot with all that has happened.' She smiled at him and reached out for his hand.

'You would never forget it; it would be like forgetting your father.'

Before she could answer they heard dogs barking and the sound of English voices. Then unmistakably as if he was in the room, Delphina heard Lorin say, 'Is there room in this bungalow for all of us? Or shall we make camp outside?'

'That devil Hartford has come,' Arnold said, springing up and leaving the room. 'Stay there. I'll see he goes elsewhere.'

15

The voices of the men receded as they moved away from the bungalow. Delphina's heart was racing but, as she told herself firmly, more in fear of Cedric Hartford than in any excitement of seeing Lorin. Her body was foolish to respond so to his voice; it was just a reaction to meeting someone from her own culture after being among people and places so different to her normal life.

She was so near to completing her task, collecting the seeds of the peony then she could go home. Nothing, but nothing must stand in her way now.

She waited a moment for Arnold to come back to her, but he did not return. He had left her room abruptly, almost shamefully, as if he had no right to be there, and she understood his feelings. Cedric would mock him as he had at the Army and Navy Stores in London make lewd remarks about his manhood. She jumped out of bed. She could not bear to think of Arnold suffering. She reminded herself about his words after Cedric had humiliated him in London, begging her to say nothing.

Then she heard Arnold calling her.

'Delphina, where are you?' His voice was brisk, business-like.

'I'm here.' She opened the bedroom door and saw him coming down the narrow passage. Tewang stood behind him.

'There you are.' He gave a quick laugh. 'I think we should move off fairly soon . . . '

'At once.' Agitation rose in her; she longed to be gone, to get to the peony before Cedric did.

'We'll move tomorrow. There is not enough room in this bungalow for everyone,' Arnold said.

'If I'm not mistaken this place has four rooms.' Cedric suddenly appeared, pushing roughly past Tewang. 'We can surely all sleep here in comparative comfort for a few days.' He peered round Arnold to see her, saying with a sneer, 'So, my dear Delphina, we meet up again. Surely you won't turn away two fellow travellers?'

'It is up to Arnold,' Delphina said tartly. 'How long are you here?' She stepped back feeling suddenly confined in this narrow dingy passage with Cedric so close to her. Excusing herself, she pushed on past him to go outside.

Lorin was there talking to Tewang. Although his clothes were creased and well worn as hers were they became him well. His face lit up when he saw it was her and, smiling, he came towards her, his hand outstretched.

'Delphina, how nice to see you again, and what a place to meet.'

'Hello.' She ignored his hand and walked away trying to subdue the sudden surge of emotion that swept through her. How could she feel such things for a man she barely knew and who would use all his charms to steal her father's peony?

Arnold and Cedric were now outside the bungalow. She heard Cedric say, 'Moving on so soon? To get Randolph's precious peony seeds, I suppose?' He said it loudly enough for her to hear. She willed herself not to react but she could not help glancing quickly at Lorin. Had she been so foolish as to say something about them to him when they met at Aurian Hall? Had she already betrayed her father?

'We only came here by chance as there was an earthquake. We move on tomorrow,' Arnold said.

'I heard about it, we were still down in the valley, but it must be time to collect the seeds. So is that where you are heading?' There was an unpleasant smile on his lips as he regarded her. She turned away to hide her agitation.

'There is no specific peony,' Arnold said calmly. 'I'm afraid Randolph was mistaken. As you know with these things, the plant sometimes does not survive. But yes, it is time for seed collecting and, like you, we will be going back to certain specimens of plants that we have found.'

Still Cedric smiled. 'Quite so. Have you found anything exciting on this trip?'

'I wouldn't tell you if I had.' Arnold strode away, calling over his shoulder, 'Come, Delphina, we have the herbarium to see to. We can't stand here gossiping all day.'

Delphina made to follow him, keeping her eyes firmly away from Lorin but she heard him say quietly, 'Do not worry, we won't interfere with your seed collecting.'

Despite her determination not to be affected by him she could not help glancing at him. He was smiling, his eyes clear and honest watching her. To her mortification she blushed. She turned away and followed Arnold and saw that he had seen the incident and was annoyed by it. His face was tense and hostile. He barked, 'Hurry up, Delphina, we have a lot to do.'

'I'll say,' Cedric said, with a smirk. 'So we'll move in here, Lorin, get some comfort. We need all the sleep we can get before the arduous task ahead of us.' He walked towards the bungalow.

Delphina remembered that she had left her journal in her bag. Cedric might go through her belongings and take it, although it would be difficult for him to decipher anything about the peony.

'Tell us which rooms are free; we will not touch yours,' Lorin said.

'I should hope not,' she said coldly, feeling Cedric's malicious eyes on her.

'You young people must get together,' he said. 'You may be married, Delphina, but there is nothing wrong in friendship. You probably have much in common that us older folk know nothing about.'

'I have no time,' she said curtly, leaving them. That was the last thing she wanted. Did he really think she'd be fool enough to tell Lorin where the peony was?

She went after Arnold quickly, and, when she drew level with him, she said, 'Wait, Arnold. I was afraid that Cedric would go into my room and read my journal.'

He whipped round, his face dark. 'What have you written in it?'

'Oh, nothing, well, only about the plants. Papa told me to keep a journal so he could read it, know what plants we have found, the conditions and everything.'

'Is it only about that?' His eyes bored into her.

'Of course.'

He sighed deeply and strode on, then he said roughly, 'I suppose you haven't disclosed the location of the peony?'

'No, well, it is disguised enough. But they will try to follow us, won't they? Is there any way we can go without them finding out where we are?'

'I don't know.'

'It is Wunji I'm afraid of,' she said. 'He might hurt you, thinking you were responsible for his beating at Rima.' She crept close to him, turning quickly to see if they were observed by Cedric and Lorin and, not seeing them, she touched his arm. He jerked it away.

'Do not touch me, Delphina.' His voice was anguished. 'We are working together, that is all, remember that.'

'Sorry, I was just going to thank you for saying Papa was mistaken and the peony is not there.' She was stung by his rejection but she realized that they must do nothing to attract Cedric's spite, though surely touching his arm was all right as they were supposed to be married.

For a moment he said nothing, then he turned to her, his face stiff with embarrassment. 'Delphina, any feelings we had were

251

only an illusion brought on by the fear of the earthquake. I am your father's friend and you are here solely in his place. We have a job to do and that is all there is to it.'

There was so much she wanted to say and yet she did not know how to say it. Instead she said, 'We must leave at once. I cannot bear to be anywhere near them. Let us find the others and get packed up. I want to leave now.'

'We cannot leave tonight,' he said, 'but we will early in the morning.'

They were outside a house, the women sat outside cooking and talking to their children playing near them. A little further away, they saw Tewang and Pasang smoking with a group of men. Their faces were grave and they were speaking angrily together. Delphina could feel the wave of hostility coming from them. Arnold said with a sigh, 'Oh, what has happened now? I hope there is not a mutiny.' He called out, 'Tewang, Pasang, can we leave tomorrow?'

They glared at him, then Tewang got up slowly and came over to him.

'What is it, Tewang? Trouble?' Arnold asked easily, but she saw the tension in the side of his mouth and his hands clench by his sides. She had never seen Tewang so angry.

Tewang spewed out his anger in a torrent

of words. He spoke in Tibetan and she could not understand what he said. Arnold listened then said gently, 'Tell me more slowly, Tewang. You must forgive me, I do not speak your language well enough.'

'A stranger has stolen statues from our temples,' he hissed. 'Some say it is you, some the others. They do not like strangers here, strangers who say they want our plants, when they take our treasures.'

Arnold put his hand on his shoulder. 'You know we did not take them, don't you, Tewang?'

'I know, but others who do not know you think you did.'

The other men he had been sitting with got up and walked slowly towards them, staring at them with their dark, inscrutable eyes. There was a feeling of menace in their movements that made her fearful. Then out of the corner of her eye, she saw Wunji leaning against the wall of the house. Surely it was he who had spread the lies about them?

Arnold saw him too and said to Tewang, 'You know that I respect you and your country and would never take anything but the plants. We must have a search at once. You with these other men can go through our baggage and the baggage of Mr Hartford to see that we do not have your statues.'

'But they could have been hidden,' Tewang said.

The other men crowded close to them, and she felt overwhelmed by their scent.

Arnold said reasonably, 'We have taken nothing. We will do all we can to help you find them.' This he repeated in Tibetan, asking them what they wanted him to do to help them.

They muttered among themselves glancing at them, their suspicion as potent as any poison. Tewang said, 'We will search your things, but even if they do not find them some people think you have taken them and have hidden them.'

'Come then,' Arnold said, 'let us go at once and look. Tewang and Pasang, I would like you to open the crates and packages. I do not want all my specimens spoilt.' He led the way back to the bungalow and after a few moments of angry muttering, the crowd followed him.

Delphina went with them. What if Cedric had taken them and put them in their belongings? She said this to Arnold.

'We'll just have to hope for the best,' Arnold said. 'Cedric is known for stealing what he can: religious statues, opium, gold if he can get it. But so many of these people are afraid of us, their fear fuelled by the monks who do not like us going to the mountains, being in the remote parts of the country. They cannot believe that we come here only for plants that have no use to them, so when disreputable people like Cedric abuse our profession by raiding their temples, all of us come under suspicion.'

Remembering the trial at Rima, Delphina shuddered. 'Will they torture us, beat us as they did to the suspects at Rima?'

'I hope not. Courage, Delphina. When Tewang has calmed down I will talk to him and he will get us away from here.'

They came to the bungalow and Arnold marched straight in leading the others. They went into his room and he showed Tewang his bags and told him to search them.

'Whatever's going on?' Cedric appeared from one of the rooms.

'Nothing to worry about,' Arnold said calmly. 'To avert trouble I am letting these men search our bags. I trust you will do the same if you want to keep them amenable.'

'Search our bags! You must be mad, man!' Cedric roared. 'I'm not having any bloody native touching my bags.'

Lorin opened his door. There was such a crowd in the narrow passage all squeezed into Arnold's room that he could do no more than open his door a crack. Delphina saw a sliver of fear cross his face. Had he stolen the statues? Was he an accomplice to his uncle's wickedness?

She fought her way through the teeming bodies to get outside and sat on the ground breathing fast. She would believe anything bad about Cedric but she did not want to think that Lorin was the same. Fear snaked through her; she had never seen the people so angry before. The bungalow was surrounded by the angry mob and she was afraid that Arnold would be hurt.

After what seemed an eternity they all came out again jabbering and jostling and, to her relief, Arnold seemed unconcerned and led them away towards their other baggage. Lorin and Cedric came out too, talking intently together. Not wanting to be involved with them, Delphina went and hid behind a ramshackle dwelling.

When everyone had gone, Delphina went into the bungalow and shut herself in her room. Her things lay neatly on the camp-bed. She began to pack them away again hoping to God that they would leave tomorrow. How she hated this place, the small, stuffy room, the dark little passage connecting all the rooms. When she had finished, she went outside again and waited for Arnold, making a pretence of reading her book, though her mind would not stay quiet and she kept looking up willing him to return.

'Is everything all right?' she greeted him, when he finally came back.

'They haven't found anything and with luck I think I have persuaded them we can leave tomorrow,' he said. His voice became bitter, the lines round his mouth biting deeply into his skin. 'Whenever that Cedric comes on the scene there is trouble. It is such bad luck that he came on us here, for seeing us together the people will think we are part of his wickedness.'

'Did they search his things as well?'

'They want to, but that does not concern me. He probably has hidden them, or given them to Wunji. Come, we must pack, get ready to leave at first light.'

'What would they do to us if they had found their statues among our things?' Delphina asked, as she followed him to the bungalow.

'They would punish us,' he said shortly, his mind preoccupied with planning their departure.

'How?'

'By blinding, I believe,' he said, and went into his room and shut the door leaving her outside in the narrow passage, the word 'blinding' filling her with fear.

16

Despite the surly grumbles from the porters, Arnold and Delphina managed to leave the village at first light. Cedric was still in bed, but Lorin was up. No doubt Cedric had insisted that he keep a watch on them. She pretended she hadn't seen him but he made straight for them.

'So you are off,' he said, his voice pleasant, a smile on his face.

'Yes, there's a lot to be done,' Arnold answered his face averted as he checked the bindings on the loads.

'I'm sorry not to have seen more of you, Delphina. I thought we might have met up last night but you were nowhere to be seen.' He came close to her and she felt her heart leap. Just before she had fallen into an exhausted sleep she had thought of him so close to her in one of the rooms in the bungalow. She looked away from him not wanting him to see how he affected her. What a fool she was playing straight into Cedric's hands by being attracted to his nephew.

'I was busy, now please leave me, we have to get on.' Her voice was abrupt.

'As you wish, I was only being friendly,' he said. 'I'd have thought that being away from people, from one's own country for so long, it would be good, a relief even, to meet up, exchange stories.'

Exchange stories, yes, find out where the peony was. 'I didn't want to,' she said, turning her back on him and walking away. She fought to keep her emotions under control. If only they could talk to each other. Even if he had not been attractive she yearned to make contact with someone English, to share the pleasures and the pain of their time here. Like her it was his first time on a trip and how interesting it would be to compare notes, but it was impossible.

It was a two-day march to the place where they were to set up a camp as base for the seed collecting.

'We have a lot to do so I suggest we do a different patch each; you know enough now to collect the right seeds, Delphina,' Arnold said.

'Fine.' She was relieved to have some time to herself and she was ashamed to admit to thinking about Lorin. They had not yet reached the place where the peony was and she tried not to think of it. What if the seed was not sufficiently ripe?

'They must be popping from the pod,' her

father had said. 'Don't be tempted to take them if they are not. There will be no point.'

The process of seed collecting had to be done carefully and methodically and she tried to ignore the agitation building up in her to get there and have them safe before Cedric came.

She worked with Tewang for many hours and when they at last got back to the camp, she saw to her surprise that Arnold seemed about to leave.

'Oh, there you are, Delphina.' His face was grave causing her stomach to cramp with fear. 'I'm going down to the village beneath us to warn them that there's been a fall of rock which has trapped the water, making a lake high in the mountains. If the rock falls they will be flooded.'

'I'll be ready at once,' she said, trying to ignore her aching bones.

'No, you stay here, get on with the work. I'll only be gone a few days. We cannot both go, we have too much to do.'

Relief and a little fear passed through her. 'Are you in any danger? Will it come down here?'

'No, not here, but it will get the village so I must warn them. Just do all you can, then when I am back we will move on to our most important quest.' His eyes crinkled with teasing amusement. He was laughing at her, but she laughed back, grateful that he would take her back to the peony. She'd hold on to that and not let her feelings of fear of being without him get to her. She'd coped the last time he'd left her, she'd do it again.

'Read the riot act to Mano please, I don't want to be knifed in my bed,' She said.

He smiled. 'I've done that. So, see you in a couple of days.'

He hovered a moment and for a second she wondered if he would kiss her, but instead he gave her an awkward smile, lifted his hand in a stiff, brisk wave and, calling to Pasang and two porters who were to accompany him, set off.

She tried to push away the feeling of isolation and fear that crept into her as she watched his sturdy figure disappear over the ridge and got down to packing up the plants to send back to England. Tewang explained to her about the fall of rock.

'There is too much water pushing on the rocks. They will slip; the water will come down, kill everyone. It is the spirits,' he said, mournfully, 'they are angry.'

'But not with us,' she said gently. 'Is it not just chance that the rocks fell in such a way as to trap the water?'

'The spirits do not like being disturbed;

somebody evil is coming,' he insisted.

Although she knew that these people, often encouraged by the monks, used the threat of bad spirits as a power over them, his words chilled her. She tried to ridicule it to herself, but it clung to her like a mist. Who knew the real truth of good and evil?

The day after Arnold had left, some porters with mules and a *gam* came up to the camp. Tewang translated telling her that Arnold had sent him up and he would see the plants safely on their way to England. He was someone they had used before and could be trusted. They had also brought some more stores with them.

'Ask him if he knows how long Mr North will be,' Delphina said, hoping he would say he would be back in a few hours.

'He come soon,' Tewang told her.

'How soon? Today?'

'No, not today?'

'Tomorrow?'

'No.'

'When then? What is he doing?' She felt impatient yearning for more interesting company.

'He go village. Tell them water comes.'

'Surely he's done that by now?' she said, in despair. The *gam* shrugged with indifference when Tewang put this to him. Then, almost as an afterthought, he took a letter from some fold in his garments and handed it to her. It was from Arnold.

See all the plants get safely off with Anu. The bloody officials here show no interest in my warning of the flood, so have sent people down to the other villages to warn them, and will go to some myself. I will be back with you in about a week. If, in the unlikely chance I do not get back, or you get bored get Tewang to take you to Darjeeling and I will catch up with you there.
  I have sent up more supplies with them. Look after yourself, Arnold.

Another week! How could she bear it? She missed Arnold more than she could say. It wasn't just his presence, so reassuring against any dramas that occurred, but she had become so fond of him. His kindness especially over giving her the peony. The peony! Another week before they got there, giving Cedric even more of a chance to get there first. She stomped into her tent and turned on some music as loud as she could to try to banish her angry fear.
The 'music box' always fascinated everyone

and it wasn't long before she heard their soft footfalls outside and excited whispers. The tent seemed in danger of collapsing with all the bodies pressed against it. A line of curious faces, their dark eyes shining with delight, peeped through the flap. Delphina turned off the music and came out, shooing them away before the tent collapsed completely.

'Have you everything properly secured?' she asked the *gam* in Tibetan, when all the crates had been tied up. She asked Tewang to repeat her request to make sure he understood.

She went over to the mules standing with their eyes and ears drooping, laden down with the crates. Apart from Arnold's name, she had put marks on some of the boxes. On one of them she'd drawn a curve like Punch's nose. This held the pressed peony. It would not arrive in marvellous shape, but it would be proof that it had been found. Then another thought hit her. What would happen if Cedric saw the crates and, recognizing Arnold's initials, sabotaged them?

'Take great care with them; do not let anyone else touch them,' she said fiercely, giving the *gam* some money and some sugar. Arnold would have paid him already but she wanted to be doubly sure that the packages would arrive safely.

'No one will touch them,' he said, looking offended at her suggestion.

The next few days dragged by. Delphina was tired after working so hard at the packing and with boredom at being without Arnold. There was no one she could have a proper conversation with and, at times, she got so desperate she would have welcomed even Cedric's arrival. And Lorin, the longer she was alone the harder it would be to ignore him. She slept quite a lot, and read. She collected more plants and drew more, determined just to fill the hours until Arnold's return. The loneliness sat on her like a huge, damp monster. Sometimes it eased a moment and she felt almost happy as she planned Arnold's return, and how she would welcome him. Then the loneliness would pounce again and devastate her.

Still Arnold did not return. The servants became restless, and one morning she discovered that three of them had gone. When she asked Tewang about it he said, 'They are stupid people. They think Mr North will not come back, so they go.'

Delphina said with as much authority as she could muster, 'Tell them that when Mr North comes back, which he will any day now, they will get extra money if they are still here.' She fought to hide from him the panic that they might all leave her alone here in this desolate place.

Two days later, there was only Tewang, Mano and two servants left. It rained all night and day. The wind blew the rain into her tent so that she had to move her clothes and bed here and there in a vain attempt to keep them dry. The stuffy smell of kerosene from the lamp made her long to go out into the air, but then she would only get wet, and sitting in damp clothes would be worse. After one night of lashing rain, she woke to silence. At first she lay there, relieved that the rain had stopped, then a bolt of fear hit her, was she utterly alone?

She pulled on some clothes and ran out. It was very early, the sky bright and clear. Everywhere was quiet save for the birds. In a panic she went to the camp and, to her relief, saw Tewang and one servant drinking tea. She joined them, pouring tea into a bowl, holding it cupped in her hands for comfort. They did not look at her and she dared not ask where the other servant or Mano was.

She bit into a biscuit hiding her agitation from the two men. She must show that she was inwardly stronger than they were. She had to know what to do, give them orders so they would feel secure with her and stay. She

266

would have to make a decision of what they were to do today.

'If Mr North is not back tomorrow we will leave for Darjeeling,' she said, firmly. She would go mad if she waited here much longer. If only he would come so she could get to the peony in time. The thought of it dominated her thoughts and dreams. This unending waiting for him to come so they could start off in that direction was driving her insane.

'Will this man and Mano stay until he comes?' she asked Tewang, relieved as Mano appeared from somewhere and squatted down beside the fire.

There was a mumbled discussion. Tewang said, 'No, the spirits will come. He will come to Darjeeling with us.' His face was sullen, making Delphina afraid if she made them stay Tewang might not come with her, or they would disappear in the night.

'We will leave tomorrow. I will pay you extra if you get me safely to Darjeeling. We will take what we can and send porters up for the rest. Understand?' She glared at Tewang.

He said bitterly, 'You do not trust me. I knew your father; I know your husband. I will not leave you.'

His words hit Delphina with mortification. 'I'm sorry,' she said, 'I know you will. It's just

I'm afraid without Arnold, and with the porters and servants leaving.'

'Mano and I will not leave you,' Tewang said, a little mollified.

'Maybe Mano should go and find where Mr North is?' she said.

Mano huddled into himself as if he could somehow escape this suggestion.

Delphina said, 'Let's wait here one more day, then decide.' She got up and left them, going to her tent to start to pack up her things. Arnold must come back today.

About four hours later she was roused from her book by the sound of people arriving. He had come at last. Her heart gave a leap of joy and relief and throwing down her book, she bounded from her tent to greet him.

Pasang, some porters and, to her horror, Lorin came into the camp. They must have met up and Cedric had insisted on travelling on with them.

Lorin came forward. 'Delphina, I'm afraid I am here alone.' He paused, his face set like granite, then the words came out in a rush as if he could not hold them back.

'There is no easy way of breaking such news, Delphina. I'm so sorry but Arnold is dead.'

'Dead?' She stared at him in disbelief. How could Arnold be dead? He would not leave her here. He would be back at any moment. This was some evil trick thought up by Cedric to get her out of the way. She glanced at Pasang. Where he was Arnold would not be far behind. But his face was impassive. She turned to Tewang; his expression was resigned, tight and stern.

Lorin came closer to her, held out his hands as if he would hold her. 'He was washed away by the flood. He didn't stand a chance.'

'The flood? But he went to warn the people. They didn't believe him.' Her eyes were wild now. Arnold wasn't dead. He was somewhere in a crevice, in a cave, safe, waiting for the water to stop, then he would come to her.

'No, they didn't believe him, so he went on with Pasang to warn people in some of the villages. But the water came down, suddenly, as he said it would. He didn't stand a chance. He was trying to save a woman who had just given birth. They were both washed away.'

'But maybe he's alive, just waiting to be picked up.' Her voice was pitiful with hope.

She saw Pasang shake his head.

'No,' Lorin said, 'Pasang saw him go. There is no hope. I'm truly sorry, Delphina, he was a very brave man.'

'Are you sure?' She snatched at Pasang,

shaking him in her fear. 'Are you sure? Can't we send out a search party to find him?'

'I am sure,' Pasang said, 'I saw him killed.'

'How are you sure? It must have been such chaos, he could have escaped.'

'Come, Delphina,' Lorin said gently. 'Come with me. Do you feel strong enough, or shall we travel tomorrow?'

'How do you know about it?' She turned on him, her pain and fear fuelling her anger. 'And where is your uncle, is he with you?'

'He is still at the village, he has a touch of fever. I had gone on and was waiting for him at the village when your husband turned up to warn everyone. I was moving on anyway. I heard of his death later and came to tell you and take you back.'

'Back where?' She must hold off this pain of grief and terror and not be tricked into losing the peony seeds.

'I'll take you back to the village, then when you have rested, I will see you get home.'

The pain was terrible now seeping in under her defences. Arnold dead. She sat down on a rock, her legs like wool. Lorin put a flask to her lips and mechanically, she took a sip. It was rich and strong and made her cough, but was like fire in her, giving her a moment's strength.

'Have some more brandy,' he said.

'No.' she pushed it away. 'Where is he . . . his body?'

'It . . . ' Lorin looked awkward, as if he wished she would not ask such distressing questions. 'It hasn't been recovered, the ravines are very deep there. It may never be found.'

'It is a good resting place for him,' she said dully, thinking that forever he would lie under the sky he loved. She hoped there would be a profusion of flowers growing around him.

Then came the picture of the circling vultures to torture her. Would they tear his flesh from his body, soar in the sky, away with him, giving him a sky burial? She tried to escape the image in her mind, and closed her eyes and would have fallen if Lorin had not caught her.

She lay against him for a moment, yearning for comfort, taking in the warmth of him, the scent of him, but all the time this terrible pain throbbed in her mind. This could not be true: it was some horrible nightmare. His arms tightened and she came to her senses. She must not stay here in his arms.

She struggled up, pushed him away. She must put her grief aside and think only of the peony.

Lorin said, 'Where are the rest of the men who were here with you? Surely Arnold didn't

271

take them all with him?'

'They've gone,' she said. 'Only Tewang, Mano and the old servant is still here.'

'Devils,' Lorin said. 'But don't worry, I'll take care of everything. I've brought a mule to carry you down to the village. It's about a five-hour trek.'

'I have walked up and down the most impossible routes. I can surely walk down to this village.'

'But the shock . . . '

She did not answer, but left him and went to her tent to pack. 'Please, Pasang,' she said as she passed him, 'could you pack up Mr North's things?'

'I am here to help you, to get you home,' Lorin called after her.

'I bet you are, home away from my peony,' she said under her breath. She turned. 'Thank you for coming with the news, Lorin. I won't hold you up any more. Tewang and Pasang will look after me. There is still a lot of work to be done.'

'But surely in the circumstances . . . and anyway I saw your plant samples coming down as I came up, so you've done that.'

She was right: he was spying on her. She wondered what Cedric would give him if he persuaded her to tell him where the seeds were.

'I am here to do a job of work. Arnold would expect me to finish it for him. You can leave me now. I am all right.' She turned her face away, willing him to go before she disgraced herself by throwing herself in his arms, begging him to take her away from all this, away from the pain of Arnold's death.

'I will not leave you,' he said, but he moved away from her walking a little up the path, then sitting down and taking out a book began to read as if he had all the time in the world.

She called to Pasang and when he came, hanging his head like a shy child, she said, 'I want to ask exactly what happened to Arnold, please tell me.'

He regarded her gravely, death to him was just going to another place. 'We went to the village. We tell the people. One man say his wife have baby, cannot go. Mr North, he goes into house. Then there is a noise.' He lifted his hands. 'Water comes like a river, pulling up plants, houses, people, pushing them with it. I call, run, but the water takes the house, rocks come too and one hit Mr North. His head, face is red.' He paused, shook his head as if to dislodge the image.

'I am knocked over, but I hold on to a rock. Water not so fast near me. I am safe, but I see

Mr Arnold go, and I know from his face that he is dead.'

'Thank you for telling me.' She struggled with her tears. 'Please, for his sake, stay with me. Let us go and finish the work he started.' She did not mention the peony, she would treat it as just another plant the seeds of which she had to harvest.

Her tears ran unchecked down her face, she felt so helpless and lost without him. She had loved him, more than she realized. She thought of her father, what would he do in this situation? He'd lost people on his trips, for the life was dangerous but he'd gone on, finished what he came to do. She would write to him. If only she could talk to him, but writing was the next best thing.

As she looked for writing paper, a flower press stacked by the wall caught her attention. She undid the tapes. One peony was hopefully on its way to England with Anu, the other lay before her, its petals now faded to a creamy fawn.

This was all she had from the expedition, a faded sliver of silk-like petals, with two leaves. What good would this do Papa? It was no better than a faded rose given a lifetime ago to a girl now long past her youth.

She heard a movement outside her tent and snapped shut the case catching the peony roughly and tearing one of its petals.

'Oh, no,' she cried out and, hearing her anguish, Lorin came in.

'Delphina, I must insist on taking you back. We can go tomorrow if you would rather.'

'Go away,' she said. 'Just go back to the village and leave me to finish my work.'

'Look,' he said, his voice reasonable, 'surely the guides can finish the rest of the seed gathering? You tell them where they are. They'll be much quicker than you will anyway, being used to the place. You can wait in relative comfort in Darjeeling for them to bring them to you.' He smiled, made a move to take her hand, then, as if he thought better of it, withdrew it awkwardly. 'I feel responsible for you, alone out here, so cruelly widowed.'

'Widowed', the word was cruel, but she would not send anyone else to get the seeds. No doubt he hoped to persuade Tewang and Pasang to tell him where they were, well, he would be disappointed.

'Let them get the seeds. Shall I bring him to you, so you can tell him?' he said.

Delphina thought about the long, weary climbs back to the peony. The unrelenting rain, the icy winds. It would be colder now that it was autumn, and without Arnold to encourage her on her way, without her determination not to hold him up, to make him proud of her, it would be doubly hard, but she must not give in and tell him.

'I've asked you to leave me. Go back to your uncle and finish your work and leave me to mine.'

'Why are you so stubborn?' he cried out, impatient with her. 'You cannot stay here alone.'

'I can and I will. Thank you for coming to tell me about Arnold's death, but I need no more from you.'

'You don't trust me, which is madness, as they are only seeds out here for all to find.' His eyes were dark with indignation, but there was a touch of arrogance there too.

'No, I don't. Now, go back to your uncle.'

'I am not at all like him,' he retorted. Then, after a visible effort to control his impatience, he said, 'I thought that when we met at Aurian House in England we got on well.' His eyes traced over her face and, despite herself she felt a sliver of warmth curl round her heart.

'That was England. I have not come here for a social life. I am working as surely you should be and I ask you to go now and leave me to it.'

17

Delphina passed the night in a confusion of pain and despair. Sometimes she railed against Arnold for leaving her, dying because of some tomfool act of courage just when she needed him most, then she scolded herself for her selfishness. As morning broke there came with it a steely determination she would go on and get the peony seeds for her father. She must persuade Tewang and Pasang to come with her; surely they would if she told them it was for Arnold's sake. But the immediate problem was how to get rid of Lorin.

She'd told him to leave and taken to her tent, but when she got up that morning she found that Lorin and his guides were still there and had made their camp apart from her. Under her irritation she felt a wave of relief.

She told Tewang to see that the camp was packed up. Lorin approached her asking how she was.

'As well as I can be. Now you are still here you can take me to Darjeeling and leave me there and I will go home.' She knew she sounded off-hand but she must not allow him one hint of her real feelings for him. She must play her part so he would not suspect that once he had left her there she would set off again to the peony.

'As you wish, but I will see you get home safely.'

She did not answer him, but when they were nearly ready to leave she asked Tewang to come and help her with something and when they were out of earshot she said, 'You must help me now, help me for Arnold's sake, will you promise me?'

He regarded her with his calm eyes thinking she wanted to vent her anger about his death. He said gently, 'It was his time to go.'

'I'm not talking of that.' Inside she railed against his stoic acceptance of Arnold's death, but she controlled her emotions and went on, 'I want to finish his work, alone without that man.' Her eyes slid towards Lorin. 'We will go to Darjeeling and pretend I am going home then you and I and Pasang and a few porters will set out to finish the work Mr North started. You agree?'

'It is too difficult for you alone,' he said.

'I will not be alone, I will be with you and Pasang, but you will tell no one and pretend that I am leaving to go home. I want no one' — she clutched his arm her face taut with determination — 'no one but us two to know about it. Will you promise me that?'

He regarded her a moment then nodded. 'They are bad men,' he said, 'they steal from us, we will not tell them.'

'Thank you,' she said fervently, tears pricking her eyes. 'Thank you.'

'I have a friend in Darjeeling,' she said to Lorin when he repeated that he would stay with her until her travel plans were made. She remembered Henry Orsin whom she'd met on the boat. He had given her his card if she should need him. 'I will stay with him and he will see me home. He is a good friend,' she went on, 'and it will be nice to spend some time with him.'

She saw a flash of jealousy in his eyes but it pushed her on. If she could get him to think that Henry was important to her then he might leave her alone. But Henry might not be there or want anything to do with her, but she'd worry about that when they got there. She felt a little ashamed when she thought of how she would use Henry, take advantage of his feelings for her to get her own way. But then, she thought, as she supervised their departure, he might not be there at all.

Lorin said gruffly, 'It is best to go home but I will see that you get safely away.'

'No, there's no need. I've told you I have a

friend. Besides what is this fever your uncle has? He might be very ill and need you.'

Lorin frowned. 'It's not exactly a fever. He . . . it's self-induced. He should be over it by now.'

Papa had told her that Cedric liked opium. With any luck he would overdose and be out of her way, she thought savagely.

They started the long march. She walked alone, thinking of Arnold and for a day Lorin left her to her thoughts, but that evening he tried to talk to her.

They sat in the pitch black by the light of the fire. She watched the flames twist and turn, feeling the pull of sleep on her but dreading succumbing to it then waking with the renewed pain of loss. Lorin's voice was soft in the darkness.

'I've never met anyone like you before, beautiful and brave.'

His voice induced a feeling of exhilaration that surged through her banishing her despair. But she must not succumb to it, she warned herself sharply. How easy it would be to be seduced by him. Her body called out for his caresses, but it was only lust and she must not be tempted. Here they were alone in the world and the loneliness of it was heightening their passion. She must not give in.

'Thank you,' she said, for she had to say something, 'but I am not brave. If I was a man this would be my profession and indeed there are some women who go on such trips.'

'But not such arduous ones. I suppose you wanted to be with your husband as you were so newly married?'

His expression was hard to read in the shadow of the flickering flames but she sensed he wanted to question her of their love.

She said, 'That's right.'

'Though your father is one of the greatest plant hunters, you must have inherited some of your love for plants from him.'

Was he trying to prize her secrets from her in this roundabout way?

'Yes,' she said tartly, 'I must have done. All my life he followed this profession and he used to come back with such stories about his finds. It was his whole life and your uncle finished it by causing him to fall off the mountain.'

'I'm sure he did not; it was an accident,' Lorin said hotly.

'An accident caused by him,' she said getting up. 'I cannot tell you what torture it is for me to see him so imprisoned, and it is for that reason I hate your uncle and all his family.' She went quickly into her tent and left him in the darkness.

They went on again the next day and though he tried to talk her she would not.

'Leave me,' she said, 'just get me to Darjeeling then you can go.'

They arrived the next day and she found a place to stay for the night telling Lorin she would get in touch with her friend and he could now go.

'I will not leave you until I know you are safe,' he protested. 'Shall I send word to your friend?' His mouth twisted at the words. He was watching her intently.

'I am safe and I ask you to go. Thank you for bringing me this far.' She went into the darkness of the house and he did not follow her.

She did not see him over the next few days and thought that he had believed her story and had gone but Tewang told her he had not.

'He is waiting for his uncle who comes here any day.'

'We must leave at once without him knowing,' she said, the fear taking hold of her. She thought for a moment of contacting Henry, persuading him to get her away, but then she thought better of it. He might be a liability, make a fuss that would alert Lorin and not let her go. 'Will you arrange it please,

Tewang? The porters can wait outside the town and I will join them.'

'His uncle is a bad man. It is better that you go home to your own country,' Tewang said.

'When I have got what I came for. You promised me you would come with me and to tell no one where we are going. I want to leave as soon as possible before his uncle comes, understand?'

At last he reluctantly agreed.

Two days later, she left the bungalow before light. Tewang led her through the town to the porters and Pasang who were waiting for her. Pasang had brought his cousin with him, a cheerful youth called Lobsang.

Delphina wore one of Arnold's jackets that he had left behind. It smelt of his familiar scent, smoke from the fires, the spicy smell of his aftershave. When she'd put it on she'd felt a rush of tears and longing for him. She could see his stocky frame outside barking orders at the porters, checking the loads. How small and weak she felt without him. But this weakness was no good. Only one thing mattered now, she must get to that peony before Cedric.

All day they marched, passing other travellers on the route. Delphina studied each group intently fearful that Cedric and Lorin had seen her go and followed her. They passed Tibetans, their sheep laden with bags of grain on their way to trade for salt or bricks of tea, and monks with their round, shaven heads, but still she studied them in case Cedric was hiding amongst them.

They spent that night under the shelter of a large roof of rock. Delphina insisted that they start off again very early the next morning. She planned to camp near to the peony so that if Cedric caught up with them she did not have hours of climbing before she reached it. It was raining now and very cold. Suddenly she recognized the tiny, stone altars set in the rocks, each with its offerings to the spirit of the mountain and knew they were nearing the deserted monastery where they had stayed before. The wind blew flurries of snow at them, the sky closed in and she prayed she had not left it too late and they would be unable to get there because of the snow.

They set up camp at the deserted monastery again and the memories of the last time she was here flooded back. It was here that Arnold had given her the peony when she had thought it had only been a figment of Randolph's imagination.

To her relief the next day dawned clear, the sun pushing through the pearly swirls of mist.

Taking Pasang, Lobsang, Tewang and a couple of porters they started off, their baggage filled with the airtight tins for the seed collection.

They walked fast along the flat path, then on up, slowing as it got steeper. It was the way the pilgrims took to another monastery that appeared to grow out of the rock high above them. The mist disappeared and the light became dazzling, the sky a rich, cobalt blue. Delphina's heart leapt at the beauty; if only Arnold and her father were here to share it, but despite her sorrow she could not stop a wave of optimism rising in her.

As they went she forced herself to stop occasionally to collect other seed capsules, instructing the others to do the same. They passed a species of primula that she remembered Arnold remarking on. She picked them for him, labelling them carefully, listing them as his discovery.

They went on until they reached the boulders. Here was the rock shaped like Punch's nose. She remembered how Arnold had led her to the peony, and dashed away the tears that threatened to overwhelm her.

'Where are you, Arnold?' she whispered. 'I do so hope you know that I have made it back here.'

'Are you lost?' Tewang asked her.

'No. I am thinking of Arnold and how much I miss him.'

He touched her arm. 'His spirit will always be here, and in our hearts.'

'I know.' For a moment she did indeed feel that he was here, that part of him would never leave her. But suddenly this feeling was replaced by one of menace. She turned round quickly, but all was deserted save for them. 'Come on,' she said urgently, 'let us collect the seeds and be gone.'

They went on until they were only a few yards from the path that led to the peony. At each step nearer to it, Delphina felt the excitement rise in her, but the agitation was there too and she could not stop herself looking round as if expecting that any moment Cedric would be there, waiting for her to lead him to the peony.

But now that she was safely here she wanted to gather the seeds alone.

'I'm fine now, I will just go on by myself as this plant is special to me. Please collect the seeds round here,' she pointed to some violas growing under some shrubs.

Lobsang grinned and hopped off down a path as if he was a child who had been given the day off. Tewang looked doubtful. His dark eyes scoured the rocks and the sky, but seeing no one about he said reluctantly, 'Do not be

286

long and do not go far so you cannot shout for me.'

'I won't, and look . . . ' — she pointed in the opposite direction to the peony — 'down there are masses of seed heads. Collect those too, please. I'd like to bring back a lot for Kew, they might employ me then.'

'Be quick, the weather may change and we must get back. I do not like it here, I feel the spirits are angry,' Pasang said.

Remembering his gloom last time she was here, Delphina said cheerfully, 'The spirits here are good, do not worry, but I will be quick.'

Pasang did not look reassured but, calling Lobsang to him, he instructed him on how to gather the seed heads, cursing him when he let some blow away.

She watched them go further down the path until they were out of her way. She ran down the path, on and on, quite forgetting in her excitement to stay within shouting distance of Tewang. Impatience mounted in her, what if it was not there? Had been eaten by some stray animal or picked for a shrine? Then there it was, heavy with seedpods though they had opened and some had scattered to the winds. She stood still a moment and worshipped it. She would never come here again. If only she could have seen the flower once more in all its glory, each petal shining as if it held the sun. She felt very humble standing there before it. A plant of such simplicity, such innocent beauty that had caused so much greed and pain.

She had done it, against all the odds she, or rather Arnold, had found her father's peony and she had come back just in time to gather the seeds before they dropped out. She thought of the joy he would have to look forward to, as this time surely it would flower for him in his own garden.

She took out a tin from her pocket for the seeds. Rocks and stones surrounded the plant for some way so that when the seeds did ripen and fall there was no earth for them to grow in. Perhaps the winds blew them away and they did find a haven to grow somewhere. She gathered the seed pods putting them into the airtight tin. When she reached the second last pod she paused; she would defy nature, find a corner of rich earth and plant these seeds for her father and for Arnold. They would grow for them, the sun in the ivory petals would be like a lamp lit for Arnold's memory.

She closed the tin and pushed it deep into her clothing. In the bulk of her clothes it would be unnoticeable. She would keep it by her at all times, even when sleeping. In her hand she held the seeds that she wanted to plant and with a last look at the peony, climbed back up to look for a place to plant the seeds.

There was a pile of boulders a little way ahead. Behind these she found the perfect place, earth, open air and yet the shelter of the boulders. She made a few holes in the earth and distributed the seeds among them, willing them to grow for her. It comforted her to think that it might be there for always, growing there for Arnold and Papa.

Then she remembered Tewang and how he might panic if he could not find her. She ran up the path and round the boulders to call for him. Cedric came round from the other side barring her way.

'Delphina. We meet again.' His voice was sickly with sarcasm, his lips curled in that cruel smile.

All the joy and pride at her achievement was crushed in her fear. Frantically she looked round for Tewang and Pasang, but Cedric catching her glance said, 'There is no one here but us, my dear.'

'That's not true, I am here with — '

He was leaning nonchalantly against a boulder as if he was enjoying the view during a relaxing ramble. He interrupted her. 'Wunji is seeing to them. I left Lorin behind. I am here alone to collect my dues.'

His voice and his expression of his enjoyment of the situation chilled her.

'You have no dues from me,' she snapped.

'Come, come, what about the peony seeds? That is the reason you are here, is it not? Surely, otherwise, you would have scampered off home, now that your husband' — he sneered at the word — 'is dead.'

She would kill him if he mocked Arnold. He would not get the seeds from her. But had he been watching her all the time? Did he know she had them now? 'I don't know what you mean? There are no peonies here.'

'I think there are. Your father is not the only one who talks of new plants. I have my spies.' He smiled. 'It is getting cold and maybe it will snow, so let us get it over with.' He held out his hand.

Perhaps she could fob him off with some other seeds, but he would surely know they were not from the peony.

'Hurry up.' He took a step towards her.

'I haven't got them. It's not around here anyway.' She looked straight at him, holding herself taller.

For a moment he hesitated and she realized with relief that despite his boasting he did not know exactly where it was.

'Where is it then? I know you will not go home without it.'

'I sent it off to England with the other supplies a week ago.'

He cursed, came so close to her she could feel his spittle on her face. 'I do not believe you. You would not trust it to the riff-raff here.'

Then she heard Tewang calling her, his voice frantic. 'Mrs North, Mrs North.'

'I am here,' she screamed loudly, 'over here.'

'Give me those seeds.' Cedric made a lunge for her, but she was too quick and dodged back behind the boulders struggling down a steeper way towards Tewang's voice. The scree on the rocks came loose and twice she almost fell but each time she managed to save herself by clutching at a shrub. She could hear Cedric behind her, but he was heavy and clumsy and could not move so fast. Then she saw Pasang standing beneath her.

'Jump quickly, jump,' he called, and without hesitating she jumped the last bit and he caught her, his body as strong and sturdy as a tree. 'Come, we must go.' He pulled her down to where the two porters cowered by the loads. Then Tewang joined them, his face grim.

'We must go, quickly,' he said, pushing her on before him.

'Where is Lobsang? We cannot go without him.' She looked around the group for him.

'He is dead.' Tewang pulled her along.

'Dead? How?'

'Come on.' They pulled her on.

'Lobsang, dead?' she repeated in horror.

'Wunji killed him.' Tewang's mouth was set in a determined line, his eyes on the path ahead.

There was a cry behind her and involuntarily she turned towards it and saw Cedric stumble, his arms flying out to recover himself. He hovered a moment, then fell over the side, out of sight.

Despite her hatred of him she paused, but Tewang seized her arm and pulled her on. 'Leave him,' he said roughly, 'we must go on.'

Delphina hurried on, shocked that the cheerful youth would sing his tuneless songs no more. She was overwhelmed with guilt; she had forced them to come here. She was partly responsible for his death, and Cedric? How far had he fallen? Was he dead, or lying injured? But she must not think of it. He had Wunji with him, and he must look after him.

They walked awhile in silence, each lost in their own thoughts. Pasang did not look at her. He walked straight and tall, his face set hard as she had often seen it as they had battled through blizzards of teeming rain. An expression of endurance, of something unpleasant but beyond one's control. Lobsang had been the one to die, not him this time. Lobsang had gone to another life. Pasang's time would come. She wished she could be so fatalistic herself.

They reached the top of the part of the pilgrims' path that led down to the deserted monastery. A group of people dressed in a sort of sacking and yak or goat's skin crossed it on their way to their shrine further up. They stopped and exchanged a few words with Pasang and Tewang.

A thin, stooped man with a bald head pushed himself forward, angrily spitting his words out of his mouth as if they were bitter. The faces of the other pilgrims were angry too. Another joined in, gesturing upwards, shaking his fist.

Tewang spoke to them. He gestured towards her and she saw a look of antagonism in their faces as they scrutinized her. Tewang shook his head denying their accusations. The pilgrims' fury obviously directed at her increased. But although their voices and faces were menacing they made no attempt to touch her. At last they quietened and, bowing to

Tewang and Pasang, they went on up the path.

When they had gone she said, 'What has happened? Why are they so angry?'

Pasang turned away and went on walking, but Tewang, his face tight with fury, threw the words at her as if they revolted them.

'Again someone has stolen things, statues, holy manuscripts from their shrine. They think it was you because you are a stranger. I know it is not.'

'Oh, Tewang, I am so sorry.' It was Cedric, she had no doubt at all that it was him.

'While one man is following us and killing Lobsang, the other is stealing from the shrine. We know who they are and they will be punished.' Tewang walked on, his stalwart frame implacable with the task that lay ahead.

18

The hostility coming from her Tibetan companions dulled Delphina's relief of having safely collected the peony seeds. She was exhausted, and her emotions dipped and swooped. Where was Cedric? Was he dead, or left wounded down some crevice? And Lorin, where was he? Was Tewang right about his assumptions that while Cedric was following her, Lorin was stealing from their temples? There were countless explorers who thought nothing of plundering the countries they visited, making the excuse that the poor of the land could not preserve them. She did not want to believe that Lorin was a thief and yet she had heard that Cedric made money this way so it seemed more than possible that Lorin did too.

They stayed that one night at the deserted monastery and all night she tossed and turned holding the precious seeds to her. She had done it, against all the odds she had done it, and now she was on her way home. Nothing more must go wrong.

The next morning she followed Tewang and Pasang wearily down the mountain on their long way back to the boat and home.

No one spoke to her, indeed they seemed to ignore her as they went. Even the songs from the porters often so cheerful now seemed more like a dirge. Perhaps they sang for Lobsang and it was his death that made them so subdued, but she sensed it was more than that. It only needed one stranger to violate their culture for them to be suspicious of them all. If only Arnold was here, he would have known what to do. He would have confronted Cedric and demanded that he give the statues back.

They arrived at last at a small village, the prayer flags flapping in the breeze, the children running out to greet them. Tewang led her to a rather dilapidated hut to sleep in, obviously used by other travellers, but now she was the only occupant. It had four dingy rooms and a long narrow passage, a few faded copies of *Blackwood's* lay on a makeshift table. It compounded her loneliness and she needed to summon all her reserves of confidence and determination not to burst into tears and beg him not to leave her alone.

'Stay here, do not go out,' Tewang said, as he left her.

'I might go for a short walk later to see my surroundings,' she said, wanting to be among the children to ease her loneliness. To distract herself from her despair she began to unpack the few things she needed for the night from her bag.

'I do not think it is a good plan; stay here.' He stood impassively in the doorway. 'I will bring you food. The people are not happy to see strangers here.'

'But they seemed cheerful enough when we arrived, running out to greet us, letting me have this hut?'

He continued stubbornly, 'I want you safe, stay here.' Then, as if he had a brainwave, he said firmly, 'Mr North would want you to stay here.'

Delphina decided it was better not to argue with him. They must be afraid of the mood of the people after the theft of their holy objects. She must not antagonize him further. She asked him if she could have some water to wash in. He agreed, used now to the strange habits of the Europeans who liked to wash their bodies instead of leaving them as they were, and went away to organize it for her.

Later, when she was washed and had changed her clothes, she disobeyed him and slipped out to explore the village. She felt too confined in this small, rather smelly hut and so desperately alone.

It was dusk and, as she walked among the small houses, the people slid away into the shadows. She noticed that some had huge goitres on their necks like some of their porters had. A small girl straggled past carrying a young goat in her arms as if it was a baby; she smiled making Delphina feel more cheerful. She put out her hand and caressed the goat's rough coat.

A group of monks loomed at her out of the dimness, shaking their begging bowls demandingly at her. She had nothing to give them so she mimed that her pockets were empty. One beggar with a thick black beard beat on a drum to accompany their chanting, the sound was mournful and sinister, adding to her feelings of depression. The beggar with the drum came close to her and she saw that the drum was made with two human skulls.

'Let me pass,' she begged, running through them and away. It was like a dreadful omen, their chanting lingering in the air, following her like a menacing bird. A huge hound bounded after her, barking furiously, then suddenly she heard an English voice.

'Go home dog, go home.' The dog surprisingly stopped, then slunk away.

Lorin came out from behind a hut. She stared at him, mixed emotions charging through her. Was Cedric here too? Instinctively she put her hand to her breast where she had hidden the peony seeds.

'Why are you here?' she saw the anger in his face. 'You told me you were going home, or were spending time with your friend in Darjeeling. But I see that was not true.'

'It is none of your business,' she retorted, 'but I am on my way home now.' She tensed, expecting Cedric to join them any second. She had seen him fall, but Lorin did not seem perturbed so he must have returned.

'Where have you been?' she asked sharply thinking of the stolen treasures from the temples.

'Around. I only arrived here a couple of hours ago. My uncle and I were working in different places. We've been here before and have our rooms already.'

Stealing in different places, she thought. She must get away from here and to the boat before them.

'If you'll excuse me I must get on.' She must find Tewang and demand to leave and get to a boat to England before them, for once on the boat she would have no protection from them.

'Why did you stay on?' he asked, his voice as cold as an interrogator. 'Was it so secret you could not tell me?'

Of course it was secret but she could not say that. 'Surely I do not have to account my movements to you?' she retorted.

'Are you here alone?' His eyes watched her warily if she might tell him of her intimacy with her 'friend'.

'I have Tewang and Pasang,' she said, and was about to embark on having Henry too when he said urgently, 'I would like to help you, Delphina. I feel that you need someone now you are alone.'

'I don't need anyone, thank you.' She must take care. No doubt he was trying to ingratiate himself with her so as to find out about the peony seeds. What would he say if he knew he was but a few feet away from them where they nestled against her breasts?

His face tightened; his eyes never left her face. 'I know it was not your fault but . . . ' He paused then went on with a rush, 'Taking the things from the temples and — '

'What?' she cried out in fury. 'What are you saying?'

'Delphina.' He raised his hand as if to ward off her anger. 'I know your husband did it without you knowing but — '

'How dare you?' she cried out. 'Arnold loved these people, respected them and their country. He would never do such a thing. It's your uncle. He has lied to implicate us and cover for himself. He has stolen these things, and maybe you have too, or at least colluded with him.'

Lorin tried to placate her. 'Delphina, listen to me. You and I are new to this country, to plant hunting. Apparently your husband made his living this way, selling their treasures when he got home.'

She slapped him sharp across his face. She saw anger and pain leap in his eyes. 'How cowardly you are to accuse Arnold when he can no longer defend himself.'

'I'm only repeating what is said here.' His eyes were hard with fury, with hurt at her betrayal. 'That is how he made his living, taking a few extra things home with him to sell to collectors of Tibetan art.'

'Who told you this apart from your uncle?'

'Some of the people, the porters, the *gam* we have.' He rubbed his cheek; she saw the red welt of her hand across it.

'They lie. It is your uncle who behaves like this. He would never dare say these things if Arnold were alive.'

Their quarrel had produced a small crowd who hid behind various buildings peeping out at them. Delphina walked away from him, seething with anger and not a little fear. Cedric had obviously put these malicious stories about to discredit Arnold, to possibly blackmail her to giving up the seeds of the peony. Now that Lorin knew she had lied about going home he no doubt imagined — possibly encourage by Cedric — that she had stayed to steal from the temples, or to collect up the things Arnold had stolen. She must find Tewang and Pasang. They would defend her, defend Arnold's good name.

'Oh. Arnold,' she whispered to the wide skies, 'I will not let you down. I will not let them think this of you.'

'Delphina, wait, listen to me,' Lorin called after her and she heard his swift steps behind her.

She turned on him in a fury. 'Let me alone, go back to your lying, scheming uncle and look for the treasures there. Arnold was a decent, honest man: he would never hurt or disgrace these people.'

It was dark now and she hurried back to her room. As she went she looked for Tewang and Pasang, but she could not see them. Her only hope was that they were at the hut. But there was nobody there. She lit her lamp and sat, terrified and furious, alone in her room, watching the flickering shadows against the dingy wall. She'd write this down, write everything in a letter to her father. She had only written a short note telling him of Arnold's death and how she was on her way home, but now she wrote down everything.

The theft of the holy treasures, her meeting with Lorin and his accusation. She would try and send this letter tomorrow, so if anything happened to her everyone back home would know of Arnold's innocence.

A young man bringing her food roused her from her task. His English was not good, but she thought he said he'd come from Tewang.

'I want to see Tewang,' she said.

He nodded.

She repeated her request, finally writing a note begging him to come to her at once and told him to give it to him.

She barely touched her meal she was so agitated. She wrote on and still no one came. She listened to the noises of the night, the wind, the wild dogs howling. She wrote on, pouring out her heart to her father writing with a kind of desperation, determined that no one back home should think ill of Arnold, telling of the plants he had found, his generosity with the peony. Suddenly she felt a shift in the atmosphere. Someone was near, moving about just outside the hut.

Tewang had come at last. She had rigged up some cloth over the window to protect her privacy, but it was possible for him to see from outside that her lamp was still lit and she was still up. Through the whistling of the wind she heard the soft sound of footsteps in bare feet in the narrow passage. But Tewang walked quickly; he would not creep like a thief. Maybe he thought after all that she was asleep and did not want to disturb her. She snatched up her lamp and, on a sudden impulse, she took up a heavy torch to defend herself, then opened the door.

It was pitch dark in the passage and, lifting her lamp, she saw a pair of eyes staring out from a dreadful, puckered face. The face was cat-like with a snarling mouth. It stood about three feet off the floor. In her terror, she jerked back the lamp and the passage was in darkness again. There was a sudden, quick movement, the shutting of the outside door. It had gone, but not before she had the sensation that there was more than just that face; there was more bulk to it, as if there were two or more beings there.

For a moment she was paralyzed with fear. Had someone come to kill her? To punish her for stealing their religious treasures? Or was it some monstrous trick played out by Cedric? But if it was why had they left empty-handed without a word?

She staggered back to her room and fell upon the bed, vainly trying to make sense of it. As her terror lessened, her thoughts became more rational. Perhaps it was a child in a mask teasing her. They were a mischievous lot; they loved to touch and pinch her quite without the restraint of children back home. Or maybe it was someone from the pygmy tribe. There were so many tribes out here, distinguishable by their shape and clothes. She heard the door open again and Tewang's voice as he came down the narrow passage.

'Mrs North, Mrs North. You want me?'

'Oh, Tewang.' She sprung off the bed so relieved to see him. 'I'm so glad you're here. I saw . . . ' The words tumbled from her in such a jumble as she told him all that had happened, that she had to start again and speak more slowly until he understood.

His face was inscrutable, his dark eyes watching her. He said, 'We know the truth, do not be afraid. Pasang and I will sleep here.'

'But this . . . this thing that came here. What was it?'

'It will not hurt you, do not be afraid,' was all he said. He went to the door and called to some youth to fetch Pasang. He arrived a few moments later and the two of them wrapped in their long cloaks that served them with so many uses, stretched out on the ground outside her hut to guard her through the night.

19

Nightmares haunted her sleep, the face she had seen in the passage grinning grotesquely at her. It was superimposed on Cedric's body swaying and looming at her as if it was suspended on a rope. She woke shaking with fear. What would the people do to her if they believed that she and Arnold had stolen from their temples? She must return home at once, leave immediately, for her own safety and that of the peony seeds.

She put this to Tewang and Pasang the next morning adding, 'But I cannot let them get away with such lies. We must tell everyone they are lying. You know Arnold would never do such a thing.'

But Tewang and Pasang just shrugged. 'Do not worry,' they said in unison. 'The spirits will punish them.'

Impatient with this theory, she went on distractedly, 'We must do something before I leave. I cannot bear Arnold's name to be so blackened.'

But they remained impassive, telling her it would be dealt with in time. They urged her to eat, telling her that they could not leave today but perhaps tomorrow. She wanted to leave at once, but she must at least stay until she had cleared Arnold's name. She explained this to them, but again, with their inscrutable expression, they repeated like a mantra that she must not worry. At last they left her, telling her they had business to attend to.

'You stay inside and pack to go home. We will come back.' Pasang said severely. Since the death of Lobsang, Delphina had felt he was angry with her, seeing her as the cause of it. How could she get round this? The language barrier between them often made her wonder how much they did understand, and if her words were misinterpreted giving further offence.

She would not have Arnold's name besmirched by such a monster as Cedric. But maybe he was dead, or anyway severely injured. She'd seen him fall and such falls were treacherous. But he had started these stories, and Lorin believed them and, even if Cedric were dead, he seemed to be passing them around. She must go and confront him, demand that he take back the lies and convince the people that Arnold was innocent.

'Wait,' she said, before Tewang and Pasang left her, 'I have a letter I want sent to my father. Please be sure it gets there and does not fall into the wrong hands.'

'Trust us,' Tewang said intently, when she handed it to him and, had she not been so agitated, she might have taken more note of his words and been comforted.

She gave Tewang and Pasang a few minutes to be out of the way before she went outside. A huge man, his muscles like coiled snakes beneath his brown skin, stood a little way off, watching her. He was bald, his features a mixture of Oriental and Asian origin. He was dressed in blue trousers, a fox-red goral skin worn over one shoulder exposing most of his massive chest. The sight of him renewed her terror. He was so vast he could easily squeeze the life from her with one hand. Had he been put here to guard her, or was he in Cedric's pay? But though he must have seen her he made no move towards her. She walked away from him determined to clear Arnold's name.

She walked with more bravado than she felt. She asked some youths where the two foreign men had rooms and one took her to a collection of dwellings and pointed one out to her, indicating that it was on the first floor.

A group of women were sitting outside the house. Their hair was braided in coloured ribbons, bright jewellery adorned their necks and ears. Their tawny faces with their black eyes were intent on their domestic tasks. They looked up at her with friendly curiosity and for a moment she yearned to sit down with them, to take up the butter churns or the kneading and shaping of the buckwheat cakes, and get comfort through her hands with the homely tasks. A child poked its face out from the folds of its mother's clothes and she touched its round little head under its rough wool cap. She envied the contentment of these women, yet in Tibet women and men were equal so perhaps they had less cause than their sisters in the rest of the world to be discontented.

Reluctantly, she left to go into the house. But she must insist that Lorin clear Arnold's name. She was convinced that Cedric had stolen the treasures and might well have persuaded Lorin to do the same, but the only way to convince the people that Arnold had no part in it was to admit to the crime themselves. It sickened her to think of what they might do to Lorin to punish him. But she must find out for certain, and if Lorin was guilty she must leave him to his fate.

She felt the tin of peony seeds at her breast. How foolish she was to confront him with it on her. She went back to the women and, making sure she was not observed, asked in her halting Tibetan the woman with the child if she could hide the tin for her for a while. The woman smiled and took it from her. The baby put out his chubby hand attracted by the glint of the tin. The mother laughed, showed it to him, then hid it in the folds of her dress.

She went back into the house and up to the door of the room the youths had indicated. She thought of Arnold; he would make her walk away, go straight back to England. She could almost hear him saying, 'What do I care what such a man says of me? Keep yourself safe, go home while there is still time.'

She thought of her father in his chair, his useless legs covered with a rug all because of Cedric; was she going to let him ruin Arnold's memory too? The anger flared in her. She knocked, then threw open the door. There was no one in the room.

In the corner was a rucksack she recognized as Lorin's. It drew her to it like a moth to the flame. She ran her hands down it and then, scolding herself for wanting to be close to him, moved to leave. But disappointment at not finding him in made her turn again to his bag. If he was a thief, might the things not be in his bag? But would he be such a fool as to hide them in so obvious a place?

She undid the strap and slipped her hand inside: clothes, a book, wash things, that was all. She re-tied the strap. She would go and find him and demand he tell her the truth. Then she saw another bag half hidden by the camp-bed. It looked roughly packed, a book and a torch jammed in anyhow. She went to it and looked inside. Among the clothes was a check shirt she'd seen Lorin wearing, it was wrapped round something. She pulled it out, fear fluttering in her heart and, unwrapping it, saw that it was a holy statue.

'My dear Delphina, welcome.' Cedric's voice was smooth, like honey drawing in the fly.

She jumped, almost dropped the statue. 'I . . . I thought — '

'You thought I was dead, but I am not. Though I am badly bruised. What are you doing here?'

'You know why I've come,' she said, her heart sick that Lorin was a thief and had the statue in his bag.

'Tell me.' He took a step towards her. Revulsion and fear prickled up her spine.

'There is no time for your tricks,' she said. 'You and Lorin have stolen the religious objects from the monastery and lied to the Tibetans, saying that Arnold had done it.'

'You are clever as well as beautiful.' He

came closer still, then, as she moved away from him, turned and went back out on to the balcony. He stared out at the range of mountains glistening under the delphinium sky. He did not speak or move, staring out with his back to her.

Anger and fear churned through her. He did not move. His broad back gave the impression that her intrusion bored him. This fuelled her anger and made her foolish. She marched closer to him and demanded, 'You will tell them what you did. You will tell them it was you who stole them. You will not put the blame on a dead man, a man with more goodness in his fingernail than you have in your entire body.'

He did not appear to have heard her. He stayed motionless, a picture of a man relaxing on a balcony, enjoying the view.

'Tewang and Pasang know it is you. They will tell the others. You will not get away with these lies.' She came closer to him.

He twitched slightly, but still he said nothing.

'You will not blacken Arnold's name. He gave his life trying to save these people that he loved. I will defend him. I'll go through one of their trials if I must, but I will not let your wickedness hurt him.'

Cedric swung round and charged into the

room trapping her against the wall and some packing cases. His eyes glinted with lust and hatred. She struggled to escape but he pinioned her against the wall, an edge of a packing case digging into her side.

'There is only one way to save your precious Arnold,' he spat in her face. 'Give me the peony seeds, then I will do it.'

'I haven't got them.' She strained away from him, the foulness of his breath making her retch.

He grabbed her upper arms, pinching the flesh hard through her clothes.

'I will have what I want. You and the peony seeds, or I will watch them punish you.' The hatred in his face was terrifying. She could have guessed he'd stoop to anything to get what he wanted, but could she trust him? If she did hand over the peony seeds would he really admit that Arnold was innocent? She kicked at him, making him lose his balance for an instant, but he quickly regained it.

'Fight all you want you . . . she devil, it excites me more.' He pressed his body against her, pulling at her clothes. Saliva was running down his chin, his demonic eyes searching her body.

Her head was reeling, she kicked him again, screaming now, at the top of her voice. Someone, one of the women downstairs, must come to help her. He hit her hard against the side of her face. She felt as if he would knock the teeth from her jaw. He yanked at her clothes scrabbling to undo her trousers. She kicked, more feebly now, fighting him off, fighting not to lose consciousness.

'I will have what I want,' he hissed, calling out obscenities now. She jerked herself away from him and, for a second, he lost his hold of her. She tried to run to the door but he was on her again.

'You won't escape me this time.' His laugh petrified her.

'Let me go.' She hit him, scratching him with her nails, then ducking as his hand whipped up to whack her again. She kicked again, managed to pull away, feeling her clothes tear in his hands.

'You're making it easier for me,' he panted, snatching at her bare thigh under the torn clothing.

Delphina grabbed at his hair, yanking it with all her strength. Cedric roared. She twisted it again, calling desperately for someone to come and help her.

He got his hand free and hit her again. She must have lost consciousness for a few seconds for when she regained it she found herself pinned against the wall by his bulk.

She was too weak, too befuddled by his violence to do any more. She tried with once last effort to push him away.

Cedric was panting heavily now his eyes frenzied with lust, his mouth wet with spittle. He pushed his mouth on hers while his hands freed her trousers, grabbed at her, twisting her flesh until the pain of it nearly made her faint again.

'No!' she screamed with her last vestige of strength, straining with every ounce of energy she had left to escape his vile hands. He was pulling at his own clothes. She laid her head against the wall in agony, her body painfully trapped by his. If only someone would come and save her.

For a long moment there was no sound save his rasping breath. She tensed herself waiting for the last violation, ready to knee him, kick him in the groin before he raped her.

She sensed there was someone else in the room. She opened her eyes and saw the hard, impassive gaze of the massive man she'd seen watching her bungalow. By his side was the face she'd seen in the hall in the dark. It belonged to a lynx that was straining from a leash held in the man's huge hand.

To her surprise the sight of them brought her no fear. They gave her extra strength. She gave Cedric a sharp push. His clothes were undone, his mind and energy intent on the act to come. He lost his balance and, in the moment his body moved from hers, she sprang away. He grabbed her arm. She pulled away, the pain was terrible like scorching rods pushed into her joints, but she stretched her body as far away from him as possible, pulling up her clothes with her other hand. Even if her arm came out at the sockets, she would not let him near her again.

At this moment Cedric, too, saw the man with his lynx. The man's eyes were fixed on him like gimlets drilling right into his brain. Only his hand moved as he unleashed the animal. With one word of command the lynx sprang straight for Cedric's throat.

There was a cry, cut off abruptly by a dreadful gurgling, a spurt of crimson blood. Delphina fell on the floor, Cedric's hand relaxed, released her.

All at once there was a lot of noise. People running in, cries of horror at the sight. Someone, she dimly realized it was Tewang, helped her up, led her away. In a daze she went with him, seeing for a second like a grisly photograph the scene in the room. Cedric slumped, covered in blood on the floor, the massive man, pulling off his lynx whose jaws dripped red, putting on its leash and leading it away from the room.

'Come.' Tewang led her out of the house and through the group of women who were standing up now, trying to get into the house to see what had happened. The one with the baby looked at her with horror and then with pity handed back the tin of peony seeds as if that would cure her pain.

As she stretched out her hand to take it she saw that her arms were red with blood. She gave a little cry, but Tewang said, 'Don't worry, we will make you better.' He said something to the women and two of them came with them. Delphina hardly knew where she went; there was a sea of faces round her looming in and away again. Then she heard her name.

'Delphina, what has happened?' Lorin was running towards her.

Tewang said something to him and led her away, her legs like cotton wool. She was too tired, too shocked to feel anything. They reached the hut and she fell upon her bed in the dingy room, shutting her eyes trying to eradicate the noise, the sight of the lynx and the blood on its jaws. Fighting to wipe out the feel of Cedric on her. She longed to wash, to fall into the river and scrub and scrub her body until the very skin that he had touched had gone.

She struggled up and demanded this, but they pushed her back and told her they would clean her, but to rest now.

She felt gentle hands wash her, dress her in other clothes. In her hand she clutched the tin of peony seeds, refusing to let it go. Then one of the women gave her a drink and she felt herself slipping away, down into welcome oblivion.

When she woke, she struggled up through the darkness and pain, and saw in her mind the puckered face she'd seen in the passage. She cried out and at once felt a cool hand on her forehead. The room was dark save for a flickering lamp in the corner. It threw shadows over the room and she could not see the features of the person who sat beside her.

'Have this drink,' a woman said in Tibetan, and she felt the rim of the bowl put to her lips. She drank again and again slipped into unconsciousness. When at last she woke it was daytime and Tewang was standing by the foot of her bed.

'Do not worry,' he said, 'it is over. We must get you to the boat and your home.'

She lay there a moment letting her thoughts come back to her, then she said, 'Does everyone know that Mr Hartford lied and that Arnold is innocent?'

'Yes. We knew always, but now everyone

knows. You were foolish to go there; we told you we would look after it,' Tewang said, regarding her intently.

'I'm sorry. I couldn't rest until Arnold's name was cleared,' she said. It all seemed such a long time ago. The she thought of Lorin. 'And the other man, his nephew, he is punished too?'

'He did not do it. We have a trial, the lamas come. The ruler comes. Wunji tells us that Mr Hartford was a wicked man. He smuggled opium across the borders and when he was caught he blamed another man. He paid someone to steal from the monasteries. It is not the first time he has done it.'

She struggled to sit up, to ease herself off the bed, but she was overcome with weakness. Then the sight and the sound like a sort of muscular warmth as the lynx had leapt for Cedric's throat, came into her mind again and she shuddered violently.

'You should not have gone to Mr Hartford,' Tewang said again. 'It is good that Wangdi followed you.'

'Wangdi?'

'The man with the lynx. He came to help find the treasures.' Tewang smiled grimly. 'When you see him be careful. He always gets the bad men.'

'Does his lynx always kill people like that?'

319

Tewang nodded. 'It kills when he tells him to. We do not argue with him. But he has never killed someone who did not deserve it.'

'But Wunji,' she frowned, remembering his complete indifference to his flogging, 'he seems not to care about pain. How did you make him tell the truth?'

Tewang grinned. 'No one, not even Wunji lies to Wangdi.'

'I can understand that,' Delphina said grimly.

There was a long pause then Tewang said quietly, 'You are safe now. Pasang and the other Englishman will see you to the boat. I must leave you. I must go back to my village.'

'Are you leaving for ever?' Delphina said, stricken that he was going. He had known Arnold and her father. He had looked after her all this time, and now, so casually, he was leaving her.

'It is time,' he said. His eyes were warm as they looked at her. 'Now you are safe. When your flowers grow in your country, you will think of me.'

'I will never forget you, any of you, and I can never thank you enough.' She got up from the bed and held out her hand to him, shy suddenly in the poignancy of the moment. He took her hand between both of his.

'You are the bravest foreign woman I have ever met,' he said. 'It has been my honour to look after you.' He released her hands, made a small bow to her.

She snatched up Arnold's travelling clock that stood by her bed and thrust it into his hands. 'Take this,' she said, 'in his memory.'

'Thank you.' He looked at it in wonder. 'I will always keep it.'

She stood looking after him long after he had gone feeling that he took something with him. The welcome perhaps, the feeling of belonging here. The time had come for her to go home and she must start on the long journey back. She would go and find Pasang, and then she remembered that Tewang had said Lorin would return with her, too. She could not see him again; there had been too much dishonesty and betrayal for them ever to feel easy with each other. She would slip home incognito, alone with the precious peony seeds taking Arnold's memory with her.

20

Delphina folded her trousers and pushed them into her bag, then deciding that as they were the best-looking pair she owned, she would wear them to travel so she took them out again, lethargic with boredom of this task. How she longed to be back in England among the cool fresh green of the countryside and the pale luminous skies. There was a sudden rapping on the door of the hut and she peered out of the window to see Lorin standing there. He saw her and moved to come in, his face was pale, tight with tension. They stood there in the small entrance eyeing each other.

'I thought you'd gone,' she said ungraciously, trying to ignore the warm relief at seeing him.

'No, I came to see when you wanted to leave.'

She would not go with him; Pasang would take her to the boat. She had planned to leave early the following morning, slip away without him knowing.

He regarded her intently a few seconds, watching her anger tense in her face.

'Delphina.' He gestured in despair. 'I know that mere apologies don't seem enough in the circumstances but — '

'They don't.' She was angry at the sudden sweep of warmth that went through her. She had hoped he had left the village, but here he was, his suntanned face leaner now, his slender body radiating strength.

'My uncle has always been thought of as the black sheep in the family, but I thought it was only because of his womanizing and his drinking. I never realized that he was a thief as well,' he went on.

'I don't want to speak of it again. Justice has been done and it's over. Now, excuse me, I want to get home to my father.'

'I can hardly wait to leave this place and get back,' he said with feeling. 'I will come with you to see you get there safely.'

'No, there is no need. If I have got round this country on my own I hardly need to be escorted to the boat,' she said firmly, hiding her face from him in case he saw her agitation. Why must her body betray her so? It must be all these months away from the warmth of her family life.

His face darkened, 'I have to get home too, at once. It is stupid not to go together. We will probably take the same boat anyway.'

'Do as you wish. If you want to be helpful,

find Pasang and tell him to come to me.'

'Pasang has gone.' He looked directly at her. 'He sent me to say goodbye.'

'Gone?' She felt a wave of hurt then suspicion crowd in. He wouldn't go and leave her. Lorin must have said something to make him leave.

'Is this true? What did you say to him?' she cried out, angry and a little afraid. Surely Lorin was in the pay of Cedric's evil benefactor, too? If he were alone with her would he steal the seeds?

'His mother is ill in his village; he had to go. I told him that I would take you safely home. He has seen to your equipment; it's packed and ready to leave for Calcutta when you give the word.'

She regarded him intently. His clear grey eyes held hers, his mouth half smiled in that way he had as though he held a secret amusement, but she must not trust him. Only a little while before she was home with those seeds; she must not lose them now.

'Why did he not tell me?' she said, thinking now of Wunji. Had he killed him as he had killed Lobsang? Made sure she was alone?

'He got word in the night and set off before dawn. I'm sorry, I told him not to wake you. I thought you needed all the sleep you could get as you've been under such strain. I'm amazed you came through it.'

She stared at him. Had he been here, too, while she was dead to the world? It was a miracle she still had the seeds, but perhaps he hadn't noticed them.

'I want to leave at once,' she said. 'Are there any of my porters left?'

'I paid them off; there is no point in having more than we need between us. My uncle and Arnold are no longer with us so we can manage with the ones we brought.'

Fear snaked through her and yet she did not want to fear him. If only she could be taken in his arms, rest her head on his breast. An overwhelming sense of longing almost made her throw herself into his arms but, annoyed with her weakness, she curbed it. She was alone with him now, even her porters had gone. She had come so far, endured so much. Arnold had died, her father made a cripple, she must not lose the peony seeds now.

'I want to set off as soon as possible,' she said firmly, 'and though it seems we must travel together, we will travel apart.' She turned and left him to go back to her room, determined he should not see her panic.

They set off early the next morning and she walked alone, deep in her own thoughts. They set up camp for the night and she stayed in her own tent, leaving Lorin to his own devices.

On they went the next day and in the afternoon when she was almost asleep, struggling to put one foot in front of the other, pushing herself on, he was suddenly there beside her.

'Delphina, please let us settle this bad feeling between us. I feel very guilty about it all. If only I had paid attention, known about my uncle's behaviour, I could have spared you so much — '

'Enough,' she rounded on him with impatience. 'It is over, and I cannot bear 'if onlys'. If only my father had not met up with your uncle on that mountain he would not now be crippled in a chair. If only Arnold had been believed about the tons of water waiting to drown everyone he would not have gone to that other village and been killed.'

'I'm so sorry, Delphina, but none of it was *my* doing.' His voice was low, insistent and the warmth of it crept into her, but she clamped down her feelings.

'Oh, leave me alone,' she said. 'It is over, all of it. My only thought now is to get home to my father.'

She pushed on, keeping her gaze ahead and she felt him drop back. They reached the train station and she sat alone staring out at the passing landscape. She recognized the places that she'd passed through with Arnold. She remembered how he had told her to cut her hair, dress like a boy to avoid unwanted attention; she remembered how he had thrown money to the beggars, how he had rubbed her aching feet with spirit and taken the leeches from her legs. It all seemed a lifetime ago, yet, as they went on she heard his beautiful voice pointing things out to her, explaining about the culture, telling her of the flowers and plants that grew in such profusion everywhere. Surely he was still here somewhere in that wild and lovely place? She hoped he was at peace at last and had found his true resting place.

At last they reached the teeming clamour of Calcutta. She was very tired and it was a relief to find a small hotel and rest there. She left Lorin to make the arrangements and he managed to get them a berth on a boat leaving in a couple of days. Delphina sent her father a wire telling him the date of her expected arrival. She spent her time sleeping and writing up her journal, trying to cram in her last memories of this place.

Once they had left Tibet and arrived in India, she felt she had left Arnold behind, but it was not until the boat steamed out into the sea towards home leaving behind the clamour and colour of India did she feel truly bereft. She stood on the deck watching the land receding from her gaze like a fading dream and thought of how much she had left behind.

The other British passengers were very like the ones on the way out. Middle-aged ladies with not much to occupy themselves other than speculating on their fellow passengers, but there was one woman, a Mrs Chapman, she rather liked, a woman with a great love of India. She was returning to England with her husband who was much older than herself and who had become ill.

'I am determined to return one day,' she confided, telling her wonderful stories of her life there.

Being with her passed the time, but as the journey went on she found herself grieving more and more for Arnold.

'It has hit home now that your travels are over,' Mrs Chapman said with sympathy when she confided in her. She was able to talk to her about Arnold and her muddled feelings.

'Love comes in all guises,' Mrs Chapman said, with a sidelong look at her aged husband sitting asleep near them.

Delphina found comfort with her and it kept her away from Lorin, but one day he persuaded the steward to let him into her cabin.

'Delphina, are you all right?'

She was sitting staring at the sea from her porthole. She did not turn at his entrance. 'I told you I was fine and to leave me alone.'

'You are not fine. Forgive me, but you cannot go on like this sitting here so alone, letting your grief eat away at you. It will make you ill.'

'I am not alone, I am often with other people.'

'Only one person. She seems nice, but I think it is time we talked. I need to know why you are so angry with me, you owe me that.'

'I owe you nothing,' she said, opening her journal and starting to write, hoping he would take the hint and leave.

'I often think of that time we met at Aurian Hall,' he went on smoothly. 'I felt a closeness with you then that has not gone away. Am I being presumptuous to imagine you felt the same?' He was standing close to her now and her body cried out for his embrace. She dug her hand hard into her breast so that the tin holding the seeds pressed into her.

'That was a different time. Too much has happened since then. Please leave me now. Surely there are other people on board you can talk to?' There were one or two pretty girls she had seen eyeing him.

'I will leave you when you have answered me properly.' He stood firmly there in the small cabin and though she would not look at him she could feel his vitality vibrating round the small space. She called on all her self-control to ignore him and will him gone.

He burst forth, 'I know you are suffering, Delphina, but no one can help you unless you let them.'

'You cannot help me. I am grieving for Arnold. I wish he was here.'

'You loved him so much?' She was stung by the surprise in his voice. 'I . . . I did not realize.'

'Why should I not love him? There was so much in him to love.'

'I don't mean it like that. You see I thought you had somehow been forced into the marriage and when we saw you at that village, well,' — he shrugged — 'you didn't seem so in love then.'

'Your foul uncle would have ridiculed our feelings, tried to make it into something sordid.' Her face twisted in anguish remembering Arnold's pain. 'He was worth more than any of you and yet we had to keep our feelings a secret to protect it, but maybe . . . ' The fire suddenly went out of her, her body sagged and her voice became small. 'It's none of your business what it was, but it was something special that would not have worked at home.'

Lorin said gently, 'What you had between you is all that really matters. But people are cruel, sometimes without meaning it. I hope I was not, Delphina.'

'But you think it strange that we might have loved each other?'

'Yes. I admit I did. You are so young, so beautiful, and he, well, it was not just his age. I know I am prejudiced, saw only that he was too old for you. I did not think of his character, of what a good man he was.' He paused watching her tentatively as if any word he said might distress her.

'Perhaps I was jealous. I thought at Aurian Hall that perhaps we had a chance. Despite the quarrel between our relatives I hoped that we might . . . ' His voice petered out. She did not answer so he went on, 'I tried to get in touch with you. I sent someone to your house, but, of course, you had already left for Tibet. I was so surprised but . . . ' he said, watching her again, 'my uncle said he was sure your father had sent you to bring back the seeds he wanted. It was a peony, wasn't it? Like the one my dog ruined.'

At his words she felt her spirit return to

her. Here it was, he was going to ask her where the seeds were.

Seeing the sudden difference in her mood, he said with a touch of eagerness, 'Did you get them? Have you them safe for your father? It is a great achievement if you have.'

'My father wanted many things and I have some of them,' she said, turning back to the porthole and the churning sea beyond.

She stared out at the glutinous sea. Why could she not trust him? It was that odious Cedric's fault, he had ruined it all, and yet she had so nearly done it, brought back the seeds for her father. She must hold on for just a little longer.

Lorin came and stood beside her. If she turned just a fraction she would touch him. She felt the power of him so close to her, but, disturbed at the desire that leapt in her she moved away and said, 'You must have found many interesting plants, why must you show such an interest in mine?'

'It is not the plants I care for,' he said defiantly, 'and you know that. You are very stubborn. We could have enjoyed this long journey together but you put up these fences between us, as if you are a nun.'

His tone infuriated her. 'So you expect me to have a shipboard romance with you, just to pass the time?'

He laughed, took a step closer to her, 'For all time,' he said.

Her heart raced, he was teasing her, enjoying having her trapped like a butterfly with a pin, she must stay on her guard.

'Tell me you never wish to see me again and I will go and leave you alone,' he demanded.

She stayed silent but moved away knowing she could not keep her feelings for him from her eyes.

'You must trust me,' he said softly, 'for without that there is nothing.' He left her, going quickly from her cabin and shutting the door behind him.

★   ★   ★

She tried to keep apart from him, but she became aware of the curious glances of the other passengers. They could not make out her relationship with Lorin: he always seemed so attentive to her while she seemed to ignore him.

'He is a good-looking young man, do you not like him?' Mrs Chapman asked her.

'He is not for me,' was all she said, afraid to let slip her real feelings under the persuasive questions from her new friend.

When at last they arrived at Southampton,

Lorin said, 'Surely you will change your mind and let me take you to your father's house? I have a car ready at the port to meet me. They will take you home.'

A sudden picture of the benefactor rose up to frighten her. What if he had sent someone to meet them, snatch the seeds from her?

'No, thank you. I told you it would be better if I returned alone.'

'But, Delphina, this feud, now my uncle is dead, surely — '

'I don't want to talk about it,' she said coldly.

'This cannot be the last time we are together. I do not believe you when you say you do not care for me.' There was a touch of arrogance in his words and she said, 'There will never be anything like that between us.'

'But when you have got over Arnold's death. You cannot waste your whole life mourning him,' he said gently. 'I feel changed, too, since I went to Tibet. I could not believe such beauty, how close it felt to . . . ' — he laughed, awkwardly — 'God, nature, the true meaning of life. Surely that is something we can share?'

It was better he thought she would not love him as she mourned Arnold. Better than thinking she was hiding the peony seeds from him. He had not asked about them again, but still every time they met she tensed, waiting for some reference to them. She only had a few hours now before she got home with the seeds. Perhaps when they were safe with her father . . . but no, she must not think of that now.

'So what will you do for the rest of your life? Sit at home with your father?'

'I don't know what I shall do. I shall see how I fit back into that life.'

'And if you do not?'

She looked at him gravely, 'I don't know. I really don't know, so there's no point in worrying about it now.'

'You still don't trust me,' he said. 'What must I do to earn your trust?'

'Just leave it,' she said, thinking back to Cedric's cruelty. Just by association with him Lorin carried with him too many bad memories. 'Thank you for bringing me this far.' She turned to leave him as the boat docked, shuddering in the water as it ended its long voyage.

'I insist that I see you safely home,' he said firmly.

'No, I don't want you to. I am sure someone will be there to meet me and, if not, I have made arrangements with Mrs Chapman. Now, please no more, Lorin. We are here.' She looked out at the busy port, the crying seagulls wheeling above the greys and browns of the landscape under a pearly sheen, quite, quite different to the dazzling colour of India. To her surprise she felt a surge of joy to be home.

'I wish . . . ' he started, his eyes lingering on her face.

'Keep your wishes, they are the only sure thing in life. Real life never works out how you think.'

'Goodbye then.' Before she could stop him he took her in his arms and kissed her cheek, holding her close.

She struggled but her body was infused with a warm longing, a longing to hold on to him to kiss his lips to never let him go.

'We love each other don't forget that,' he said and suddenly released her walking fast away from her.

She watched him go. Surely he would turn once more to look at her but he did not and she lost sight of him in the crowd. Her body soared and swooped like the sea. He had taken liberties with her; she could be angry but in her heart she knew he was right. Nothing could come of it, however.

Mrs Chapman called to her and she collected up her things and went down the gangplank to the waiting throng below.

'Delphina, here, over here.'

She saw Philip Stacy, and then Carson and her father in his chair. Philip came to her and hugged her.

'You are back. How happy we are. When he got your wire your father insisted on coming, so I thought I should come, too, to drive him.'

'Thank you.' She felt shy suddenly with him, unsure of herself. She ran to her father, tears and laughter on her face. He was older, more fragile, yet his eyes held such strength and joy. She bent and kissed him and felt his weak arms round her.

'Oh, Papa there has been so much,' she said.

'I know, my darling, but you are safe.' He kept his eyes on her, holding her hand as if he could not believe she was really there. She saw the question burning in his eyes and, taking the seed tin from where she'd just put it in her bag placed it into his trembling hands.

'Here they are.' It seemed such a simple act to hand them to him like a souvenir after a holiday instead of all the hardship and the suffering she'd endured to get them. All the tears and the love too, another life.

'I'm so sorry about Arnold, I shall miss him.' Randolph said, watching her, a mist of tears in his eyes.

'I'll miss him too,' she said.

'Good riddance to that Cedric though,' Randolph said smartly, as if he wanted to change the subject. 'I can hardly wait to hear it all, my darling, but come, you must be tired, let's get to the car. Carson will see to your luggage.'

Philip turned the chair towards the car and she followed feeling strangely alien, apart from them all. Her father let go of her hand but held the seed tin close to him.

She looked back and there was Lorin watching her. Their eyes met and she knew suddenly that he understood her confused feelings. That part of her was left behind in Tibet soaring free among the savage beauty and the flowers. But she saw his expression as he looked at Philip and heard his silent question.

'Is he the man you have come home to? Is he the reason you will not admit to loving me?'

21

It was so good and yet so strange to be back home. How often had she imagined being here when she was stuck in a wet tent stinking of kerosene, with her bowl of yak tea and a mess of plants and meat for dinner. How she'd dreamed of the smell of beeswax, flowers, and good food. The bliss of running hot water, soft towels, linen sheets and now here she was back at last and despite all her suffering she had brought back the peony seeds.

But she soon found out that although Randolph had put on a great show when she arrived home he had become much weaker — so weak that he had asked his sister Charlotte to come and live with them.

She was a tall woman, soberly dressed and soberly minded, and he'd never really got on with her so he must have been desperate to have asked her to come.

'Has he been very ill?' Delphina asked her aunt, when Randolph had gone to bed and they sat together one evening. 'He never said anything in his letters.'

'He wanted you to fetch that blessed flower

for him, though I thought he was touched' — she looked disapproving — 'sending you all that way, with Lord knows what dangers. So he wouldn't tell you. He didn't want you to worry and come back before you found the plants. He suggested that I stay here, make my home with him . . . with you.'

Her heart sank knowing how her aunt would take over the house make it boring with her routines, but she could say nothing she was so tired, She would wait to question it when she was rested.

Randolph spent a lot of time in bed, but now she had returned he seemed to be brighter. He kept the peony seeds by him while he planned with Ely how to plant them, the earth outside was still too cold, and they discussed planting them inside.

The second day she was home, Ely came into the kitchen and asked to see Aunt Charlotte, his face creased with anxiety. Delphina was there telling Mrs Crane and Elsie about her adventures.

'What is it, Ely?' she said

'Someone 'as been in me potting shed, been through everything, left a dreadful mess.'

Aunt Charlotte who frowned on gossip and had come to shoo Delphina away, was just in time to hear his remark. 'Are you sure it's not that good-for-nothing boy?' she said sharply.

Delphina stared at him, fear clutching at her. Surely Lorin had not come to try and find the seeds?

'Let me see,' she said.

'Make that boy clear it up,' Aunt Charlotte said. 'As if I haven't enough to do getting this house straight, I don't want to deal with the garden as well.'

Delphina saw Elsie and Mrs Crane exchange glances, no doubt they were being kept up to scratch.

'I want to see what's happened and please, Aunt Charlotte, don't tell Papa and worry him,' she said going out with Ely.

'It's not Tom,' Ely said with impatience, as they walked down the path to the potting shed behind the shrubbery, 'though 'e is untidy, the padlock's broke. Someone is looking for something — perhaps them seeds you brought the master.'

She fought to curb her mounting agitation. She had an odd sensation that they were being watched. Was someone spying on them waiting to see where they planted them only to steal them in the night? They reached the potting shed, panes of glass slanting down from an old wall. The door hung open, the padlock had been sawn through. Had Lorin done this? Even though she would never see him again, she could not bear it if he had done this. Inside the shed, all the carefully labelled pots were tossed around, earth and small seedlings littered the surfaces and the floor. Nothing had been left undisturbed, boxes of fertilizer, bags of special composts all ripped open their contents spilled everywhere.

'Oh Ely, what a mess,' she cried out. All his hard work to grow unusual, delicate plants from seed was ruined. She bent down and picked up a tiny plant. 'Maybe we can re-plant some of these. I will help you.'

Ely looked near tears. 'Savages,' he muttered. 'Who else would do this but savages.'

All day she worked with him trying to salvage something, determined not to tell her father anything. With luck, by the time the good weather came, some of these plants would have grown.

'It's them peony seeds they're after,' Ely kept muttering. 'We should send them away, get Kew to grow them for us.'

'I have already sent them some, but Papa so loves to have them by him to watch them grow.' She did not add that looking forward to them growing might prolong his life.

'It's not safe; you'll be murdered in your beds,' Ely said mournfully.

The next day a letter came from Kew, announcing the safe arrival of the plants she had brought back from her trip.

'Well done, my darling,' Randolph said, reading it in his chair by the window. 'I think it's time Ely planted these, started them off inside, to get them ready for this summer though they won't flower so soon.'

'I wonder if it would not be safer to send them straight to Kew. I mean,' she went on, seeing his surprise, 'Ely is marvellous with plants, but they might need special conditions we do not have here.'

'I want to grow them here, watch them day by day. Ely can do that.' He frowned, and she had not the heart to tell him how afraid she was that Cedric's benefactor was still after them, no doubt having been briefed by Lorin as to their whereabouts.

How sad that she could not trust him, but perhaps she told herself vainly, he did not know how evil this benefactor was, but then why was he trying to steal them from her? What was he being paid? She thought of Aurian Hall, still unsold. Was it for that he was prepared to steal?

Philip Stacy was a constant visitor and very attentive to her.

'I cannot believe you survived such a journey,' he said, his eyes glowing with admiration. 'Achieved so much despite terrible ordeals. I am so glad to see you back safely, I worried for you every day.'

'You needn't have done.' She wondered if he now expected her to repay his anxiety by marrying him. He had not asked her, but he had made a few remarks on settling down. How easy it would be to marry him. He was a kind man and she was fond of him, but her body still leapt and sang when she thought of Lorin; she must wait until those feelings died.

Philip brought back Prima and once or twice she rode her, but her heart was not in it. She could not bear to go near Aurian Hall and bring back the memory of that one wonderful day she'd spent with Lorin. One or two friends asked her to parties, but she told them she could not come. She was afraid to leave the house for long, still feeling she had to guard the peony. One morning, Carson reported seeing a man in the garden the night before when he was locking up. He'd run away when he saw he'd been observed.

Lorin rang, but when Carson came to tell her he wanted to speak to her, she refused to speak to him, irritated with herself at the surge of sudden joy that sprang in her.

Seeing her reaction, Aunt Charlotte remarked acidly, 'Someone special, had a lovers' tiff?'

'Nothing like that at all. Do not take anymore calls from him, please, Carson. I do not wish to speak to him.'

'You must start to see your friends, go out again,' Aunt Charlotte scolded her, impatient with her moods. 'You must not become like your father always planning a trip away, not wanting to socialize. You must marry, settle down. I think Philip Stacy will be a good match for you.'

'I do not wish to marry, Aunt Charlotte,' she retorted, thinking that she wanted her out of this house so she could control it. 'Just leave me, please.'

'It's those wretched seeds, quite an obsession with both of you. It's time you planted them, see if they come to anything.'

'We'll do it when it is time,' she said, wondering if Aunt Charlotte was a threat to them, too. With her mania for tidiness she might well throw them out.

After much thought she went to her father. 'Papa, I am afraid for the safety of those seeds. I think we must plant them and hide them somewhere safe until they grow. I think we should sow them away from here where no one can find them.'

'What nonsense, my darling. Cedric is dead, who will take them now?'

'His benefactor. You said he would stop at nothing.'

Randolph frowned. 'Has he shown any sign of taking them? Well, has he? You're hiding something from me, Delphina, I can see it.'

She sat on the floor and laid her hand on his knee and told him about the potting shed and Carson seeing an intruder near the house.

'And you never told me? I'm not an imbecile, you know. I need to know. So it's his nephew, that young chap who came here. He must have come to look for it.'

She flinched at his words, but she must face it. He and Cedric had set out together to bring back the peony seeds and Lorin would be expected to finish the task.

'So we must hide them until they are grown,' she said. One plan she had was to plant them when it warmed up at Aurian Hall, somewhere out of the way where they could grow undisturbed.

'I will think on it.' He took the tin from the table where it lay and held it to him. 'They will have to kill me first,' he said, his knuckles white with the effort of holding it tightly to him.

The shock of her revelations made Randolph ill and he was confined to bed.

One morning, Aunt Charlotte announced

346

cheerfully to Delphina, 'I've received a letter from an old friend of your father's. He's asked you to lunch. He has some plants for Randolph and he wants you to choose them. He'll send a car. It would do you good to go. You must get out. I've told Randolph about it and he wants you to go.'

'Who is it? I don't want to go,' Delphina said, without interest.

'Daniel Shawcross. He lives near the sea.' She picked up the letter again and peered at it.

She remembered Daniel Shawcross; she'd liked him. He had a famous garden. Perhaps she could confide in him. She'd see what her father said.

'Go and see Daniel,' Randolph said from his bed, and, 'though it's strange he doesn't come here himself or even telephone, but maybe he can't leave his beloved garden at this moment. Tell him I want to see him the minute he can get away.'

'I will,' she said, reluctant to go. 'I'd like to hide those seeds first in case someone comes.'

'They will be safe with me, but if it will make you happier I will put them out of sight.' They lay now on his bedside table. 'Enjoy yourself and get him to show you round the garden and tell me how it is growing.'

The next day Daniel Shawcross sent a car for her. Delphina dressed carefully in a blue tweed suit with a flared skirt and a fitted jacket. Perhaps everyone was right and she needed a break from here. What would be better than a day with Daniel in his wonderful garden?

A black Rolls Royce glided up the drive driven by a liveried chauffeur.

'What a car. My dear, how smart. I didn't realize he was so rich. No doubt he did the sensible thing of staying put and growing things to sell instead of gallivanting round the world.' There was a reproach underneath Aunt Charlotte's enthusiasm, as she ushered Delphina out of the house towards the car.

'Nor did I?' Delphina was puzzled. Daniel had money but she had not thought him the sort to splash out like this; he was always building new glasshouses or making some shrubbery with his money.

The chauffeur, a sallow, dark-browed man, stood to attention and opened the back door.

Something was wrong; Randolph didn't have friends like this. And that letter, didn't Aunt Charlotte say she had received the letter from Daniel? Why had he written to her and not directly to Randolph? She backed away from the car about to question Aunt Charlotte more closely, but her aunt, thinking

348

she was shy and to encourage her, pushed her forward, and the chauffeur taking her arm, propelled her inside and shut the door.

'No, I'm not going. I've changed my mind, let me out.' Delphina tried to open the door, but it was locked. The chauffeur jumped back in and the car sped away.

She banged on the glass partition between her and the driver, but he took no notice. Vainly she looked to attract her aunt's attention, but she had gone back inside. The doors and windows were locked. There was no way she could escape.

She lay back in the leather seat, her heart pounding. This was not Daniel's car. Had he even asked her to lunch, or was he, too, after the peony seeds? No, of course not. This was the doing of Cedric's benefactor. How could she have been so off her guard to fall for this trick? What would he do when she got there? She remembered Arnold's anguish when he had told her of Selena's death. Would he kill her too?

They drove for over an hour and she spent the journey partly in terror, partly thinking up ways to escape. She thought of Lorin. Would he be there, would he help her, or was he part of this too?

The car slowed down by some massive wrought-iron gates. The chauffeur hooted the horn impatiently and a man came running to open them, peering into the car as he did so. They swept through and Delphina heard them clang shut with a terrifying finality behind her. Anger seeped through her fear, but she must keep her mind clear, take note of where she was and try and escape.

They drove up a tree-lined drive and stopped outside a huge grey stone house. Two footmen came forward and opened her door. One footman leant in and said, 'You have arrived.'

Delphina hesitated. If she refused to get out of the car they would drag her out. Better to play into their hands, pretend to be docile. They might become less vigilant and give her a chance to escape. She got out, shaking off their hands impatiently. She walked up to the open door looking around her trying to memorize the landscape. Inside was a large hall with suits of armour and a ring of firearms high above the fireplace. There was a heavy feeling of oppression. Another man, dressed in a dark suit like an undertaker waited for her.

'This way.' He led her down a corridor his hand not quite on her arm but near enough to grab her if necessary. He opened a highly polished wooden door at the end.

It was such an effort not to scream and

run. She looked around her. The room was decorated in deep-red silk like blood, the long windows looked out on to a magnificent garden. The furniture and pictures were priceless. In one cabinet she saw some statues she was certain came from the temples in Tibet and India.

'So you are Randolph's daughter?' a thin voice, like the wind creaking in the shutters, addressed her.

She did not answer, but examined the small, yellow man dressed in an oriental robe who sat in a gilded chair.

'Stand in the light where I can see you. My sight is not so good these days,' he commanded.

She studied him carefully, seeing his water-coloured eyes staring at her, his thin brown hair, obviously dyed, greased flat to his head. She felt a jolt of revulsion; he was yellow from sickness. Apart from his clothes there was nothing oriental about him at all.

'May I introduce myself? My name is Edwin Keating. I've heard all about you, Delphina.' His voice grated through her. 'You owe me something, I understand.'

'What do you mean?' Her voice was sharp with fear but also anger and disgust at this toad-like monster, responsible for causing so much pain, squatting in his chair, staring at her with those colourless eyes.

He smiled, though the curve of his thin mouth added a sinister look to his face. 'The peony, my dear. The ivory peony.'

'It is not yours. My father found it and then Arnold North. It is not yours.'

'If I was younger, and not so sick, your temper would amuse me.' His words oozed like slime into her. 'I want that peony. I collect them. You can see them in my garden. I paid Cedric a lot of money to get it for me.'

'You cannot have it. I have sent the seeds to Kew,' she said, defiantly.

'All of them? Did you not even keep one to put on your father's grave? I hear he has been going downhill these last months.' He smiled again, spite in his eyes.

'They are all at Kew. You have no right to them. Arnold found them, strictly, they belong to him.'

'And he is dead, too. But then,' — his voice hardened menacingly — 'so is Cedric.'

Delphina bit back her retort of him deserving it. He was a thief and in the pay of this evil man, and now, like Arnold's love Selena, before her, he had caught her.

'How is Daniel Shawcross involved in this?' she demanded. Was there some awful coven of them, all plotting to steal from the plant hunters?

'He's not, but I know he is a friend of your father's. I'm quite pleased my little ruse worked sending you an invitation from him. I knew Randolph was ill and wouldn't come, but I also knew if I mentioned he wanted to give him some plants he would persuade you to go.'

'So you forged the letter and sent it to my aunt?' she spat at him, but at least Daniel was not in his pay. 'You will never get the seeds, so let me go home,' she demanded.

'That's right. I'd heard she had taken over running his house and she would not know who it was from. You owe me a lot, my dear. The cost of the whole trip, Cedric's death. You lost me a good man.'

'He was a wicked man,' she burst out. 'He stole from the temples; he paralysed my father; he would do anything to get what he wanted.'

'He did it for me, and for the money I gave him.' There was anger in those icy eyes. 'I get what I want in life. I have no time for smug feelings of honesty and goodness. I *will* have that peony, my dear, and you will stay here until I get it. Now go.' He flicked a small hand at her and turned away.

'If I stay here how will you get it?' she tried, thinking if she got out of this room, she could somehow escape him.

'I have ways of getting what I want.' His eyes were like steel rods pinning her to the wall.

The butler and a footman came back and, taking her arm, frogmarched her out of the room. She struggled to break free.

'Haven't you killed enough people?' she cried at him.

Edwin Keating merely smiled, flicked his hand to dismiss her as if he was bored with her.

22

The two men holding her, picked her up by her arms and pulled her from the room, their grip like a vice.

'You'll never get it, never,' she shouted, as she was dragged away.

They went along the corridor, down some stairs and, reaching a door, opened it and pushed her in roughly, locking it behind her.

She rubbed her arms, looking helplessly about her. There was nothing she could have done. When she had tried to resist they had just picked her up by her arms and carried her here.

There was one dim bulb laced with cobwebs hanging from the ceiling so she could just see her surroundings. It was a small room in the basement of the house. There was one window above her with a grille over the outside. The walls of the room were very thick. There was an empty packing case, a table, a chair and a rug, and a grubby-looking mattress on the floor. Putting the rug over the mattress she flung herself down in despair. There was no escape. Now having seen him, she knew that Edwin

Keating had no mercy, he would get what he wanted from her. No one would hear her screams, or find out that she was here. He had laid his trap well, finding out that her father was too ill to talk to 'Daniel' on the telephone and had been taken in by the letter.

But Keating was old and very sick, that might be his weakness, for he would not have the physical strength to do much to her himself. But this did not ease her fear; perhaps he got his pleasure from watching other, stronger men torturing his victims.

She lay there many hours hearing nothing. She saw from the window the dusk slip into night. How long would they keep her here? Or would they wait until the darkness to carry out whatever evil they had planned? Surely Papa would by now be wondering where she was and have got someone to telephone Daniel? Would he guess what had happened? Would he send the police to get her? But Keating must have thought of this. He might have telephoned Aunt Charlotte again, made up some story of her staying there a few days. She lay like a wounded animal, curled up on the floor, deep in despair.

It was pitch dark, only the light from the moon shone through the window at her. A shadow moved across it startling her, she was sitting now against the wall, knees bent to her chest. There was a grating sound as if someone was tampering with the bars.

They had come as she had dreaded they would. Though why through the window and not the door? She shrank back into herself, tried to block her ears against the scraping by the window. Then she heard a tapping on the glass. It stopped came again. In mesmerized panic she looked up. A figure was pressed against the window. It tapped again, this time more urgently.

It was a trap, she was sure of it, but something made her go closer to the window. The person had a torch, he shone it on his face. It was Lorin.

She stared at him helplessly. Was he part of this evil place? Had he been sent to lull her into false security to get the peony from her?

He tapped again, gestured to an iron bar held in his hand, then inside the room, then at the window. She was puzzled, then she saw in the dim shine of moonlight he was pointing to the old rug on the mattress. He wanted to break the glass and she must deaden the noise with the rug. Quickly she picked it up and folded it, but she could not reach the window without standing on something. She tried the chair but that was not high enough, the table was too rickety to stand on. Franticly she heaved the empty packing case under the window and put the chair on that and clambered up with the rug.

As she did this she wondered again if it was some kind of trick and they would break down the door and grab her while she was balancing on the chair, but if it was she'd risk it. She did not want to believe that Lorin would hurt her.

She held the rug close to the window bracing herself for the force of the iron bar. He hit the glass and she felt it shatter, nearly losing her balance. She heard Lorin say desperately, 'Hold it again, higher up.'

She strained upwards again her arms screaming out with pain. He broke the top half of the window, but the force of it toppled her off the chair and on to the floor.

'Delphina, get up quickly. We haven't a moment to lose.'

She scrambled up, located the chair and put it back on the case and climbed rather unsteadily on to it.

'Give me your hand.'

He had removed the iron grill and he grabbed her hand and pulled her out through the jagged hole in the glass on to the ledge.

'Keep holding my hand and run as fast as you can. We can't hang about. Understand?'

She held tightly to his hand as if she would

never let it go again. There was a sound and he motioned to her to stand still. They listened intently, her nerves stretched to breaking point. The silence was broken by a crunch of footsteps on gravel just to the left of them. They were lost.

Lorin put his finger to his lips to warn her to be quiet and pulled her quickly away from the house. There was a shrubbery a few feet away and they dodged into that. The branches tugged at her clothes, snagging her stockings.

'Run, as fast as you can,' he commanded suddenly, and, pulling her with him, she ran, her heart pounding, her breath tearing at her chest, her toes trying to cling on to her shoes. They left the shrubbery and were out into an open space. There was a shout, and suddenly the whole place lit up as huge searchlights bit into the darkness.

'We're nearly there,' Lorin gasped. 'You must run faster. They have dogs.'

Every fibre in her body shrieked for her to stop, to drop down to rest on the ground, but he urged her on. Her feet were agony. There was shouting, pounding feet, the bark of dogs behind them. She had a quick mental picture of the lynx jumping for Cedric's throat as she forced her body on.

'Here.' Lorin pulled her through a gap in a

fence on to a road beyond. The harsh light from the floodlights shone on a car. 'Get in.' He opened the door and ran round to the other side. Delphina scrabbled in, locking the door behind her.

Lorin struggled with his door a moment, then threw himself in. He turned on the engine. It spluttered, died. The shouts of the men came nearer, their feet pounding on the road. One reached the car, banged on the roof of it, then lifted a stick to smash the glass. Lorin cursed, tried the car again, it jerked forward then away, leaving their pursuers shouting after them.

Delphina couldn't speak. She lay back in her seat, her eyes closed, her breath coming in painful bursts. She was overwhelmed by the shock of the chase and their close escape. Lorin drove on, faster and faster through the night.

After what seemed like forever she opened her eyes and said, 'How did you know I was there?'

'I rang your aunt insisting on speaking to you, to warn you to take care. But she said you'd gone out to lunch with Daniel Shawcross.'

'That's what I thought I was doing, but it was a trick. But how did you know that?' Sorrow stabbed at her. He must have known, perhaps he had even forged the letter inviting her.

'Daniel Shawcross has gone to London. He has meetings at Kew all this week.'

'So how did you guess where I was?' She had to ask, find out once and for all what his role in all this was.

'I met Edwin Keating a few times with my uncle. I knew he paid for our trip, but although I didn't like him I thought he was just some rich eccentric who paid people to bring back plants for his garden. It was not until we were in Tibet that I began to wonder and when I returned and . . . ' His face became stiff and her heart fell again. Was he going to confess he was in his pay?

'And what? I must know everything,' she insisted, sitting up now and watching him, his face a play of shadows in the darkness.

'He asked to see me when I returned, indeed he had a car waiting for me at the port. He questioned me about you and Arnold and this peony. I said I didn't know about it, but he insisted that it was his and that your father had stolen it. He wanted me to get it from you.'

'You will never get it,' she cried out. 'Let me out now, for whatever you do to me I will never let you have it.'

'Oh, Delphina, do you still not trust me?'

He slowed down the car and turned to her, 'I don't want it. I remember your anguish that day my dog destroyed it. It is yours. I will not take it. I told Keating this, so he tried to blackmail me by saying I had stolen the statues from the temples. I refused to help him, but I guessed he'd try some other way to get them so I rang to warn you but you wouldn't speak to me. I was determined to try again and some stroke of luck I rang today.'

'Tell me this, did you break into our potting shed?'

'No.' He looked puzzled. 'I have done nothing to try and find the seeds and I won't. They are yours and you must keep them.'

'But still, how did you know where I was?' How she longed to trust him.

'Keating insisted that I bring you to him. He pretended he wanted to give you some plants for your father. I refused, saying I didn't know where you lived. That's why I telephoned to warn you. I never thought he'd move so fast. I only saw him the day before yesterday.' His face was grim as he turned to her. 'Did he hurt you?'

'No. But I was afraid he would. He . . . Oh God, he's done so many dreadful things . . .' She closed her eyes. 'But how did you know where I was? That house is enormous.'

'I had to give it some thought. I broke the fence and left the car ready to drive away. But . . . ' He paused. 'Let's say I had to use a little force to find out where you were.'

She shivered. 'I don't want to know any more. It's just such a relief you came in time.'

'I should have kept more watch on you. I wish I'd known what danger you were in from him and from Cedric. I'm sorry I didn't do more to protect you.'

He turned down a lane and stopped the car. The grey dawn light picked out the flint-scattered walls of a square house. They sat awhile still not speaking as if once the car door was opened the terror of the past hours would pounce on them. Delphina also felt that once outside the car she would have to face up to the reality of their situation together.

'Where are we? I thought you were taking me home.'

'No, I think you will be safer here. They might go to your house so I am going to telephone now, tell them what has happened and suggest they call the police if anyone should come.'

'They might be there already.'

'Remember I have already warned them, but I tried not to worry them too much about your safety. If they had called the police God knows what Keating might have done to you before they came.' He put out his hand and touched her arm.

'Please trust me, Delphina. I know it's a lame excuse now, but I didn't know Cedric had set out to steal the peony from you. He did tell me that your father had stolen plants from him and put them down as his discoveries and that he owed him a great deal of money, but I didn't realize the gravity of it.'

'But did he not talk of the peony and how he wanted it?'

'Not really. He'd mention one plant and then another. I regret I did not take it seriously enough. He'd send me off to plant hunt, something I was glad of, but when I returned he was often dopey with opium. Once or twice I did question him over things . . . why he was sending sacks of plants across the border for instance. He always had an excuse. Now I know those packages contained opium, or stolen objects from the temples, on their way back to Keating. I don't want to excuse him, Delphina, but I think the opium turned his mind, made him behave as he did. After all, he needed money to feed his addiction back here.'

She shivered, seeing again that frenzied face as the lynx had pounced. 'For me there are no excuses. I will never forgive him, especially for what he did to my father.'

'Will you forgive me?' The words lay between them, thrown down like a glove in a duel. She moved restlessly as if the words had spikes on and were chafing her.

'Let's go in,' he said before she answered, getting out and opening the door. 'This house belongs to a friend who's away; we'll be safe here.' His voice was deceptively light, as if his question before was unimportant.

Weak and dazed, she followed him into the house. He snapped on the light bringing to life the long pale room with a beamed ceiling. There was a massive grey marble fireplace at one end of the room and large comfy looking sofas and chairs crying out to be sat in.

She sank gratefully on to a chair while Lorin lit the fire.

'I'll make you some coffee and sand-wiches,' he said. 'You must be starving. Are you cold? Do you want a hot bath?'

'Later, I just want to sit here,' she said, his words, 'will you forgive me' ricocheting round in her head.

He was back in a moment with some rather thick ham sandwiches and a cup of coffee. He sat down opposite her pretending not to watch her while she ate. 'I've telephoned your house and told them you are safe, but to keep a watch out. The man who answered — '

'Carson.'

'Carson said you had better ring your father yourself or your aunt when they are up.'

'Thank you.' She glanced at her watch. 'I will in a couple of hours.'

They sat in silence eating their sandwiches.

He said at last, 'That young man who came to meet you. I saw how he looked at you. Are you going to marry him now you are back?'

There was a slight edge to his voice and she said, 'Philip is a good friend.'

'And will you marry him for your father's sake as you married Arnold?'

His voice was very quiet his eyes eloquent with suspense.

'No. I went through a form of marriage with Arnold as my father didn't want to upset my mother's smart relatives. I grew to love him, he had suffered so much. That devil Keating killed the girl he loved. Keating and Cedric have a lot to answer for.' She thought of her father and his crippled body, and Selena's tragic death that had blighted Arnold's life.

'I am learning more and more about him and my uncle and it disgusts me,' Lorin said with vehemence. 'We could have had so much, shared the wonders of that trip if — '

'I also couldn't understand,' she said

quickly, to stop his words, 'how you had enough money to talk about buying Aurian Hall. I thought it must have been paid to you to get the peony from me.'

Lorin sprung up from his chair. He leant on the mantelpiece staring into the fire. 'My father left me some money. I told you I wanted to buy an estate. But I can only afford a run-down estate, one that I will restore. I want to turn it into a nursery, like Daniel Shawcross has, turn it into a business.'

'And will you?'

'I don't know. It depends on how things go.'

The look he gave her filled her with warmth, but still she stalled, ashamed of her suspicions of him. She said to justify herself. 'I thought Keating and Cedric were using you to get the peony from me. You must see how hard it was to trust you. Will we ever be safe? Cedric may be dead, but that monster Keating is still alive, he won't rest until he gets it,' she said, starting up in her chair, as if even now there was no hope for them.

'Keating has terminal cancer, and has only a short time left to live. But I will keep you safe, you and the peony, until he dies.' With one step he was beside her, kneeling down in front of her. He took her hands and kissed them, holding them against his mouth a moment. 'I should have followed my instincts and known what Cedric said about you and Arnold could not be true. Then I could have protected you from all this.'

'I think I managed well enough by myself,' she said fighting to control the surging desire rising in her, but he saw it in her eyes and in the restlessness of her body.

'Will you ever admit to yourself that we belong together, that you knew that from that day at Aurian Hall? I detest that peony, it stands in our way. Why can't you realize that I don't care for it, I don't want it. I see it no more worthy than any other plant, but you have this obsession for it as did your father and indeed my uncle. Think how much happier we'd all be if it had never been found.'

'You can't say that, I've been through so much to get it,' she cried out. Her anger was not with him, but with the truth of his words. Her father's accident was caused because of it, if Lorin had not rescued her who knows what terrible fate she might have suffered at Keating's hands and perhaps even Arnold's death could have been prevented if they had left the peony alone.

'And I have been through so much to get close to you. Are you going to throw this away too, all for a plant?' He got to his feet and walked away from her to stand by the mantlepiece leaving her bereft.

The room was filled with silence but she knew this was her last chance. Her mission was over. She had brought back the ivory peony and that must be the end of it.

'You're right,' she said at last, 'it's just been so hard not knowing who to trust.'

He came to her then and pulled her up into his arms. 'You can always trust me,' he said, 'you could have done so from the first. Come,' he smiled and kissed her lightly on her mouth, 'we have all day and all night too to settle our differences, and also catch up with the love that has been between us all this time.'

We do hope that you have enjoyed reading this large print book.

Did you know that all of our titles are available for purchase?

We publish a wide range of high quality large print books including:
Romances, Mysteries, Classics
General Fiction
Non Fiction and Westerns

Special interest titles available in large print are:
The Little Oxford Dictionary
Music Book
Song Book
Hymn Book
Service Book

Also available from us courtesy of Oxford University Press:
Young Readers' Dictionary
(large print edition)
Young Readers' Thesaurus
(large print edition)

For further information or a free brochure, please contact us at:
Ulverscroft Large Print Books Ltd.,
The Green, Bradgate Road, Anstey,
Leicester, LE7 7FU, England.
Tel: (00 44) 0116 236 4325
Fax: (00 44) 0116 234 0205

Other titles published by
The House of Ulverscroft:

THE BEST-KEPT SECRET

Mary de Laszlo

Cornelia, an innocent seventeen-year-old, is to leave the sheltered atmosphere of her Catholic boarding school and spend a year in Paris. First, though, she must meet the redoubtable Aunt Flavia, who proceeds to transform the schoolgirl into a beautifully presented young woman. Next it is school at Mademoiselle Beatrice's, where Cornelia meets other English girls, most of whom are just as naive as she is. Then there is Laurent, without whom Paris would never be Paris. So begins the happy initiation which will change her life forever.

DANCING ON HER OWN

Mary de Laszlo

Miranda is single and entirely happy on her own, with her career as a fashion journalist, her lovely flat in London, her hobbies. Seeing the mess some of her girlfriends have got into, she is sure she doesn't want to marry. Miranda certainly has no intention of getting involved with a married man, until she meets Jack. Jack's marriage has been a sham for years: he instantly recognises Miranda as the partner he needs, and Miranda sees how her life could be endowed with a richness she had never believed possible. But someone needs Jack more than Miranda — his vulnerable dyslexic son, Tom . . .

THE WOMAN WHO LOVED TOO MUCH

Mary de Laszlo

Ever since they were little girls, Grace's cousin India has got what she wanted. Yet pretty, privileged India has always been secretly jealous of Grace. So when Grace falls in love with charismatic Jonathan Sheridan, India knows she must have him — the fact that Jonathan marries Grace only sharpens India's desire to wrest him from her. Grace knows how much India wants her husband and she is so anxious to keep him that she fails to see the weakness in their relationship that one day will jeopardise all she has worked so hard to preserve, all she loves so much . . .

BREAKING THE RULES

Mary de Laszlo

Growing up watching her father tire of a steady stream of wives, mistresses and, heartbreakingly, his children, Cecily Forester learnt that when a man grows bored with a woman he'll leave her. Which is perhaps why she chose to marry solidly reliable Edmund. But as Cecily nears middle age, she finds herself cast loose from the marriage she believed would last forever. When the emotional loss of her husband is followed by devastating financial disaster, Cecily begins to see that breaking the rules bred into her since girlhood may be the only way to survive . . .

THE MORNING PROMISE

Margaret James

Rose Courtenay's wealthy parents expect her to marry a neighbour's son and then settle down in Dorset. But the outbreak of the Great War offers Rose an unlikely opportunity to escape . . . Longing for adventure, she trains to be a nurse and is sent to France where the stark reality of war forces her to grow up fast. And then she falls in love with a man she can never marry. As the war ends, Rose must make the most difficult choice between her family, wealth and comfort, and the man she loves.

THE WINDMILL

Stephanie Gertler

Olivia and Carl appear to have the perfect life: a son and a daughter, weekends on Cape Cod and satisfying jobs as professors at Belvedere College in a picturesque Massachusetts town. Until, one day, the seemingly dependable Carl disappears, leaving behind only a cryptic note . . . Alone and terrified, Olivia relives the pain she felt when she lost her first husband. While Carl travels back to his childhood hometown to confront the demons he has always hidden from his wife, Olivia must take a journey of her own to make peace with the memories that haunt her . . .